AN ANOMALY NOVEL

SHADES

OF

TREASON

SANDY WILLIAMS

.✸ ✹ ✸.

SHADES OF TREASON

ISBN: 9780996323116

Cover Art: Damonza.com
Developmental Editing: Red Circle Ink Editing
Copy Editing: Victory Editing

To my brother, the Marine.
Thanks for "letting" me steal Timothy Zahn's Heir to the Empire.
It made me fall in love with science fiction.

ALSO BY

SANDY WILLIAMS

The Shadow Reader
The Shattered Dark
The Sharpest Blade

PRAISE FOR THE SHADOW READER NOVELS

"Combines top-notch writing and world-building with characters you'll adore…and the star-crossed lovers may just break your heart… If you enjoy fae urban fantasy, then don't miss this splendid debut. Loved it. Can't wait for the next book."

—Ann Aguirre, *USA Today* bestselling author of *Endgame*

"A fresh take on the fae, packed with suspense, surprises, and real moral dilemmas. Sexy and fun, this is a must for anyone who likes their fae modern, their stakes high, and their property damage extensive."

—Seanan McGuire, *New York Times* bestselling author of the October Daye Novels

"When facing this stubborn, smart escape artist of a heroine, watch where you walk, as every foostep leaves a shadow and every shadow tells a long-time reader like McKenzie Lewis the truth… whether she wants to know it or not."

—Rob Thurman, *New York Times* bestselling author of *Slashback*

"A compelling, action-packed follow-up to *The Shadow Reader*. Fans of urban fantasy should definitely pick up this series and give it a try."

—Fiction Vixen Book Reviews

"Prepare yourself to swoon, to cry, to smile, to hold your breath, to lean in close to your book. Just prepare yourself."
  —Goldilox and the Three Weres

"Be prepared for nonstop action, intrigue, and a few bombshells that will leave you dying for book three."
  —All Things Urban Fantasy

ACKNOWLEDGEMENTS

To my readers: You are the most patient readers in the world. Thank you for waiting for my next book, and for being willing to try out my "urban fantasy set in space." I hope you love this book and these characters as much as I do.

To the pioneers of indie publishing: You guys are amazing and brave. I've learned more from you in a few months of reading your publishing journeys and business practices than I did in all my years of traditional publishing. I admire your courage, your belief in yourselves, and your professionalism.

And a big thank you to my publishing team:

My husband, who continues to support me through my ups and my downs.

My friends and family, who are always eager to learn how the writing is going.

Rene, who once again prevented my hero from being an a-hole. You always tell it like it is.

My betas: Rachelle, Shelli, Carolyn, Ed, Tricia, Ami, and Leah.

Jessa Slade, my developmental editor, who provided a speedy edit despite a broken arm, and who helped me make this a better story.

And Anne Victory, my copy editor, who endured all my misplaced commas and crazy sentences. You boosted my confidence in this project and made the book meet the high standards I expect from myself. It was a pleasure working with you!

SHADES

OF

TREASON

CHAPTER
ONE

WHEN COMMANDER RHYS "Rest in Peace" Rykus walked back into her life, Ash smiled because she knew it would piss him off. He was an intimidating SOB, always had been, and it took an effort not to give in to habit and stand to salute him. It helped, of course, that her wrists were shackled to the arms of her chair.

Rykus didn't say anything when he entered her stale-aired prison, so Ash echoed his silence. The room's low ceiling accentuated his height and broad shoulders. He outweighed her by forty, maybe fifty pounds now that he'd completely gotten over his old shoulder injury and packed on more muscle. The way his crisp black uniform embraced his frame drew her gaze, but she was a bit disappointed that he was clean-shaven. She'd always liked it when stubble shadowed the planes of his face. She'd told him as much once during training, and he'd sent her on extra weighted runs as punishment. Though she'd ended up sore, stiff, and tired as hell, it had been worth it to get under his skin.

She had to get under his skin now because she could already feel his presence scraping away her resolve. The Coalition wanted her to talk, and she'd been programmed years ago to respond to Rykus's voice. She had to escape soon—now—because if she didn't he'd trigger that brainwashing and command her to give him the cipher the Coalition so desperately wanted.

Keeping her smile in place, Ash turned her attention to the two men flanking him. The first waited beside the door, his gaze locked on her, his hand resting ready on his gun. The other man wasn't armed. Instead of a weapon, he carried a bio-scanner and med-sack. He dropped the sack on the data-table in front of her, yanked out a blue aerosol bottle, then sprayed both his hands with liqui-glove. With short, rough movements, he treated the cut on her temple.

Ash lowered her gaze to the table, but Rykus's stare drilled into her. She didn't have to look up to imagine his expression. After a year of training under his command, she'd memorized the harsh set of his jaw and the dark, I've-been-to-hell-and-back depths of his eyes. The force of his scowl could shatter heat shielding if Rykus was so inclined, but he usually kept his anger in check. Usually. Ash had a talent for setting him off.

He sat in the chair on the other side of the data-table, the only piece of furniture in the cell besides her chair and the sleep-slab that was now folded into the dull gray wall.

She took a moment to steel herself against her loyalty training, then met her former instructor's eyes. "It's been a while, Rip."

When the medic went still beside her, she forced a laugh. "Guess the commander doesn't go by that name much around here, does he?"

Ah, there it was, the telltale tightening of the skin around Rykus's eyes. No one else called him Rip—at least, not to his face—but she was the one who'd given him the nickname back when she was his cadet. She figured she might as well use it, especially if it would throw him off-balance. For the Coalition's loyalty training to fully kick in, Rykus's words had to be spoken in a precise tone and cadence. When he was angry or—dare she suggest it—aroused, his voice dipped. It was a slight, almost unnoticeable change, but it was enough to let her fight and occasionally overcome the compulsion in his commands.

"Still," she said to the medic, "he is the only man in the entire federated military to show up alive and well to his own funeral. He never told us anomalies how he managed that." She tilted her head to the side and pitched her last words as a question.

Rykus just sat there staring through her. Her faith in her plan wavered. Maybe she shouldn't push him away. Maybe he could help her. If he ordered her to report what happened on the mission to Chalos II, maybe she could break through the telepathic stranglehold preventing her from explaining everything.

But as soon as the thought entered her mind, her heart clogged her throat. She could almost hear her subconscious cautioning against the idea. Something bad would happen if Rykus commanded her to speak. She was certain of it.

She made her tone casual, her expression unconcerned. "Tell me, Rip, how are you liking this plush new command?"

Still he said nothing.

"Not much for conversation these days, are you?"

He didn't even blink. When had he become so fucking impenetrable? Used to be she could make him angry with a few take-me-to-bed glances, but maybe his triggers had changed. Or maybe, since she was no longer his cadet, he didn't give a damn about her anymore.

Her stomach twisted like a transport on a bad reentry into atmosphere. She blocked out the sensation, the odd little mix of hurt and devotion. It was just the loyalty training urging her to please him. It didn't mean anything. Never had, never would.

The medic finished treating the cut on her head, then swabbed the broken skin on her knuckles. Even though her escape attempt had failed, she'd managed to land a few solid hits before she went down. Rykus had taught her well.

The medic put away the disinfectant and picked up a bio-band. He stared at the device, then frowned at her chair-shackled wrists.

"You can unbind me," Ash told him, innocence dripping from her tone. "I won't try anything. Promise."

He glared, shook his head, then stepped back to look at her bare feet. She'd regained consciousness without her boots and without the knife she'd confiscated from one of the guards she'd taken down during her transfer to the ship.

He strapped the device to her ankle and switched it on. It wouldn't do him any good. Her physical injuries were superficial, and she'd already been scanned a dozen times since her arrest. The bio-band wouldn't tell the doctors what was really wrong with her, and she couldn't tell them herself. She'd tried. Over and over again, she'd tried, but Jevan, the deceitful, manipulative bastard, had screwed with her head.

"I didn't train a traitor."

Rykus's voice rebounded off the walls and struck Ash in the center of her chest. She kept her focus on the medic, hoping the bio-band didn't pick up an increased heart rate.

"Tell me what happened."

He didn't command her to speak, thank God. He never did at first. If his habits hadn't changed, he'd ask her once more before he tried to force a confession.

She made her hands loosen their grip on the chair arms. "Guess you're not as good at reading people as you thought."

A low blow, one that should have hurt, but Rykus didn't even twitch. Damn it. Had she lost her touch?

"You need to start talking." His tone turned brutal, bruising. "The Coalition is sending their best man to interrogate you. He won't be gentle."

Ash saw her opening and made her voice a low purr. "You know I like it rough, Commander."

A sharp and sudden inhalation was the only sign he'd heard her words. Ash kept her half smile plastered on her face despite the painful twist in her stomach. She'd already lost her comrades, her career, her reputation, everything. She might as well act like the arrogant bitch he'd always thought her to be.

Rykus leaned forward. "This is the last time I'll ask. Tell me what happened."

"Tell me what you believe."

She hid a grimace when the words left her lips. She didn't want to know if he believed the accusations. If he did, it would hurt. If he didn't... Well, it would make it that much harder to push him away.

Seconds ticked by. Ash wanted to slouch in her seat, but she kept her chin lifted, her eyes on Rykus's.

Finally, he came to a decision and jabbed at the data-table. "Let's start with your team."

Their images appeared on the table's surface. The universe pitched into an angle that was all wrong. It didn't feel like they were dead. It felt like she could call them anytime, especially since the pictures had been captured weeks ago, just days before they'd left for Chalos II.

"You're accused of executing five men, each with a single shot to the head. You worked with them for the past year, some even longer than that. Yet when asked why you murdered them, you gave no comment."

Emotion scraped Ash's throat raw. Those men were her family. She would have given her life to save them. Instead, they'd given their lives to save hers. And to save the Coalition. They'd all taken an oath to preserve and protect it.

Rykus flattened his hand on the table, and the images changed to show a series of decoded transmissions. "Your file contains over thirty records of communications with known Saricean agents. In them, you reveal classified information. Your leaks ranged from incidental supply shipments to the name and coordinates of a shuttle carrying Senator Ben Playte." Rykus pinned her with one of his destructive glares. "Playte was assassinated three days after the Sariceans received this document. When asked if any of these were forgeries, you gave no comment."

He swiped his hand across the table's surface, flinging her service record in her face.

"Since your graduation, you've received top reviews from every commander you've served under. They've stated that you're 'a superb soldier,' 'unwavering in your mission,' and 'dedicated, if a bit cheeky.'" He looked up. When she raised her shoulders in a shrug, his expression hardened. "There are some blips in your attendance the past six months. Times when you didn't answer your summons, showed up late to debriefings, or didn't make an appearance at routine, required meetings. When your interrogators asked your whereabouts, you gave no comment."

Six months ago. That's when this had started. That's when she'd met Jevan and become a fool.

"You still have no comment?" Rykus asked.

She stared at the table. She'd deny it all if she could, but she knew better than to try. She couldn't speak of anything that had happened since she met Jevan. When she tried, she blacked out. No one noticed. She always stayed upright; her eyes never blinked, never lost focus, but seconds, maybe minutes would pass before her brain started functioning again. If someone was interrogating her, they assumed she was ignoring their questions.

"Do you know why you were brought to the *Obsidian*?" Rykus asked.

She pressed her lips together. The Coalition wanted the information her team had copied from the Saricean databanks on Chalos II. That had been their assignment, and they'd completed it without a hitch. It wasn't until after they withdrew from the planet that Trevast, her commanding officer, had sat down and analyzed what they'd stolen. He'd cursed. Then he'd looked at his team and told them telepaths were real and that they'd infiltrated the Coalition's government.

She'd laughed. They all had.

Telepathy was a fiction, a farce, a fabrication for the gullible. It didn't exist.

She looked back at Rykus. His mouth tightened into a frown, a frown which gave her flashbacks to the harsh, hellish days training under him on Caruth. "Did you change the encryption on the files, Lieutenant?"

The truth clawed at her throat. A private yacht had intercepted her team's shuttle before they could make it to the rendezvous point. It hadn't broadcasted an ID or a Mayday, and they hadn't been near any mapped routes. There was only one reason for the yacht to be there, and when it fired upon them without any provocation, Trevast had shoved a comm-cuff with the stolen data into Ash's hands. He knew she was an anomaly. He knew what she was capable of. He knew she was the only person on the team who could re-encrypt the Sariceans' files with a different cipher before their attackers boarded, and that's exactly what she'd done. It was in her head now, and both the Coalition and Jevan would do anything to rip it out.

"You'll be charged with treason if you don't cooperate." Rykus's words were softer than his expression, and the loyalty training pulled at her again.

She was damn sure the medic's bio-band was picking up the thudding of her heart. She had to get control of this conversation and get rid of Rip Rykus.

She leaned forward as far as her restraints would allow, waited until Rykus did the same, anticipating her confession. Their heads almost met in the center of the table, and Ash breathed in deep, exhaled slowly.

"I've always loved the smell of your aftershave."

Rykus exploded, launching his chair across the floor. The medic scrambled out of the way when he rounded the data-table. "I'm the only person in the Coalition who wants to help you, and you're playing your goddamn games."

His hand went to her chest and shoved with enough force to send her and the chair toppling backward to the ground. The impact knocked the breath from her, and she choked trying to reinflate her lungs.

Rykus kneeled beside her, pinned her. "*Give me the cipher.*"

She sucked in a breath as the compulsion snaked through her. She'd been successful though. His pitch was a little off, his voice a little too tight. She fought against the need to obey him—battled against it—but he hovered above her. His eyes demanded the truth, and her control began to slip. Desperate, she worked enough moisture into her mouth to spit in his face.

She saw his chest rise and fall, heard the huffs of his angry breaths. Slowly, he stood. He said nothing as he wiped his face with his sleeve, nothing as he bent down to heft her upright. In fact, she was pretty sure he wouldn't have said anything at all if a guard hadn't entered with a tray of food.

Rykus stopped the woman, stuck the knife, spoon, and fork in his pocket, grabbed the tray, then dumped its contents across the table, effectively ending Ash's next escape attempt before she had the chance to implement it. "She can eat like a dog."

CHAPTER

TWO

RYKUS KNEW ADMIRAL BAYIS would be waiting in the brig's security room, so he forced his fists to relax, his jaw to unclench, and he put on a cool, controlled façade to disguise the turmoil banging around in his chest.

"Interesting woman," Admiral Bayis said. He stood in the observation room down the corridor from Ash's cell, staring at the security vid that showed brown gravy dripping off the data-table and onto the floor.

"She is," Rykus agreed, though the assessment was an understatement. Ash was more than interesting. She was intriguing, infuriatingly insolent, and one of the most cunning and determined soldiers he'd ever trained. He hadn't seen her in three years, but she hadn't changed. As the medic unstrapped the bio-band, Rykus watched Ash's face and felt that old, uncomfortable ache in the pit of his stomach. Her smile was the same; so was the slight tilt to her head and the spark in her green eyes. He'd grown to hate that expression, to hate the way she always looked like she knew a secret. He'd punished her for it, kept her up through the cold nights at Caruth's poles, run her into the ground during the planet's blistering summers. He'd tried everything that was permitted to make her tap out of the program, but that half grin never wavered.

And she still had that damn braid. It was barely visible beneath the rest of her dark hair, but the end of it draped over her right shoulder, a blatant sign of defiance.

"Has she broken the loyalty training?" Bayis asked.

"I'm not sure," he managed to say, ignoring the quick, sudden tightening in his gut. He'd left Caruth because of the loyalty training. He and the other three lead instructors had been told the program would insure the anomaly's mental stability—something that had been an issue in the past—but after the soldiers were put in the psyche-mask and indoctrinated, the side effects had become evident. Loyalty-trained anomalies would jeopardize everything to follow their instructors' commands. That had never sat right with Rykus, even when I-Com explained that, unless something went wrong, he would never again come into contact with any of the anomalies he trained.

Bayis clasped his hands behind his back. "If the Sariceans have broken the programming, the doctors will want to study her. They're already asking she be sent to the institute."

Of course they were.

"The institute will botch up her mind," Rykus said. "We need the cipher, not a brain-dead zombie."

"Can you make her talk?"

Rykus stared at his former cadet. "I don't know. Even with the loyalty training, she was a difficult cadet. Manipulative. She stretched the rules, tested limits. Plus she's stubborn. Unmovable when she sets her mind to something."

"Perhaps she's always been a Saricean agent then?"

Bayis was thinking out loud—he didn't intend the question as an insult—but it cruised too close to Rykus's flight path anyway. He'd spent four years of his life on Caruth, training cadets whose combined psyche and medical exams came back a hundred points higher than normal. He schooled them in martial arts, taught them to fire every weapon in the Fighting Corps' arsenal, and made them experts in tech-apps, systems engineering, cryptography, and hack-sig. He and the other instructors on Caruth had weeded out the cadets who couldn't handle the pressure and those who had questionable moral compasses. They were all damn good at their jobs, but a few anomalies slipped through the other instructors' filters. The Senate Intelligence Committee had insisted on the loyalty training. They'd wanted dependable soldiers and a guarantee that their investments wouldn't snap or go rogue.

They'd wanted a fail-safe.

"I don't think so." He should get a medal for his even, controlled tone. It would have been more deserved than the last one he'd received. "Ash never hid her opinions. If she had a problem with something, she'd tell you, no matter how much you might want her to keep her mouth shut. That's why her behavior makes no sense. She's not talking, and that's not like her."

"You said she's manipulative."

"Yes," he said. "But I could always see through her charades. I know her, Admiral. I trained her. I spent two years learning her strengths, her weaknesses, her little quirks. She couldn't hide something like that from me."

Bayis's eyes snapped to his. "Fraternization between ranks is discouraged—"

"I know."

"And she's one of your anomalies. It would be more than discouraged between you. It would be—"

"There's nothing between us," Rykus bit out. He held Bayis's gaze until the admiral relaxed and turned back to the security vid.

Rykus looked at the vid too. There had never been anything between him and Ramie Ashdyn, and not just because a relationship would have resulted in a court martial. No, he knew better than to get involved with Ash because Ash played games. She was an unrepentant tease. It had taken him months to find the woman she kept hidden behind her flirtations, but eventually he had found her. She wasn't a traitor. At least, she hadn't been.

Now?

He watched Ash stare at the gravy dripping off the edge of the data-table. Now he didn't know what he believed.

When Ash's guard and the medic approached the cell's door, Bayis stepped forward and entered a code into the console beneath the screen. The door slid open, allowing the two men to exit the cell. A minute later, they emerged from the corridor. The admiral acknowledged their salutes then waited until they left before speaking.

"Oh two hundred on the sixth," he said, keeping his voice low. "Operation Star Dive is a go."

The only outward reaction Rykus gave to those words was a small nod, but his insides felt pelted by bullets. After months of political posturing, gambles, and deals, the Senate Intelligence Committee had finally come to a decision. They'd given a go date. In three days, Rykus would lead a contingent of soldiers in a daring, deadly assault on an enemy shipyard. In three days, the Coalition and the Sariceans would be at war.

"She could save lives?" Bayis asked.

Rykus followed his gaze back to Ash.

"Many lives," he said. He hadn't shared the exact projections with Bayis. Rykus was in charge of the *Obsidian's* Fighting Corps so it was his burden to bear, full gravity, not the admiral's, but the numbers haunted him. Blowing up the shipyard was the easy part of the mission. It was the second phase that would be costly. I-Com wanted Rykus and a select group of soldiers to take over a nearly complete Saricean warship and bring it back to Coalition space.

In one piece.

The last time Rykus had taken over an enemy vessel...

No. Going back to the past wouldn't do him any good. He had to focus on the present and on the future. And if he wanted the majority of his soldiers to make it through the mission alive, he needed the Saricean files decrypted. They contained the schematics for the shipyard. Intel gave him and his men a general idea of what to expect when they arrived, but experience told him general wasn't good enough. A corridor with three doors instead of two could be the difference between life and death. He needed details, and the key to getting them was shackled in the *Obsidian's* brig.

"Are we certain she changed the cipher?" he asked Bayis.

"None of our algorithms fit the digital signature, and Colonel Evers said she never denied the accusation."

"Evers? How did he capture her?"

Bayis's lip twitched into a smile. Evers was Fighting Corps, but even the admiral knew the man was an idiot, an idiot who had his sights set on a political appointment to I-Com.

"She didn't fight his men when they boarded."

"What?" Rykus bit out.

"She didn't resist arrest."

That didn't make sense. If Ash had killed her teammates and had time to re-encrypt the files, she would have tried to escape before she was escorted onto the *Anthem*, the ship that had brought her and her deceased teammates back to Coalition space. The fact that she hadn't meant...

"She wants to be here," he murmured.

His murmur was, apparently, loud and clear enough for the admiral to hear.

"Two escape attempts suggest otherwise. Evers said they almost lost her just before they rendezvoused with us. She took down three of her security detail, nearly killed a fourth."

"They underestimated her."

"Yes." Bayis turned to face him fully. "I'm putting you directly in charge of her security. I know the myths surrounding anomalies are exaggerated, but the enlisted ranks are superstitious. I don't want her guards getting trigger-happy if she tries something again."

And she *would* try something again, Rykus was sure of that.

"What's the ETA on the interrogator?"

"He's coming on the war chancellor's shuttle with the crypties and a medical specialist from Caruth. They should be docking soon." The admiral paused and his brow furrowed as he studied Rykus again. "You think the interrogator can get the cipher in time?"

"I think he'll have a better chance of getting it than the crypties will have of breaking in."

"They're not here to decrypt the files," Bayis said. "They're here for you."

Rykus resisted the urge to pinch the headache growing between his eyes. The two crypties—Cryptologic and Information Warfare specialists—would be part of his assault team. Their job was to infect the Saricean ship—one which might possibly be equipped with new weapon or defense capabilities—with a data-virus that would give the Coalition control of navigation and enviro. The pair was supposedly the best in Coalition space, but Rykus had glanced at their bios. They'd been transferred too many times to be the best. Most likely, they were adequate and dispensable.

He just hoped they had combat training.

"I'll meet with them tonight." He turned back to look at Ash, who still hadn't touched the slop of food dripping off the table. "I want to read through her file again, see if anything seems atypical." Atypical for Ash, at least. "Maybe I can pinpoint when her aberrant behavior began."

"Would it help to use someone close to her for leverage? Threaten them?" Bayis waved the comm-cuff fastened around his wrist over the sensor in the wall console, then typed in his security code. "I believe the addendum to her file mentioned a fiancé."

Rykus was damn lucky the admiral wasn't looking at him. If he had been, he would have seen Rykus's mask shatter for an instant as cold, hard shock knocked him off-orbit.

"Yes. Here it is," Bayis said. "His name is Jevan Valt, a legislative assistant for the senator from Rimmeria. Record says they met last year. He put in a notice of pending marriage about two months ago with his employer—it's required by the senate—but he withdrew it after Ashdyn's arrest. He doesn't think he revealed any classified information, but he's working with Coalition investigators to be sure."

Rykus yanked an invisible blade free from his gut. It never should have wedged itself in there to begin with. Ash had never been his—had never been anyone's—and it was best that way. But maybe that's what bothered him. He never thought she'd allow herself to be shackled to any man. This Valt character couldn't have known Ash at all if he thought she'd settle into a marriage. His cadet wasn't wife material.

And his cadet wasn't a traitor.

Rykus's headache throbbed again. This time he did reach up to pinch the bridge of his nose.

Treason. The word cut like shrapnel. He didn't want to believe it. He'd rather Ash be certifiably insane. The loyalty training was supposed to prevent that, but the program was only four years old. It was possible it hadn't solved the problem with anomalies, and if it didn't and Ash's mind had broken, she would be sent back to Caruth for evaluation at the institute.

Rykus dropped his hand to his side. "Who's the medical spec—"

The admiral held up a finger and tilted his head, listening to someone on the voice-link looped around his right ear.

"Yes," Bayis said. "Yes. Good. I'll meet him in my office." He focused on Rykus again. "The war chancellor's shuttle just docked. I need to brief him on Lieutenant Ashdyn and our preparations for Star Dive. He'll want to speak to you as well."

Rykus locked his jaw shut.

"He'll *insist* on speaking with you," Bayis said. "He came all the way from Meryk to make sure this operation goes smoothly."

"I don't have time to waste on that politician."

"Commander." There was no rebuke in Bayis's tone. He knew Rykus's opinion of Chancellor Hagan. After the infamous hearings three years ago, nearly everyone in the Coalition did.

"I have Ash's records to review, two crypties to brief, an assault plan to triple-check, and I need to meet with Brookins to make sure he isn't having issues with the excess crap I've delegated to him."

"Your XO can handle it." Bayis turned toward the brig's exit.

Rykus walked with him past the security desk then out into the *Obsidian's* gray-and-white corridor. He almost tripped over a broken sensor box. *Utilitarian* is how fleet described this ship. If they meant she was useful as a salvage ship, Rykus would agree, but he had his doubts as to whether the ship would hold together under fire. Multiple ceiling panels hung open, spilling the *Obsidian's* innards into the air.

Rykus ducked beneath a tangled mess of wire. "You sure she's going to be operational in three days?"

"She's not that complicated a ship," Bayis said, a tight pinch in his voice.

Rykus snorted at that. The *Obsidian* was an ugly box with bulky engines, bulky weapons systems, and most importantly, bulky, outdated computer systems. The latter was the reason they'd pulled the ship out of a museum—a physical, dirt-anchored *museum*—and were retrofitting her for Star Dive. The war council had decided to send an old, brainless warship into the Sariceans' territory so the enemy wouldn't be able to ransack the systems of the Coalition's newest, sleekest sentient-class ships.

The plan would be called genius if it worked. If it didn't work...

Well, Rykus would most likely be dead if the plan failed. The war and the future of the Coalition would be someone else's problem.

He and Bayis walked past the loud *clank, clank, clank* of a spacer pounding a wall panel back into place; then they stepped into the *Obsidian's* central lift. Gears ground as it fought the artificial gravity. Rykus glanced at the admiral, but Bayis kept his attention focused on the lift's oil-smeared door.

"You could always turn the gravity off," Rykus suggested.

Bayis's eyebrows lowered a small, almost imperceptible fraction. He waited until the lift doors groaned open before he responded to Rykus's comment. "I'll be sure to tell the war chancellor you're looking forward to meeting with him."

If Rykus hadn't had a mother lode of responsibilities weighing him down, he might have laughed. Instead, he acknowledged Bayis's victory with a nod that said point-to-you.

They parted ways, and Rykus walked half the length of the ship—not a quick jaunt—before he stopped in the middle of a cross-corridor. He wanted to hole up in his quarters with Ash's file, but if he did, he'd pass out. He hadn't slept in well over twenty-four hours, not since he'd learned what Ash had done.

What Ash had *allegedly* done.

He needed a good shot of energy to make it through the rest of his shift. He could take the lift down to the *Obsidian's* gym, work off some excess tension until he cleared his head, or he could pump himself full of caffeine in the officer mess hall. The noise and the conversation of the latter might be a good distraction, so he hooked a right turn at the cross-corridor —

And nearly ran into a face from his past.

CHAPTER
THREE

K ATIE?" HE SAID, making her name a low rumble to disguise his surprise.

"Commander Rykus." She didn't look at the curious spacers who glanced their way. He did. He glared until they continued on with their business, then he turned his attention back to the woman he'd almost married.

"What are you doing here?" he asked. Then he noticed her med-sack and grimaced. The medical specialist from Caruth. She'd come on the war chancellor's shuttle and was here to evaluate Ash. He should have been prepared for the possibility she would arrive.

"I was summoned." She kept her tone professionally neutral. Obviously, Katie had been prepared to see him.

He dug through his memories for something to say, but they were buried beneath too many layers of numbers and tactics and training-sims. He couldn't push the upcoming mission from his mind any more than he could push away Ash's alleged betrayal.

"I didn't know you'd made medical specialist," he said, settling on the first safe topic that came to mind.

"I was promoted two years ago." Katie smiled. It was a pretty smile, one any man would beg to see on her lips, but there was something hesitant about it too, something pensive.

Had it been that long since he'd spoken to her? They'd separated—more accurately, Katie had left him—three weeks after Ash's class of anomalies graduated. He'd been immersed in training and testing the two years they'd dated. He hadn't had time to focus on a relationship that had been falling apart for months.

"I should have called," he said.

"I wouldn't have answered."

He took the punch without comment. He deserved it. Katie Monick was a beautiful woman. Intelligent. Compassionate. *Passionate*. He hadn't treated her right, hadn't given her enough attention.

A moment of silence stretched, became awkward. She seemed to be waiting for him to say something, but he didn't know what she wanted to hear. When he didn't speak, she sighed, and when her chest rose and fell, the overhead lighting reflected off her insignia.

"Well, a belated congratulations then. The promotion was well deserved."

She shrugged. "I decided to focus on my career after we… Well, I decided to focus on my career."

"That's good. Very good."

Hell. He'd dated this woman for two years. He should be able to carry on a better conversation than this, but he was exhausted, frustrated with Ash, and worried about Operation Star Dive. He wasn't at the top of his game.

"Yes." Katie stepped to the side of the corridor so a few spacers could pass more easily. "Things are going well. How are your soldiers?"

So that's how it was going to be, a slip back into an old habit. The last few months they were together, all they could find to talk about was their work. He'd talked in vague terms about his cadets; she'd talked in vague terms about her patients.

"They're fine." They were fine today. In three days? Computer models said up to forty percent of them would be dead.

Unless Ash gave him the cipher.

"You've read the anomaly's file?" he asked Katie.

She shook her head. "It's classified. I didn't get it until we docked."

Then she wouldn't have a preliminary assessment of Ash's mental state. He wanted someone to tell him he hadn't missed something important during

Ash's training. If he missed something with Ash, he might have missed it with others. The training the anomalies received and the booster they injected biweekly gave them the capability to kill and destroy with remarkable efficiency. Even with the loyalty training, Rykus and the other instructors were careful about who they accepted into the program. They didn't want the wrong man or woman to graduate and join the ranks of the Fighting Corps.

He felt Katie studying him. When he looked up, some of the stiffness in her posture melted away.

"You're not personally responsible for every anomaly you've trained."

He was responsible for this one. The loyalty training hadn't taken hold of Ash like it had the other recruits, but he'd thought her smirking, her bending of rules and regulations, was just one of the many quirks the soldiers sent to him so often had. Every cadet who'd been under his command was a little crazy, a little off in some way. All anomalies were.

Exhaustion pulled down on his shoulders. He forced himself to straighten. "I was heading to the officers' mess. Join me for coffee?"

Katie hesitated. "I need to read Ashdyn's file."

"And you'll need to interview her fail-safe."

Again, she gave him a slightly sad smile, but she nodded and turned left toward the lift that would take them up a level to the mess hall. The doors slid open when they approached. He gestured Katie inside. As he followed her in, he took note of the curves beneath her snugly fitted uniform and the blond hair that—as per regulation—she'd twisted into a long, loose braid.

"It's good to see you again," he said.

She turned so quickly he almost ran into her. "Don't," she said. "It's not fair."

"Fair?"

The doors slid shut behind them.

"My feelings for you never changed, Rhys."

"Neither did mine."

"I know." She closed her eyes briefly, then let out a sigh. "That was the problem. I thought they would after a while, but… well, they didn't. All I ever was to you was a pleasant distraction."

"You were much more than that, Katie."

She shrugged. "A good friend then. A sister."

He almost choked. "We slept together."

"I know," she said pointedly.

He was about to object again when the lift doors slid open. A pair of spacers stepped aside so they could exit. Now wasn't the time or the place for this discussion. Besides, maybe she had a point. Maybe she had been only a distraction to him. He'd sometimes needed one after dealing with anomalies all day. He sure as hell had needed one after dealing with Ash.

Off-duty spacers and soldiers crowded the room. A few men and women acknowledged his presence with a nod, but most were absorbed in conversations or focused on the wide screens that played vids of the latest news reports from around the Known Universe. When Javery, Rykus's home world, appeared behind a reporter with a marquee that read KU Breaking News, he focused all his attention on finding a table.

Katie eyed him as she sank into a chair near the rear wall. "The Coalition isn't going to be able to convince Javery to join, is it?"

"Not with my father whispering in the prime minister's ear."

"Has the senate asked you to speak to him?"

He grunted out an affirmative, then tapped on the table to bring up the menu.

"*Have* you spoken to him?" she asked.

"Once or twice."

"Once or twice in the past few months? Or the past few years?"

He looked up from the menu. "He wants the Coalition to fail, and he tried to sabotage my career."

"He apologized—"

"Only after he thought I'd been killed. Caruthian brew?"

Katie pinched her mouth shut at the abrupt subject change. Then she relaxed and said, "With *radda* leaf."

"You have capsule sickness?" he asked, his tone softening. Most people could traverse the universe on a tachyon capsule without a problem as long as they didn't move when the capsule entered and exited the time-bend, but Katie had never been one of those individuals.

"The leaf will help," she said.

So would sleep and electrolytes, but he dutifully keyed in her order and requested the same, minus the leaf, for himself. A *bleep* acknowledged his request and confirmed a debit from the account linked to his comm-cuff.

"You've spoken with Ashdyn?" Katie asked.

"Yes," he said. Then he added, "It didn't work."

He didn't have to explain what "it" was. The only reason Ash was on board the *Obsidian* was because he was her fail-safe and should have been able to command her compliance. It was merely convenient that he was also the officer in charge of the assault on the shipyard.

A groove formed between Katie's eyebrows. "No one told me she'd snapped."

"She isn't acting like she has," he said. "Admiral Bayis thinks the Sariceans broke her loyalty training."

"They broke—" Katie cut off her words when a squat metal box on wheels rolled up with their order. Rykus passed Katie her coffee and cupped his own steaming mug between his hands, letting it heat his palms. When the bot retreated, Katie said, "You can't break the loyalty training without breaking her mind."

"She isn't showing any signs of snapping."

"She inexplicably murdered her team," Katie said. "I'd say that's a sign."

"The Sariceans could have gotten to her before she came to Caruth." He pulled his coffee mug closer. "Maybe they found a way to prevent the loyalty training from taking hold."

Katie stirred the steaming black liquid in her mug with a straw and studied him. He met her blue eyes, kept his expression rigid and stony.

"You think she's innocent." She sat back in her chair and chewed on her lower lip.

"She's not denying the evidence."

"But you don't believe it," she said.

Honestly, he didn't know what he believed. The evidence was irrefutable. It would be crazy not to see that it all pointed to Ash, but maybe that's what bothered him. It was too obvious, and Ash wasn't careless. If she truly was a Saricean agent, she would have covered her tracks. She knew how. If she would just explain her behavior or tell him she was framed, he might believe her. He'd at least try to help. So why the hell wouldn't she talk to him?

"I don't think she's snapped," he said. By default, that made Ash a traitor. His words and the unspoken conclusion hung between them.

"Her mental breakdown could have been temporary. I'll be able to tell you more after I evaluate her." She took the straw out of her coffee and set it aside. A few seconds later, she said, "They still talk about you on Caruth. Your tap-out rate hasn't been broken yet."

He acknowledged her words with a grunt, then took a sip of his drink, letting it burn down his throat. He'd had a talent for identifying the cadets who would walk to the data-con in front of the barracks, tap in their ID-sigs, and quit the training program. Roughly two percent of the population of the Known Universe was identified as anomalies each year. Out of those, less than one percent agreed to travel to Caruth and let themselves be brainwashed into obeying the commands of a stranger. And out of that one percent, very few were women. That's why there'd been so much pressure from the intelligence committee to pass Ash. No woman had ever completed the training, and they yearned for an anomaly with one more weapon in her arsenal.

Ash was exactly what they desired: beautiful, lethal, and supremely intelligent. More importantly, she was willing to submit to the loyalty training. Only the desperate agreed to go through that terror and give up their free will.

Was Ash desperate enough to commit treason? She was from Glory. Few people survived on that planet without losing their souls.

"How's the new instructor working out?" He took a long draught of his coffee and let the bitter liquid chase away all thoughts of his cadet.

CHAPTER

FOUR

THE SLEEP-SLAB WAS HARD and lumpy, and the transparent blanket too thin for Ash to sleep well. She tried resting on her side so she could use her arms as a pillow, but the metal support beams hurt her hip, and her cuffs dug grooves into her wrists. They didn't want her to be comfortable. Probably didn't want her to get much sleep at all.

She must have drifted off for at least a few minutes though. When she became aware of her surroundings again, she felt somebody watching her. She knew it was Rykus by the smell of his aftershave, but she kept her eyes closed and focused on recapturing the elusive memories from her dream.

Jevan, her deceitful, manipulative farce of a fiancé, shouldn't have stepped onto her team's shuttle—he shouldn't have been carrying a gun and grinning—and for the first time in her life, Ash had frozen. She didn't think that was possible, to be struck immobile by fear. Maybe she'd still been rattled from the stun grenade the boarders had thrown into the shuttle, but she'd let him approach. It still hadn't clicked—she hadn't made all the connections, not until Jevan picked up the comm-cuff that held the stolen data she'd re-encrypted.

Jevan's presence wasn't a coincidence. Jevan was an enemy.

A spy.

A telepath.

And Trevast hadn't been joking. He'd *known*.

Cheerfully, Jevan had duplicated the Sariceans' files, but his smile disappeared when he discovered he couldn't access the data. He'd turned to her and demanded the cipher. Ash had glanced at her team lead, but Trevast had shaken his head. A second later, Jevan put a bullet between his eyes.

There were more bullets, more threats, a plea for his life from the youngest member in her squad. She'd almost given Jevan the key then, but Chakin— for two minutes her commanding officer—ordered her to keep silent. Jevan turned, raised his gun again, and Chakin's brains scattered across the dura-steel tiles.

The dream, the memory, blurred after that. She remembered her ears ringing and the room spinning as her fiancé took her face between his gloved hands. She remembered him looking into her eyes as he'd done a hundred times before, but this time, the gaze was different. This time, it was penetrating.

She'd fallen to her knees. She felt his touch and heard his voice, but didn't understand his words. Something *moved* in her mind, and despite all her training, she was helpless.

But Jevan wasn't able to rip the cipher from her mind. She knew that only because he was pissed when the CSS *Anthem* came within scanner range. He'd grabbed her by the hair, dragged her toward the docking tube. At the last moment, she'd recovered enough of her senses to fight, to shove him out of the shuttle and seal the emergency-tube hatch, then she'd crawled back to her comrades with Jevan screaming profanities in her mind.

"The rate of your breathing has changed, Ash. You're awake."

Rykus's voice pulled her out of the memory. She opened her eyes to slits. "You getting off watching me sleep, Rip?"

A part of her hated to provoke him, but she had no choice. If he stayed— if he forced her to give him the cipher—the Coalition would gain access to the Sariceans' files and to the information that would rip the Coalition apart. Ash wouldn't let that happen. The KU needed the Coalition, and she'd vowed to preserve and protect it.

"Get up." Rykus leaned against the data-table in the center of the room and crossed his arms over his chest. The dark gray dress-downs he wore didn't disguise his physique; it accentuated his biceps and the powerful muscles in his shoulders. He was fully capable of hauling her ass out of bed.

"We could have more fun over here."

Maybe she should have lifted her blanket or patted the sleep-slab to make her point. His eyes didn't narrow and his strong jaw didn't clench. Not good. She'd have to be even more forward to get to him. She didn't want to go that far. She'd reined in her behavior since she'd graduated—Trevast just hadn't been as fun to torment as Rip. Plus, Trevast and the rest of the guys were like brothers to her, and it was somewhat awkward to flirt with family around.

They *had* been like brothers to her. She fought back the anguish threatening to cloud her mind.

"Get up. Now," Rykus ordered.

Next time, he'd *command* her compliance. She was surprised he hadn't stormed in and immediately done so. Surprised and a little dismayed. He was treating her as if she were still his cadet. The instructors on Caruth had a code: they respected the anomalies' right to free will, only using compulsion if they had to. Rykus shouldn't be extending that courtesy to her now though, not after the way she'd treated him yesterday.

She sat up and turned toward him, letting her long legs dangle over the edge of the sleep-slab. The room spun when she did, and she felt a not-so-gentle pressure at the base of her skull. Her hands and feet prickled, but just as quickly as they came, the sensations vanished.

"You can talk to me or you can talk to the interrogator. He's waiting outside."

She focused on Rykus again and hid her anxiety behind a half grin. That drew a reaction. His lips tightened just perceptibly. They were nice lips even though they didn't smile often. Soft too, she imagined. It was a shame they'd never kissed, but Rykus wasn't one to violate protocol.

"Come here." He turned to tap in a command on the data-table.

Damn, his back was tempting—for a number of reasons, actually—but she wasn't going to attack her fail-safe. The loyalty training discouraged it.

He threw a glare over his shoulder. "I said come here."

Apprehension coiled in her stomach. He was too in control of himself. The compulsion would work if he used it, and once it took hold, his next orders would be all but impossible to resist. Ash had to set him off.

"Are you married, Commander?" She tilted her head and let her long bangs fall across her cheek.

"You don't know when to stop, do you?" His tone was even, unaffected. Hell, maybe she *had* lost her touch.

She raised her cuffed hands—damn, her wrists were sore—in a semi-innocent gesture. "What? I just want to know if you're available."

He moved fast, grabbing her arm and yanking her off the sleep-slab. Her neck popped from the whiplash, then she was shoved facedown over the data-table. Her nose pressed against an image of Trevast's corpse.

She tried to move away, but Rykus held her down. Trevast's body was more real than the one from her dream. She could almost smell it, could almost feel the blood congealing between her fingers.

"This is cruel, Rip." She hated the way her voice cracked.

He pressed down on the back of her head, preventing her from turning away. "You don't want to see your handiwork? I thought you'd enjoy it. They found you bathing in their blood."

Her heart hurt, physically hurt. Back on the shuttle, she'd crawled across the slick floor to Trevast. He'd still been breathing, still been able to talk, to tell her not to decrypt the files for anyone. *Will destroy the Coalition*, he'd said. Then he'd grabbed her shirt and whispered, *Fashions. Fight.*

Trevast's mind had been muddled by his impending death. He'd merged together their previous argument over her not-quite-regulation camouflage and an order for her to fight. She'd demanded *he* fight, and she had tried to save him. She would have saved all of them if there'd been a way, but the others were already dead, and he was too weak. He'd lost too much blood.

Rykus's grip on her neck tightened. "He had a family. You met his wife, even gave his five-year-old son a present for his birthday last month. That's what Lydia said when she was told you killed her husband."

The table image changed, and she stared into the glazed eyes of Kris Menchan. *Kris.*

"He was the newest member of your team," Rykus continued. "He graduated three months ago. You were his mentor. Taught him a lot of the things I taught you: how to drop-kill surveillance systems, how to subdue captives. But you didn't teach him how to avoid a knife in the back, did you?"

"Go to hell, Rip."

Ash wouldn't cry. She *never* cried.

She managed to twist enough to hook her left foot around his ankle. She kicked forward, forcing him to shift to maintain his balance, then she dropped her shoulder and slipped out from under him.

Rykus's time away from Caruth hadn't diminished his ability to kick ass. He evaded her spin kick and the fist she aimed at his chin. Her next move slipped through his defense, but only because he allowed it. He took the blow on his chin, then used his close proximity to swing the blade of his right hand into her shoulder, sending a jolt of sharp pain from her neck to her lower back.

Her knees gave out. She rolled when she hit the ground, but Rykus didn't pursue her.

"On your feet," he ordered.

She complied but circled away from him, giving her body a few seconds to recover. She'd sparred with him before, but never when she felt like this: angry, frustrated, and burning with the need to beat the ever-living hell out of something.

"Did you betray them for money?" he demanded. "You were close to bankrupt two weeks ago. Now you have a year's salary in your account. Did the Sariceans pay you?"

Rage scalded her veins. She wanted to tell him where he could shove his accusation, but she'd tried to tell others the truth, that she lived on very few credits each month and sent the excess money back to her home world. She'd blacked out before she spoke a syllable of the explanation, and the investigators hadn't been able to trace the money. None of it ended up in legitimate bank accounts. She sent it to Glory's precinct bosses. It was bribe money. She paid the bosses to leave the Coalition's humanitarian aid workers alone.

Those aid workers had saved her life and her soul. Ash did everything in her power to do the same.

Rykus took a step forward, stopping beneath the not-quite-hidden security camera in the ceiling. He must have noticed when she glanced up because he shook his head.

"It's not going to happen, Ash. I ordered them to stay out."

She suppressed a grimace. He knew her too well. She'd never get off the *Obsidian* with him supervising her imprisonment. But she would try. She and all the other Caruth-trained anomalies didn't know how to give up.

"They'll come in if I drop you."

His laugh was short, mocking. "You're good, but I know all your moves. You'll never be able to take me hand to hand."

Ash refused to acknowledge the truth in those words. Trevast had told her to fight. The order might have been shrouded in the confusion of his impending death, but she intended to carry it out. She wouldn't let the stolen files destroy the Coalition she'd sworn to preserve and protect.

She let Rykus approach even though it was foolish to let him get close. She landed a few punches, got one solid kick through his defenses, but he was too strong, too experienced to damage. He knew her weaknesses, knew she was limited in her moves by her restraints, and he was too damn perfect to make a mistake.

He didn't pound her face in like he could have—like he probably should have—but he slammed her to the floor and pinned her arms over her head.

She stared defiantly into his eyes. "Congratulations, Commander."

"You think I enjoyed this?" he demanded. The way he held her wrists made her restraints dig into her raw and swollen skin.

"You've been waiting for an excuse to take me down for years."

"Tell me what happened on that shuttle."

She shook her head. He shook her.

"Tell me!"

When she refused a second time, she expected to be jostled again, but his grip on her loosened, the anger whooshed out of him, and his body relaxed against hers. She realized a moment too late what would happen next.

"Did you execute your team?"

His tone and cadence were perfect. The loyalty training slithered through her body, and a familiar warmth surged in her bloodstream. Her veins felt foreign, like they were strings extracted from a puppet, and she had no choice but to speak the truth.

But she couldn't. Something else seized her—a different compulsion, a different command—and an indescribable panic settled in her chest.

Ash couldn't comply with both orders.

She *had* to comply with both.

Her vision blurred, and when she opened her mouth to tell Rykus she hadn't killed her teammates, the only sound that came from her lips was a scream.

CHAPTER

FIVE

RYKUS RELEASED HIS CADET, arms raised as if he'd just blown his cover on an op, but as soon as he let go, Ash's fingertips dug into her temples. He hovered at her side, stunned, until her screams faded and the seizure began.

He gave her more space, his heart free-falling into his stomach. He hadn't pressed an attack during the fight, only deflected her punches and kicks. Nothing looked broken, but her back arched and her arms flailed at her sides. When she slammed her head into the ground, then into the leg of the data-table, he gathered her into his arms.

"Medic!" he shouted at the room, holding her tight. "Shh, Ash. It's okay. I've got you. I've got you. It's okay."

Her tremors turned into trembles, tiny shudders that were vaguely familiar. He remembered holding her when she'd stumbled inside his office one cold night on Caruth. He had ordered her to sit outside and count stars. She'd been pressing her luck for too long and he'd finally had enough. While there were a million things he could have punished Ash for—her flippant speech, her lackadaisical attitude, her open flirtation with him—he'd lost his temper over the most simple, stupid transgression: her hair. She'd shown up late after a weekend leave, and her wavy locks, soft and shining in the artificial lights, had spilled over her shoulders.

He should have ignored the infraction because, once he confronted her, she knew it was the perfect way to shatter his composure. She insisted on wearing her hair any way she liked. He insisted on her following regulation and braiding it. Since Ash and the other cadets hadn't been put in the psyche-mask yet, he'd ordered her out into the night. She remained there for hours, long after a blizzard covered the compound in ice. The weather had turned early. He hadn't realized it until, half-frozen, she'd shuddered her way into his office, not repentant *per se*, but much less blatantly insolent. He'd wrapped his arms around her, warming her with his body heat while he called for a medic. After that her protests became smaller, more measured. From that point on, she'd pulled back her hair, but she'd twisted only that small, almost-hidden portion of it into a braid.

He let that braid slide through his fingers now as he rocked her, and finally, her eyes fluttered open.

"Hey," he said, going still.

She swallowed, focused on him, and swallowed again. "I'm so fucked, Rip."

"Tell me how to help." He brushed hair damp with sweat from her forehead, then let his fingers trail down her cheek, smooth except for a red welt beneath her right eye, probably from when she hit the table. She had a beauty mark to the left of her mouth. Rykus had always been tempted to run his thumb over it—he thought it too strategically placed to be real—but he wouldn't let himself touch it now. It seemed… inappropriate.

"Just… go away." Ash's tone was halfway between a plea and an order.

"That's how you want me to help?" He slid his hand down her arm.

She nodded.

He wanted to ask again if she had killed her teammates, but he hated using compulsion, hated it so much he'd left the anomaly program because of it. And what if she seized again? He didn't want to hurt her.

Searching her eyes, he looked for more answers. This close, he could see a touch of hazel in the green irises. She seemed to be focusing better. Color was returning to her cheeks too, but she looked vulnerable without her signature half smile.

The clank of the door unlocking drew his attention. It slid open and Katie entered the cell. She set her med-sack on the data-table. When she lifted an eyebrow his direction, Rykus became all too aware he was still holding Ash in his arms.

"She had a seizure," he explained, shifting Ash's weight so he could get them both on their feet. He half carried her to the chair on the other side of the table, then took a step back and frowned. It wasn't like Ash to let herself be helped with anything, not without some wisecrack or brazen remark. Even after the Dead Man's Circuit through Caruth's sunbaked mountains, she'd reserved enough breath to suggest skinny-dipping with him in the Liera River.

Katie opened her med-sack, took out a bio-band, then bent down to strap the device to Ash's ankle.

"Chief medical specialist," Ash said, her voice raspy. "I'm moving up in the world."

Katie straightened. "I'm Dr. Monick. I just arrived from Caruth."

Ash started what might have been a nod but cut it short. He saw something move through her eyes—a hint of fear maybe—then she dropped her gaze to the data-table. "I haven't snapped, Doctor."

Ah, the institute. Anomalies would do anything to avoid being sent back there. That's where the Coalition hooked them up to machines and brainwashed them into being loyal, and that's where they would return if they lost their holds on reality. No anomaly wanted to become an experiment, but the whole KU knew the damage they could do if they snapped. The last time it had happened had been back before the loyalty training, and twenty-six people, mostly women and children, had been slaughtered on the shopping deck of a civilian tachyon capsule.

A few days ago, Ash had inexplicably slaughtered her team.

Rykus looked at his cadet, saw her staring off at nothing. He was supposed to cull the individuals who couldn't take the mental pressure. Had he overlooked Ash's signs of stress?

Katie took out a tablet and stylus, then tapped on the screen. "Your vitals match the ones taken yesterday. Everything looks good. Perfect really, except for your superficial injuries." She paused. "Your previous medic didn't note the swelling under your right eye or the bruises on your arms."

"She hit her head when she seized," Rykus said. The bruises, he suspected, were his fault. He hadn't been gentle when he'd deflected her attacks.

"When was your last booster, Lieutenant?" Katie asked.

Ash leaned back in her chair and settled her shackled hands in her lap. Something in her demeanor made Rykus uneasy. If Ash had snapped—or even if she hadn't and was, instead, a traitor—Katie was standing too close. Ash could lash out with a kick strong and accurate enough to break a person's neck.

He took Katie's arm and moved her out of striking range.

Ash noticed, and the first sign of a smile tugged at the corner of her mouth.

She turned her attention back to Katie. "A week before my last assignment. So, around ten days, I guess."

Katie transferred her frown from him to Ash. "Your last assignment *ended* ten days ago."

Ash blinked a few times. After a long pause, she asked, "How long was I on the *Anthem*?"

"Eight days," Rykus answered. "You don't remember?"

Commander Evers's report said the *Anthem* had boarded Ash's shuttle twelve hours after her team began their mission. The warship then rendezvoused with the *Obsidian* twenty-five hours ago, and Ash had been transferred here. If she'd injected the booster a week before her last mission, it had been almost twenty days since she'd had it.

When Ash didn't say anything else, Katie asked, "Are you having any headaches? Any blurred vision?"

Ash still didn't answer; she just sat there staring with an apathetic look on her face. It was the expression Rykus taught his cadets to adopt if they were captured and questioned by an enemy.

"This isn't an interrogation," he told her. "She's trying to help."

Another long blink, then Ash rolled her eyes toward him. "I know."

Katie pursed her lips. "I think it's too soon for you to be experiencing withdrawal symptoms, but I'll have a booster sent up."

Could that be what this was? The bimonthly injections curbed mental and physical fatigue. They made anomalies stronger and quicker than the average soldier. They made them heal faster. The Coalition would have fed the drugs to all its enlisted men and women, but normal humans couldn't take them. They seized and, if they didn't get immediate medical attention, they fell into comas. Anomalies were different though. Their bodies handled the chemicals, and though the injections didn't make them superhuman, they certainly gave them an edge.

They'd give Ash an edge over most of the *Obsidian's* crew and over his soldiers. The latter would be assaulting a Saricean shipyard in less than three days.

The ship's gravity pressed down on his shoulders, and his chest felt tight. No matter how much watching Ash seize had bothered him, he had a duty to the men and women under his command. He had to do whatever it took to bring as many of them back alive as possible.

"No," Rykus said. "No booster."

Katie tapped something into her tablet. "You're not in charge of her care, Commander."

"Thank God," Ash muttered.

He fought the temptation to turn a cold, hard glare on his cadet. Instead, he kept his gaze on Katie. "I'm in charge of her security. I won't risk her escaping."

Katie glanced up from her tablet. "And I won't risk her health."

"A few more days isn't going to kill her."

"If she's already experiencing withdrawal symptoms," she said, her blue gaze unwavering, "it might."

It wouldn't. Anomalies might be addicted to the drugs, but every one of them should be able to make it three or four weeks without serious complications. "I won't approve it, Dr. Monick."

Katie's chin jutted out slightly. Hell. She'd completely and thoroughly adopted Ash as her patient. Katie wouldn't back down easily. She could be damn stubborn when it came to anything medical.

"Then I'll go through Admiral Bayis," she said.

"*He* won't approve it."

Her eyes narrowed. She held his gaze for another few seconds, then reached up to click on her voice-link. "We'll see."

She left a message to speak to the admiral. In his peripheral vision, Rykus noticed Ash tilt her head to the side. He could practically hear her snap the pieces of a puzzle together.

"You two have a history together." A smile stretched across her face. "I thought I was the only woman for you, Commander."

He ignored her. Obviously she was feeling better.

Katie said nothing as she bent down to unstrap the bio-band from Ash's ankle. When she straightened, she frowned at Ash's shackled wrists.

"Not pretty, are they?" Ash commented.

Rykus took a step forward, saw they were swollen and purple.

"Not at all," Katie agreed. "How long have the restraints been on you?"

"Since I was detained."

Katie chewed on her lower lip, then turned to him. "Can you take the restraints off?"

He started to say he could, but something held him back. Ash's wrists shouldn't have been as swollen as they were. Tender and a little bruised? Okay. But this? No. This stunk of premeditation.

Nice try, Ash.

"You'll have to treat her with the cuffs on."

"Her wrists are so swollen the restraints are cutting off her circulation. If I don't treat her, and treat her properly, her hands are going to rot off."

"You really wouldn't want that, Rip." Ash's smile took on a seductive and suggestive edge.

Katie frowned. "Is this normal behavior for her?"

He should have let Ash bash her head into the table.

"Unfortunately, yes," he said. "Although she usually spreads out her... comments."

Ash swung her gaze to his. "*Flirtations*, Commander. I usually spread out my flirtations."

"She knows how to get under your skin." Katie let out a short, humorless laugh as she retrieved gauze and disinfectant from her med-sack. "Take off the restraints. I'm sure you can handle her."

"I'll loosen them, but they're not coming off." He kept his eyes on Ash as he pressed his thumb against the print-lock sensor. He wasn't overreacting. Ash might not try anything with him there, but if Katie or one of the medics fell for her tricks when he was gone…

He'd have to review the precautions listed in her file, maybe add a few more restrictions. He'd do it as soon as they were done here.

The mechanism connecting the cuffs unlatched. He fastened the security bracelets encircling her wrists to the locking devices in the arms of her chair, then loosened them one notch, which barely allowed them to slide over her swollen skin.

"I like her, Rip," Ash said.

He ignored her provocative grin, walked behind her chair, and stood, making sure she felt how close he was. Even if the Sariceans had somehow broken the loyalty training, Rykus was an imposing man. He'd cowed anomalies long before the Coalition decided the instructors should become fail-safes.

Katie pulled up the room's other chair. The door to the cell slid open, and Admiral Bayis entered.

"Sir," Katie said, halting her descent into the chair and straightening instead.

"You had a question, Doctor?" Bayis stopped beside the data-table.

"Yes, sir. Lieutenant Ashdyn suffered what appeared to be a seizure. Withdrawal from the booster could cause this. I want to give her an injection to see if it prevents another occurrence."

"She's had one episode?" Bayis asked.

"When you have no previous history of seizures, one is significant, sir."

Bayis glanced at him. "You're against it?"

"Completely," Rykus said, though that might have been stretching the truth. He didn't want Ash to seize again—he wanted her to get better—but the booster would give her strength and confidence. If he wanted the majority of his soldiers to return alive from Operation Star Dive, he needed that damn cipher.

"Then she doesn't get it," Bayis said.

Again, Katie's chin jutted out. "I treat anomalies every day. I'm capable of handling her."

"Rykus is in charge."

"But Admiral—"

"No." Bayis held her gaze to make his point. "Finish your evaluation, Doctor. The interrogator is ready to question her. Commander"—he turned to Rykus—"I'd like to speak with you outside."

Rykus nodded, then said to Katie, "Tighten those cuffs before you leave."

After one last glance at an all-too-innocent-looking Ash, Rykus followed Bayis out of the cell. In the room at the end of the corridor, a petty officer sat behind a desk, watching a wall full of security vids. Two guards were on duty as well, but it would take them half a minute to get to Ash's cell. An anomaly could wreak a lot of havoc in that amount of time.

"I take it the compulsion didn't work again," Bayis said.

"No." Rykus focused on the admiral. "She seized when I tried."

"Is that normal for an anomaly who has snapped?"

"Not exactly," he said. "The majority of unstable anomalies seized at some point, but as far as I know, compulsion didn't cause it."

"Could she have faked it?"

"Faked it? N—" He stopped. He remembered her scream, the way she'd shook in his arms, how she'd opened her eyes and focused on him as if he might be her savior. It all seemed genuine, but if he took himself out of the picture, considered her record, who and what she was, he had to hesitate. Ash was a chameleon. She knew what to do and say to get what she wanted from just about anyone.

Bayis turned. He didn't say anything, but the corners of his eyes crinkled.

That crinkle irritated the hell out of Rykus. "I'm not questioning your accusation just because she's a woman."

"I'm not suggesting—"

"You're thinking it. She was one of my cadets, Admiral. I'm her fail-safe. I have a responsibility to her just like I have a responsibility to every other anomaly I've trained, whether they've been brainwashed or not." He'd taken an oath to look out for their well-being. That's all he was doing. "But, yes, she could have faked it."

And if she had, it was looking more and more likely that she'd committed treason.

His hands clenched at his sides. Despite the evidence, that conclusion still didn't feel right.

After another weighted pause, Bayis said, "That's what I told War Chancellor Hagan, but he doesn't believe she's a traitor. He said the loyalty training is infallible and that she's snapped. He thinks we should send her to the institute and be done with it."

"He doesn't know a goddamn—"

"I know," Bayis said. "But he has the final say in what happens. When the interrogator is finished with her, she'll be transferred to Caruth, whether she's committed treason or lost her mind."

The thought of one of the Coalition's trained interrogators getting access to Ash made Rykus's stomach churn.

"What if there's a third option?"

Bayis stared at him, his expression unreadable. Rykus made sure his thoughts were hidden as well. It wasn't as easy as it should have been to do. Conflicting thoughts and theories and feelings ricocheted off each other. When he threw in the need to gain access to the Sariceans' files, it made his head one galactic mess of a place to live.

"I'm listening," Bayis finally said.

"Blackmail." Rykus put forth the first idea he latched onto. "Or she's protecting someone." That felt closer to the truth. "Or protecting something."

"You're grasping at stars."

"Something isn't right here."

"Perhaps you're looking too deeply for an explanation," Bayis said. "Sometimes the simplest explanation is the most accurate."

"Then why isn't she denying the charges? She isn't suicidal. There has to be a reason she's not answering our questions."

"No, Commander." Bayis turned away from the security vid. "There has to be a *way* she isn't answering *your* questions. A loyalty-trained anomaly shouldn't be able to ignore her fail-safe's orders."

The muscles in Rykus's back and neck tightened. He tried to make his body relax, but Bayis's words were true. She shouldn't be able to ignore him.

He'd screwed up, overlooked signs of her mental frailty or treasonous motives, and because of that, five good soldiers were dead.

And more would die soon if he didn't get access to those files.

Bayis drew in a deep breath, then let it out. "Maybe there is another explanation, but without evidence, we have to assume she's betrayed us." He paused, and Rykus saw the gravity of his next words in his eyes before he said them. "If it's proven that she hasn't snapped, Rykus, people will start mining deeper for an explanation. They'll stop asking her questions and will start asking you."

Rykus let out a sharp, short laugh. "Hagan's already starting the rumors, isn't he?"

Bayis's mouth flattened into a line that all but confirmed Rykus's words.

"Just give me some time before you send in the interrogator," he said. "I'll find answers."

The admiral turned away to face the security vid again. "I can give you three hours. Lieutenant Ashdyn is scheduled to capsule out at oh two hundred. You need to come up with an explanation before then."

CHAPTER

SIX

THE SLICK, COOL GEL the doctor painted over Ash's swollen wrists eased the pain. It would reduce the swelling too. In time. Time that Ash didn't have. Not with the interrogator ready to begin his work.

She glanced at the med-sack on the data-table. The name tape on the sack's side read K. Monick. The initial tapped against a compartment in Ash's mind.

Katie. She was almost certain that was the doctor's name. She'd heard it years ago on Caruth. Rykus had been canceling dinner plans because of "problems with the cadets." That wasn't the complete truth. That night, Ash had been the only cadet causing "problems."

"Is something funny, Lieutenant?" Katie asked.

"No, ma'am." Ash let her smile linger even as the doctor retightened her cuffs. Sometimes a smile was all that stood between Ash and despair.

Katie retrieved a blood-band from her med-sack, then wrapped it around the crook of Ash's right arm. "You still look at Commander Rykus with respect."

Ash gave the doctor her best if-I-did-it-was-an-accident expression.

"When he's not looking at you, of course," Katie continued. "I think it's difficult for you to disobey him."

Ash snorted. It was more difficult than she would ever admit.

"And if it's difficult for you to disobey him, then it's likely the loyalty training is still in place."

Ash wanted to nod so badly her right leg started jumping. She bit the inside of her cheek to keep her mouth shut and lowered her gaze to the floor. She couldn't say anything, not even something mundane or unrelated to Katie's unspoken question. The wrong word or inflection might send Ash into another blackout. Since she'd been arrested, she'd experimented with hundreds of words and phrases, thousands maybe. Some of them barely made any sense at all, but the result of trying to speak the truth was always the same. Her blackouts weren't triggered by what she said. As near as she could tell, they were triggered by her intentions, and so far, she hadn't been able to accidentally point a finger at Jevan.

"Rykus doesn't think you committed treason," Katie said, frowning at her tablet.

Don't move. Don't speak. Don't breathe.

Ash did those three things fairly well, but she couldn't control the way her heart pumped warm blood through her veins. If Katie's words were true—and, damn it, Ash wanted them to be true—her fail-safe believed in her. Despite everything, he believed.

"Anyway," Katie said, "I still have some tests to run. Make a fist, please."

Ash complied, clenching her left hand. Her wrist ached despite the healing and numbing effect of the medical gel. Katie shifted the blood-band around Ash's inner elbow until a sensor beeped. When Ash felt a sharp prick, she relaxed her fist, letting the band draw her blood.

"A blood test won't tell you if I've snapped," Ash said.

Katie unstrapped the band. "I'm hoping it'll help identify the cause of your seizure."

Wouldn't that be nice?

"Since you're so concerned about my well-being, why don't you ask the interrogator to wait on the results?"

Katie met her gaze. "You have something Commander Rykus needs."

Again, she had to swallow down what she wanted to say. She couldn't risk another blackout. They were getting worse, leaving her with headaches and a general feeling of weakness. She needed to keep her mind clear. At least for a few more hours.

When Ash gave no response to her words, Katie said, "I'm hoping the results will appease the doctors at the institute."

A cool, ghostlike sensation started at her scalp, then slid down her spine. She would *not* return to the institution. She'd rather die.

"There's nothing to study." Ash kept her tone light. The last thing she needed was for the Coalition to learn just how badly she did not want to end up a lab rat.

"You're wrong about that. If you've snapped, they'll want to know what went wrong in your head. If you're a traitor, they'll want to know how you broke the loyalty training."

"You think I've broken the training?" Ash asked carefully. Her head throbbed, but she remained conscious.

Katie placed the blood-band and her other supplies back in the med-sack.

"There's no other explanation for why you would kill your teammates and not respond to your fail-safe's command. Unless you have one you'd like to offer?"

Ash's corpse would have scars on the inside of her cheek, she was biting it so hard and so often. Her headache sharpened. Anything she attempted to say now would trigger a blackout.

The metallic tang of blood invaded her mouth. Silently, she watched Katie stand.

"As your treating physician," the woman said, sounding and looking one hundred percent like a detached, unemotional medical specialist, "I recommend you answer the interrogator's questions. *All* of his questions. It would be in your medical interest to do so."

Katie grabbed her med-sack and exited the cell.

Ash's gaze shifted from the solid steel door to the idle data-table. The images of her teammates were gone, leaving behind a dark, scratched, and smudged surface. Her soul felt the same way. No one could see past the evidence to the truth. She didn't blame them. If she'd been in their place, studying the documents and data that Jevan must have had planted, she would have condemned herself too.

A clank rang out from the front of her cell. A second later, the door slid open. A man dressed in a black uniform stepped inside. Even if Ash hadn't expected him, the crossed daggers over his heart gave away what he was.

Ash let her shoulders droop, making herself look small and, she hoped, fragile.

There's no need to go through this. The words trumpeted through her mind, and the ghost-fingers she'd felt earlier tightened in her hair. She shivered, then pushed the feeling aside. She wouldn't give this man the cipher. It might lead the Coalition to the truth about what had been done to her, but it would also lead to suspicions and accusations that would rip the alliance apart. Besides, Jevan *wanted* her to reveal the cipher. That was the only reason she was able to. He'd tugged and pulled and prodded on that part of her mind so hard it didn't matter that the files might clear her name. He wanted something in them badly enough to risk letting her live. Ash would make him regret that decision. Somehow.

The interrogator took a black glove out of the case he carried. When he pulled it on, she caught a glimpse of the silver circle in his palm.

Nausea churned in Ash's stomach. It was a nerve-disc. Anomalies were introduced to those fun little devices during resistance training. They hurt like hell, made you think your flesh was on fire—melting, charring, dripping off—but they did no lasting damage.

She closed her eyes. Her heart thumped too quickly in her chest, and she knew the interrogator could see her quick, shallow breaths, her near panic. She didn't want to go through this. The resistance training hadn't been pleasant, but she'd known then that everything would be okay. She didn't have that assurance now.

The interrogator approached, then lifted his gloved hand. She clenched her teeth together, determined not to scream. Her resolve shattered the instant the silver disc touched her skin.

◆ ◆

"OKAY," ASH RASPED OUT MINUTES, hours, an eternity later. "Okay."

Sweat drenched her body, and her chest heaved, sucking air into lungs that felt too sticky to expand.

"Okay." She rocked back and forth, hot and cold, trembling and numb. She couldn't scream anymore. Her throat was too raw, too parched. She squeezed her already-closed eyes shut harder.

"You're ready to enter the cipher?" her interrogator asked, monotone.

Ash tried to force out a yes with her nod, but she only managed to repeat *okay* over and over. She hurt too much to form any other word. She couldn't think, couldn't breathe, couldn't see.

She raised her head, desperate to make him understand she'd had enough. She'd do whatever he wanted, just so long as the pain—

The pain had… It hadn't stopped. It had ebbed. Her skin still felt like it was on fire, and moving even a little hurt—so did not moving at all—but the interrogator no longer touched the nerve-disc to her skin, and the reprieve allowed her mind to function again.

She'd made him stop two, maybe three times before, promising to enter the cipher into the data-table. Each time, she'd meant her words, but once she reached this point, the point where she was once again capable of thought, she changed her mind. She focused on her team. They were her brothers, the only family she'd ever had, and the only reason she'd been adopted into their ranks was because the Coalition had accepted Glory into its membership. She'd been on the edge of losing her soul completely on her home world, but an aid worker had given her food and a cot to sleep on, not just once, but a dozen times, and every morning she woke up safe and secure in their shelter, the flag of the Coalition was hanging in a window, backlit by the dawn.

Ash focused on the small flag sewn onto the interrogator's uniform. She'd vowed to preserve and protect the Coalition. Only a small number of people would give their lives for it. Many would like to see it ripped apart. All they needed was a reason, a conspiracy. Learning that telepaths existed and that they had infiltrated the Coalition would make them suspect everyone. The senators already fought and argued and threatened to secede. She wouldn't give them more fuel to burn their ties.

Sweat stung her eyes, resurrecting tears which had dried up eons ago. She was just catching her breath when the interrogator moved toward her.

"No more delays." He gripped the pinky of her right hand and broke it. Ash cried out and doubled over.

He slammed his fist into her face, knocking her back against her chair.

She blinked, trying to force the black splotches out of her vision, trying to pull her thoughts back together.

He reached for her hand again.

"Okay!" she gasped. Breaking bones was a psychological tactic—it disturbed an individual a hell of a lot more to see a crooked, flopping finger than it did to see unblemished skin—but that knowledge didn't render the tactic ineffective.

"I don't believe you," he said in his cold, dead voice. He reached into the case sitting on top of the data-table. When he faced her again, he held a hammer. Hope dislodged from its tiny corner in her heart and fled. This truly was the end then. She wouldn't be able to escape after he took that to her. After he broke more bones.

The data-table was on; the time blinked 2200. She'd been with the interrogator for almost an hour. Her body felt like it had been beaten and bruised and broken for so much longer than that. She had to make her plan work now. *Now*, before she lost the last of her strength.

As he raised the hammer up, Ash screamed. Not in fear or panic, but in a raw, determined fury.

The security bracelets bit into her shackled wrists as she yanked her arms backward. Her wrists were swollen, but not as much as before. The medical gel did its trick, and it made her skin slick enough for her hands to slip free.

The hammer slammed down, catching only the side of her left hand. She ignored the bright burst of pain, threw an uppercut that caught the interrogator on the chin. He stumbled and the guard by the door drew his weapon.

"On the ground! Now!" the guard shouted.

Ash dropped to her knees immediately, hands raised. He held a Maven 660. It wouldn't burn a hole through the hull of the ship, but it would burn one through her.

"Don't move!" he ordered, striding forward until the barrel of his gun pressed into her forehead, a move meant to intimidate her into surrendering.

His mistake. She grabbed the Maven and redirected the line of fire over her shoulder.

The guard jerked the gun back. She held on, let him pull her to her feet, then she pushed forward and landed a kick to his groin. When he doubled over, she followed up with a knee to his nose.

Adrenaline and the familiarity of a move she'd practiced over and over again on Caruth dulled her pain. She turned, the guard's gun in her good hand, and pointed it at the interrogator.

Fifteen seconds, her mental clock told her. This was already taking too long.

She backed toward the cell's exit, weapon locked on the man who'd hurt her.

"Lieutenant Ashdyn." He didn't sound cold and emotionless now. He sounded scared. Big bullets of sweat beaded on his forehead.

"Walk forward," she ordered. When he didn't comply, she fired a blast that tore through the flesh of his upper arm. He cried out, clutching it.

"If you value your life, move. Now."

Blinking rapidly, he approached until he was half a pace away.

Just in time. The door clicked behind her.

Two guards rushed in to save their comrades' lives. But their entry was unplanned and uncoordinated. Ash had already circled behind the interrogator. They couldn't shoot her without hitting him.

But *she* could shoot *them.*

SEVEN

RYKUS TOOK A SIP OF HIS THIRD cup of coffee, but the words on his screen remained blurred. His mind was fuzzy, split between his responsibilities as the commanding officer of the *Obsidian's* contingent of soldiers and his limited amount of time to determine if his anomaly deserved to become a lab rat. He hadn't gotten anywhere with her files.

Rotating his left shoulder, he stretched the artificial ligaments in the reconstructed joint. He'd have to make sleep a priority soon. He couldn't lead his soldiers in the shipyard assault fueled only by stimulants. That's how mistakes were born, and during the mission, he couldn't afford to be anything but precise and perfect. If he wasn't, too many lives would be lost.

Too many lives will be lost anyway. He scowled at the numbers again, but they weren't intimidated.

"Ninety-five percent is more accurate than most raid ops get," his XO said, sitting across from him and staring at the same data.

"The schematics aren't even seventy percent accurate." Rykus tossed his stylus onto his desk. It was a hunch, a gut instinct that told him this thoroughly researched mission the Intelligence Committee had concocted was destined to turn into an epic disaster. The council thought they had every door, every corridor, lift, and stairwell mapped within inches of their actual locations. But Rykus didn't trust their calculations. He wanted information from real sources, from eyes on the ground or from the Sariceans' own data-banks, not from some researcher's made-up algorithm.

"Sometimes I-Com gets things right," Brookins said.

He met the other man's gaze. Clay Brookins had been his XO for the past two years. Before him, Rykus had gone through half a dozen officers, all men and women who did nothing but agree with him. They thought his appointment to the anomaly program and his status as a war hero made him infallible. He wasn't, and he needed an XO who would punch holes in his plans. Brookins was that man.

He also happened to be the only anomaly on the ship. Not one of Rykus's cadets, and not loyalty trained, thank God. But that's what made him an asset. Every anomaly thought his time on Caruth was the toughest, his instructor the most demanding. Brookins had made it clear he thought Rykus was overrated. He'd stated up front that he'd rip apart every one of Rykus's ideas. He'd go out of his way to disagree and would be hell to work with. Rykus had held out his hand and said, "Welcome to my team."

"Everyone knows the risks," Brookins said.

Rykus glared at the other man. "They haven't seen these numbers."

"Not the risk of the specific operation, but the risk of doing nothing." The anomaly's expression was hard, unforgiving. "The Sariceans don't have to like the Coalition, but their raids on our member worlds are unacceptable. Their disregard for human life—for anyone who doesn't believe in the sanctity of their home world—is unacceptable. We shouldn't just be raiding this shipyard. We should take the battle to Saris—"

"That won't happen," Rykus said, cutting him off. Brookins wasn't the only one in the Coalition who felt that way, but attacking Saris would stir up the Known Universe. Native Sariceans weren't the only ones who believed Saris had been visited by a god or the gods sometime in the past. Billions of others, all scattered through the KU, believed it as well. The Coalition wanted to defend its member worlds against Saricean aggression, not start a religious war, and right now, I-Com and the senate thought the best way to do that was by launching a preemptive attack on one of the Saricean shipyards.

It better be worth the cost.

Rykus leaned back in his chair. "Personnel and equipment for the operation is the same whether we get more information or not. Make sure everyone has what they need, including adequate sleep."

"Does that last part apply to you, sir?" Brookins asked.

The look Rykus settled on his XO made Brookins's eyebrows rise; it was supposed to make him snap his mouth shut and give a curt "I'll make sure it's done, sir."

"I'll get some sleep when you get out of my office," he said.

Brookins didn't stand immediately. He maintained eye contact for a good five seconds, long enough to prove he was leaving because he chose to, not because Rykus had given him an order.

The small act of defiance reminded Rykus of Ash, and when Brookins finally exited, Rykus swiped his hand across his screen, returning to the evidence that had been gathered against his cadet.

It was all blatantly irrefutable. There were encrypted communications with Ash's ID-sig, classified data stored in her comm-cuff, and numerous references to her contact with Saricean agents. Every single piece of evidence should have raised alarms. Why hadn't they? The Coalition's intelligence community couldn't be *this* inept, could it?

He swiped to the next file, Ash's financial records. They were the most damning of the evidence. Anomalies were some of the highest-paid people in the military. That's why many of them were willing to travel to Caruth, go through the hell of training, and become dependent on the boosters that fueled their minds and bodies.

Others went for different reasons. About a third of them craved the challenge. They wanted to become the ultimate warriors.

The rest of the anomalies, the majority of the ones who made it through the training, were there because they believed in the Coalition. They were willing to sacrifice their free will and their lives to protect it.

That's why Ash had signed up. She'd never cared about the money. She'd cared about the Coalition.

But maybe she'd begun to care about money.

Rykus sat straighter in his chair and frowned at the transactions. Every month, the majority of her paycheck disappeared into an account the Coalition hadn't yet been able to trace. The money Ash lived off was minuscule, barely above poverty level on most planets. At least, it had been up until the day her teammates were murdered. On that day, the equivalent of a standard year's salary showed up in her account.

And intelligence had linked the source of those funds back to a Saricean financier.

He stood, knocking his chair away from his desk. The evidence *proved* Ash had committed treason. Why the hell couldn't he convince himself to believe it?

More theories, more scenarios, kicked around inside his head. None of them fit the evidence. None of them explained Ash's behavior. None of them erased the feeling that he was missing something crucial.

He couldn't think in his office anymore, so he confirmed the two meetings he had scheduled later that day, ignored a message from his father to call, then logged out of his computer and headed to his hole in the officers' barracks. His room was a square box, barely big enough to fit a bed and small desk. It was extravagant compared to most crew quarters though. The rank and file shared holes only slightly bigger than this one with five other men or women. Rykus had privacy.

Heading to his desk, he untucked his uniform and took off his comm-cuff. His door pinged while he was rolling up his sleeves. He turned, and the ship announced his visitor as Dr. Kathryn Monick.

"Allow entry," he said.

Katie stepped into his quarters. He expected her to tap the door-hold button—rumors spread when a man and woman were alone in the same hole, no matter how innocent the visit—but she let the door slide shut behind her.

She stared at his disheveled uniform. "I didn't wake you, did I?"

He shook his head. "Haven't had a chance to sleep."

She pursed her lips and nodded, but her eyebrows crooked in a familiar expression.

"What?" he asked, tucking his uniform back in.

"Nothing," she said far too slowly.

"Katie."

"You're having trouble sleeping."

"I said I haven't slept, not that I'm having trouble."

"Oh." Her tone made it sound like she knew something he didn't.

"Oh?" He frowned. "Why are you here, Katie?"

"Why did you leave Caruth?"

"Caruth?" The question struck him like undocumented space debris. "Is this visit business or personal?"

"Business." Her right thumb rubbed over the surface of the comm-cuff strapped around her left wrist. "Mostly."

On his best days, he didn't have patience for this kind of thing. Today wasn't one of his best days. "Everyone knows why I left. I didn't approve of the loyalty training."

She gave a little shrug, and there was that expression again, the one that suggested he wasn't being honest with her.

"If you have something you want to say, Katie, just say it."

She looked away and nodded, but not as if she was agreeing with him. It was more like she was agreeing with her own thoughts, whatever they were. When she met his eyes again, her expression was calm, certain.

"I always thought there was another woman."

Rykus stared. He couldn't possibly have heard her correctly. "What?"

"When we were together," she said. "I thought there was someone else."

He still couldn't believe her words. He had never, not even once, been unfaithful to a woman. That Katie could accuse him of it *now*, after almost three years apart, suggested she didn't know him at all.

"Tell me you're joking." His voice was so low, so icy, he was surprised she heard him.

"I'm not saying you acted on those feelings, but…" She walked to his desk and waved her comm-cuff over a sensor. The terminal logged her in, and the screen brightened, showing overlapping line graphs which were shaded in different hues of blue.

"The darker color is your vocal imprint from Caruth," Katie said, pointing. "This is what your voice looks like when you engage an anomaly's loyalty training to give commands. The lighter blue here"—she moved her finger to indicate the zigzag just below the upper line—"is from earlier today when you ordered Ash to give you the cipher."

The difference was almost insignificant, but it was there, a subtle dip it seemed, in his tone. Maybe a small variance in his inflection. He knew the graph was significant, but he filed it away in his mind, still caught up on Katie's insinuation. He was so damn tired of people accusing him of having feelings for Ash.

"That doesn't mean I'm in love with the woman," he said, not bothering to keep his irritation in check. "And she has nothing to do with the reason I left Caruth."

Katie faced him. "You decided to leave *after* Ashdyn's class graduated. You could have left before the senate implemented the loyalty training."

"I objected to it before. I didn't leave then because I gave it a chance. Then I saw what it did to the cadets. One command from me made them ignore their needs and their safety." Not only was that wrong, but it was dangerous. Rykus and the other instructors were well vetted by the Coalition, but if a new instructor came along and abused his position…

"You've seen the loyalty training in action too," he said, softening his voice. "You've seen the way their personalities change."

Katie's blue eyes met his. "Did Ashdyn's personality change?"

"Ash was always—" He cut himself off. Ash had always been a pain in his ass. Apparently, three years apart hadn't changed that.

"I don't know," he said, a weak answer, but it was the truth. Ash had always hidden behind her half smiles and her flirtations. That didn't change after the loyalty training. But every once in a while, when Ash was exhausted or unguarded, she'd looked at him like he was more than just her instructor. Were those glimpses of her calculated? Sometimes he'd thought so. He'd thought she was letting him see a vulnerability in order to manipulate his emotions. But other times?

Other times, he thought what he saw was real.

"You've only attempted to use compulsion twice," Katie said.

"I haven't used it more than that because I'm trying to find out what the hell is wrong with her, and I respect her free will." He held up a hand to stop her reply. "And before you say that's because I like her, it's not. I'd do the same for any one of my recruits."

"Yes," Katie said. "I'm sure you would have held them the way you held her when she seized."

"Seeker's God, Katie, I—"

She held up her hands in surrender. "I'm done. I won't say anything else."

"Don't even think it. You and Bayis both are reading too much into her flirtations."

"Bayis thinks you're in lo—"

He flashed her a look that would have made most men snap their mouths shut. Katie just twisted her lips into a halfway-apologetic smile and shrugged.

Rykus turned back to the data-screen, stared at the disparate graphs, and forced the tension out of his body. "The vocal imprints," he said. "Do you have one from just before she seized?"

"Yes." She unhooked and flattened her comm-cuff, turning it into a small tablet. She tapped in a command, then waved the device over the desk's sensor again. "That's what's interesting."

The imprints matched perfectly, overlapping at almost every leap up and down. At least he'd gotten the tone and cadence right once.

"The compulsion triggered the seizure?"

"Possibly." Katie sat on the edge of his bed. "Or it could be a coincidence. It could be withdrawal from the boosters. It could be a sign of mental deterioration or an unrelated medical condition we haven't identified yet."

He turned away from the desk, felt the muscles in his face tighten. "You're trying to make this not my fault."

Katie shrugged. "It might not be. She isn't acting like an anomaly who has snapped."

"Which leaves one conclusion," he said, frustration making his voice harsh. "She's a traitor."

"You still don't believe that, do you?"

"I don't have a choice." He gripped the back of his desk chair. "Unless you have evidence of something else?"

"Not yet. I'm still looking."

He stared at his display.

"I think she does it on purpose," Katie said after a moment. "Ashdyn's learned how to get under your skin, so she provokes you. She flirts. She says things just to make you lose your temper, all so she can wiggle out of the compulsion."

He gave a short, humorless laugh. Yeah, that sounded like Ash. She had an uncanny ability to see what set a person off. He'd seen her use that skill to her advantage before. That's how she survived the first few weeks on Caruth. The recruits in her class were susceptible to her charades. When they sparred, she made them think she was weak, fragile, feminine... until she managed a perfectly timed, perfectly placed kick that laid them out cold.

Unfortunately for Ash, the anomalies learned quickly. They didn't underestimate her twice, and she spent most of her time on Caruth getting her ass kicked. She never gave up though. Rykus had to intervene more than once to prevent her opponents from permanently injuring her. She was an impressive woman, an impressive woman whom he *did not* love.

He straightened and faced Katie. "You're here because you want me to try to command her again."

"Ashdyn is my patient," she said. "And they're hurting her, Rhys."

"Hurting her?" His gaze jerked to the time on his comm-cuff: 2205. "I have another hour."

"Another hour?" Katie asked.

"Yes. Bayis gave me... Never mind." He picked up his comm-cuff and fastened it around his wrist. "When did the interrogator go in?"

"Right after I left."

Katie's words lacerated his chest. He'd been drinking coffee and staring at a screen while Ash was having who the hell knew what done to her below-decks. If he'd known, he would have...

He didn't know what he'd have done—tried more threats or compulsion or *something*.

"Where are you going?" Katie asked when he headed for the door.

"I'll talk to h—"

His comm-cuff pinged. The message said Bayis was calling. Good. Rykus had just been about to call him.

Pulling his voice-link out of his pocket, he slipped it over his ear. "Admiral—"

"Commander Rykus," Bayis's too-calm voice said. "Lieutenant Ashdyn has escaped."

CHAPTER

EIGHT

IT FELT LIKE ASH HAD spent her entire life in a box and was being let out to stretch for the first time. Her muscles loosened as she moved, as she stole a uniform, a voice-link, and a comm-cuff, all in just under five minutes. Still, her body demanded more action. It wanted to run, to fight; it didn't want to kneel in a maintenance closet prying at a panel with a knife.

The knife point skated across the bulkhead. Ash wiped her sweaty palm on her pants and tried again. She didn't have time for clumsiness, but the pinky of her left hand was broken and her right one wouldn't stop shaking. Honestly, she was lucky she was able to do any of this. If her last booster wasn't lingering in her system, and if the doctor hadn't painted her wrists with the slick medical gel, she'd still be trapped in that damn chair.

But her breaking point wasn't far off. How long before her body gave out, she didn't know. She shouldn't be experiencing such severe withdrawals so soon, but that's what the weakness and the shaking felt like. She needed an injection before it all got worse.

Unfortunately, an assault on the drug locker wasn't part of her present itinerary. Getting into the head on the other side of the wall was. It would take her to another corridor, another room, another plan. After that, she'd get off the ship, deal with her addiction, and track down her soon-to-be-dead fiancé.

Her stolen voice-link clicked. She paused, listening to the transmission, and heard a spacer issue an advisory on a "dangerous escapee." Rykus would know about her now. Was he already tracking her? He was the biggest obstacle in her plan. He might figure out what she was doing. He might help the spacers recapture her. He might command her to…

She closed her eyes, fighting against the loyalty training that urged her to turn herself in. It was never comfortable, doing something Rykus wouldn't like. It felt like she had her skin on backward, like all her movements were wrong and she was struggling against a current.

She blew out a breath. If Rykus knew why she was doing this, he wouldn't be angry.

The chains tying her to her fail-safe loosened. She focused again on the stubborn panel she needed to pop out. Rykus's presence was inconvenient, yes, but give her ten more minutes, and he could do nothing to stop her.

Her hand jerked when the blade slipped under the panel. A satisfied smile spread across her lips. It dissolved a second later when she felt the air press against the back of her neck.

She heard a whisper and spun, bringing her knife around while she reached for the gun holstered on her hip.

No one was there. The maintenance closet was as dark and empty as when she first entered.

She wet her lips. She almost wished someone *was* there. This was the third time since her escape that she'd heard a whisper and felt a presence. If she'd believed in ghosts, she would have said the *Obsidian* was haunted. That would have been preferable to the alternative.

Her head felt like it was being squeezed in a hyperbaric chamber. She endured the pitching moment of dizziness, then turned back to the wall, trying but failing to ignore the fear that clung to her like the halo around a sun. Anomalies who had snapped heard voices. They saw things that weren't real. They harmed people who were innocent.

What if all this was a hallucination? Would she know if she'd lost her mind? Maybe she'd imagined Jevan and the other men. Maybe they'd never stepped foot on the shuttle and *she* had killed her team. Maybe she'd soon be talking nonsense about fashion and fighting like Trevast had when he'd been on the precipice of death.

She tightened her grip on her stolen knife.

No. It couldn't be possible. She might be an anomaly, but she was only one person, and her teammates weren't incompetent. They would have stopped her before she was able to kill even half of them. She hadn't snapped; she'd just been a fool. Jevan had pried into her mind. He'd known exactly what to say to keep her close these past six months. He'd kept their relationship casual, struck up conversations on how to improve the lives of people on Coalition worlds. He'd even donated funds to humanitarian organizations on Glory. He'd manipulated Ash into trusting him.

Opening her eyes, she stared at the loose panel. There was no time to linger on the past. No time for regret or weakness. In ten minutes, Ash would be off this ship, and then she'd make Jevan pay.

She let out a slow, centering breath, then slid the wall panel aside.

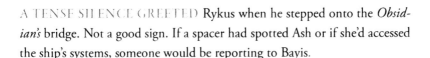

A TENSE SILENCE GREETED Rykus when he stepped onto the *Obsidian's* bridge. Not a good sign. If a spacer had spotted Ash or if she'd accessed the ship's systems, someone would be reporting to Bayis.

The admiral stood at his command console in the center of the room. His hands were clasped loosely behind his back, but from the way the entire crew on deck kept a professionally neutral expression and locked their eyes on the status screens, it was obvious Bayis was anything but calm. Perhaps that was because he wasn't alone at his console. War Chancellor Hagan was there as well.

Had Hagan ordered the interrogator into Ash's cell? Bayis had given Rykus more time. It wasn't like the admiral to change his mind, especially not without notifying Rykus first.

"Admiral. Chancellor," Rykus said, keeping his tone the same for both men's titles. They turned, and he met Hagan's cool gray eyes. The war chancellor was close to his father's size and age—late fifties, most likely—which made him one of the youngest war chancellors in the Coalition's three-hundred-dred-year history. Rykus hadn't liked the man before the anomaly hearings, but he despised Hagan now. Not only had he advocated for the Caruth anomalies to be brainwashed, but he wanted the few individuals who showed *any* sign of mental instability, whether they completed the program or not, to be sent to the institute where they would be dissected and studied. All without any solid proof that they would eventually snap.

The man was immoral and pure politician. Neither the Fighting Corps nor the Fleet had a high opinion of him.

Rykus focused on the admiral. "What happened to my three hours?"

Bayis's mouth tightened. "There was a miscommunication. Can you find her?"

For one insanity-laced moment, he didn't want to. He stood there staring at Bayis, hoping Ash would disappear until he had time to fully analyze every piece of evidence brought against her.

Then Chancellor Hagan shifted, and Rykus remembered Bayis's warning. This wasn't the time to question Ash's imprisonment. If she escaped, Hagan would make sure Rykus answered for it.

"How long has she been free?" he asked.

"Almost ten minutes," Bayis said. "We've sealed off deck two."

"She won't be there now." He focused on the schematic of the ship on the central console. In the month since they'd come on board the ancient vessel, the layout had become familiar, but he hadn't looked at the design from the perspective of someone trying to escape.

"I shut down the lifts," Bayis said. "I have men stationed at every stairwell, emergency ladder, and—"

"It doesn't matter," Rykus interrupted. "She's an anomaly. She's found a way out."

"Are you saying she can walk through bulkheads, Commander?" Chancellor Hagan turned from the forward viewscreen to address him.

"In a way, yes."

"Explain," Bayis ordered.

"Anomalies study spacecraft designs. *All* the designs—the Sariceans', the Coalition's, even the designs of the individual planets that aren't part of our organization. Ash knows the layout of this ship better than we do, Admiral. She could be anywhere."

"Engineers built partitions between the bulkheads," Hagan said. "Even in these old designs. She can't move between them."

Rykus ignored him. The brig was located on deck two. Below it was engineering and storage. Above it were the crew quarters and hangar bays, and above that, the rec deck, kitchens, and mess hall.

"I'm assuming you've lost security feeds."

"For half the ship, yes." Bayis's voice was tight. "We're working to get them back."

That was Ash's doing, and if she'd gained access to security, she could gain access to other ship functions. "I suggest you cut off remote log-ins to the *Obsidian*. Anomalies are trained in hack-sig. She's stolen a comm-cuff, probably a voice-link too."

"She'll try to get off the ship," Hagan put in.

Bayis glanced at the chancellor, and his nostrils flared slightly, a clear indication he didn't want the man on his ship. Hagan used to command the Fifth Fleet, and Bayis couldn't be comfortable having the man breathing over his shoulder.

"All outbound flights are terminated," Bayis said in a calmer tone than Rykus would have managed.

Rykus stared down at the command console. He had no patience for the war chancellor. Somehow, he had to find Ash. The problem was, he wasn't an anomaly. He didn't have every detail of the ship's schematic memorized.

Brookins would though.

He tapped on his comm-cuff to call his XO when a tone chimed across the bridge.

"Sir," a spacer called out. "Three life rafts have launched from deck two starboard."

"Order standby fighters to their birds," Bayis said. "Deploy when ready and engage to cripple."

"Aye, aye, sir."

The admiral's command and the spacer's response were calm, professional. Rykus sealed off his own emotions and studied the forward viewscreen. Three bright orange life rafts veered away from the *Obsidian*. The small craft had limited maneuverability. They were designed to move fast over a short time period, just long enough to get away from a damaged ship or from a skirmish, and while they were equipped with some defensive weaponry, they didn't have enough to divert an opponent who was set on retrieving them.

There was no way Ash was on one of those rafts. They weren't covert. She'd know Bayis would notice. She'd know she wouldn't make atmosphere before the admiral deployed his fighters.

Before he deployed the fighters.

Ah, hell.

"Admiral—" A siren cut Rykus off.

"Admiral," a spacer called out. "Unidentified warships have appeared in-system. They've engaged the *Centennial.*"

"Ephron Station is reporting additional bogeys, sir."

"Close-range radar picking up two vessels approaching at point-five light."

Rykus took a step back from the command console as the bridge erupted into a flurry of activity. It took several seconds for the situation to sink in, to recognize what was going on and who had just invaded their star system. When the truth finally stabbed through his mind, his gut plummeted like a jump from a sub-atmo fighter.

The Sariceans had just launched a preemptive attack against the Coalition.

The Sariceans had started the war.

———◆·◆———

ASH WATCHED THE LIFE rafts shrink to tiny dots as they shot away from the *Obsidian.* She didn't expect Bayis to shoot them down. He still needed her to decrypt the files. Plus her supposed death would have made things too easy for her, and she was fairly certain the gods of the universe weren't finished putting her through hell yet. So when one of those life rafts did explode, she blinked. She stared harder, convinced her vision was failing her. Then, seconds later when more explosions brightened the life systems chief's office viewport, she cursed. She'd only released three life rafts. There were five explosions out there.

Chewing on her lower lip, she focused on the unconscious chief's desk terminal. She'd remained virtually invisible since escaping her cell, covertly passing through bulkhead after bulkhead until she'd pried open a panel to the LSC's office. She'd forced him to initiate an emergency drill for the three life rafts, an action that didn't raise any alerts until after those rafts shot out into space. A simple diversion code she'd inserted into his terminal made it look like they were fired off from their pods, not fired remotely. Bayis didn't know where she was right now. Plugging into the desk terminal to determine what the hell was going on outside might change that.

Ash couldn't risk it. She needed to drop down to the flight hangar, which just so happened to be right under her feet. It was the best chance she had to—

An explosion rang through her ears. She was on the floor, something wet and sticky running from her nose.

Blood. Had to be.

She forced her eyes open. Her vision blurred, blackened, then came back red.

Emergency lights.

Alarms blared through the ship. She was on her back, staring up at a metal beam that, had it not hit and crushed the LSC's desk, would have dropped one fatal inch and hit and crushed her head.

What the hell was going on?

She gritted her teeth, then rolled to her stomach. The room kept rolling. Staring at the floor, she willed her vision to level out. When it finally did, she crawled out from under the beam.

Her entire body hurt, but only her left pinky and perhaps another bone in her hand were broken. She was lucky. So was the LSC. He was unconscious right where she'd left him, and he looked unharmed as well.

She controlled her breathing and let her gaze sweep the chief's office. The damn beam had fallen onto the room's blast hatch. There were only two such hatches hidden underfoot on this part of the ship. She'd already loosened the floor panel's screws, but there was no way she'd be able to move that beam and slide it aside. Her route to the flight hangar had just been cut off.

She quickly amended her original plan and grabbed two oxygen masks out of the emergency cabinet. She fitted the first over the LSC's face and the second over hers, then double-timed it to the door. She had to put her full weight against it to shove it open, and still she barely managed to move it.

Good enough. She reached behind her back, drawing the stolen Maven she'd tucked into her waistband. She was about to step into the corridor, but the gun's weight didn't feel right in her hand. She looked down, saw that the battery pack was crushed.

She squeezed the grip in her hand.

Piece-of-crap machinery.

Dumb-as-dirt spacers. Fleet refused to allow personnel to carry decent weapons on board their vessels out of a superstitious paranoia that they'd blast holes through the bulkheads. They wouldn't. Ships were made out of tougher material than that.

Ash chucked aside the useless Maven. Energy-based guns were lethal, but damn fragile. She wanted her weapons and armor back.

She wanted a lot of things back.

Her jaw ached from grinding her teeth. She drew in a deep, centering breath, and reminded herself that only ship security and top brass carried weapons. As long as she avoided them, she wouldn't need a gun. She hadn't planned on killing anyone anyway.

She faced the tiny opening to the corridor again, squeezed through it—

—and stepped into chaos.

More flashing lights. Dust and debris everywhere and people—some with O2 masks, some without—stumbling across the dura-steel tiles. The whole wall opposite the LSC's office was peeled open. No one emerged from those rooms. That left at least half a dozen administrative officers dead.

Do you really care if they die?

That thought felt foreign. Of course she cared. Despite what people thought, she wasn't the enemy, and she owed her life to the Coalition. She was following Trevast's order and trying so damn hard to—

Someone grabbed her arm. She locked her hand on the man's elbow but caught herself before she dislocated it, realizing her O2 mask provided a perfect disguise. He couldn't have any idea who she was.

"Move!" the man ordered, his words muffled by his own mask. "Admiral's gonna seal off this sector. Go!"

"Yes, sir," she said, but he was already turning toward another man.

"Neeson! Where the hell is your O2 mask?"

The dazed man stumbled. He was young. Half his face was covered in bright red blood, and suddenly Ash wasn't staring at a spacer named Neeson. She was staring at Kris Menchan, the teammate she'd mentored. His mouth opened and he spoke. She couldn't hear his words, but she could read his lips: why. Why hadn't she saved him?

Her lungs stopped working. She couldn't breathe, couldn't move, and the uniform she'd stolen became heavy and sweltering, sticking to her sweat-covered skin. Why hadn't she saved them? She should have been able to. The Coalition funneled billions of credits into the anomaly program. She was supposed to be superhuman. She shouldn't have been brought to her knees by a simple stun grenade and the presence of a politician's aide.

The ship rumbled around her, shaking her back to the present. The *real* present. The tremors running through the *Obsidian* now weren't secondary explosions. The ship was under heavy direct fire.

Her voice-link gave three quick beeps, signaling a ship-wide message.

"A fleet of Saricean warships has appeared in-system," Admiral Bayis's calm, measured voice said into her ear. "Our priority is to protect the civilian population on Ephron followed by the two tachyon capsules and the military installations. Every available pilot, proceed to your fighters."

Damn it, damn it, damn it.

She'd finally escaped from her cell and the fucking Sariceans showed up. If there was one person remaining on this ship who didn't think she'd betrayed her teammates and the Coalition, they'd change their mind now, especially since this attack was a guaranteed ticket off the ship. Her original plan—to hijack one of the fighters Bayis would send after the life rafts—was risky. This new setup was damn near perfect. The confusion of battle and the damage to the *Obsidian*—and undoubtedly to the fighters sent out into space—would erase all trace of what happened to her.

She hammered her fist into the wall. She didn't like this. The timing was too coincidental. Had the Sariceans discovered her team's data grab and decided to retaliate? Trevast was certain they'd made it in and out undetected, but maybe they'd learned about the security breach later? Why else would they attack now?

It's so very obvious the Coalition is planning a preemptive strike.

Ash stumbled into the broken wall. Shards of ice raced down her neck and spine. Her heart rate quickened, and her lungs rasped empty despite the air she sucked in. She'd suspected the Coalition might be planning a strike—it was the logical reason for her team to steal the shipyard schematics—but she didn't *know* that. The voice in her head couldn't be her own.

The smoke filtering through the almost-deserted corridor stung her eyes despite her O2 mask. She squeezed them shut, then concentrated on the elusive, ghostlike presence that had been nudging her for the past few hours.

"Who the hell are you?" She didn't have to worry about any spacers hearing her. They'd cleared out of the corridor already.

Finally figuring it out? It took you quite a while.

She wasn't hallucinating this. Someone was speaking in her head.

Was it Jevan? She couldn't tell. The words were clear, but they weren't attached to a voice.

More pressure surged through her head. It felt like someone was jabbing their fingertips into her temples. She pushed away from the wall, started scrambling toward the end of the corridor as if she could escape the thing shadowing her. She *needed* to escape it. She needed to escape this damn ship.

The smoke filling the corridor made it almost impossible to see. She felt the heat from the hatchway the rest of the spacers had rushed through.

The hatchway she was now stumbling toward.

Stopping abruptly, she cursed, then drew in a deep, smoke-laced breath. She was acting without thinking. She had to get it together and get the hell out of here, and that hatchway wasn't the right choice. There was another option, one she'd dismissed before making her way to the LSC's office because there would have been too many spacers to subdue.

The officer's mess. It should be evacuated now, and like the LSC's office, a blast hatch was built into the floor. It would drop her down just outside the flight hangar. She could still escape, and maybe—just maybe—once she was off the ship, the pressure in her head would go away.

She crouched low and felt her way along the wall. The red emergency lights did little to light the corridor, and the black smoke twisted and hissed overhead. By the time she reached the open doorway to the officer's mess, she was certain she could hear someone speaking again. Maybe the telepath. Or maybe there was interference on her voice-link or on a speaker relaying alerts and ship-wide messages. Whatever it was, she'd reached her destination.

Coughing, she crawled to the center of the room. She quickly found the tiny grooves in the floor and took out the multi-tool she'd stolen from the LSC's office. Within seconds, she had three screws out. She fitted the multi to the fourth, had started to unscrew it when the hisses and whispers became louder, clearer. She finally made out the calls for help.

She squeezed her eyes shut. She wasn't the only one who hadn't escaped this section of the ship. They were all sealed in now, and the spacers were panicking. They didn't know about the blast hatches—this was an old vessel—and they would succumb to the flames.

It wasn't her problem.

It really wasn't.

The last screw loosened, and she slid the floor panel aside, revealing the heavy metal blast hatch below. She gripped the bright yellow wheel in the center with both hands, then strained to turn it.

One of the people calling for help was a woman. Ash tried to ignore her along with the others. It probably wasn't Katie, and even if it was, it shouldn't matter. What mattered was getting off this ship.

The hatch groaned as it ever so slowly turned.

The woman yelled again.

Damn it, the voice sounded like Katie. The blood in Ash's veins quickened, her breath steadied, her muscles tensed—all signs her body was primed for action.

Primed to save the doctor.

She recognized the pull of the loyalty training. She should have expected it. People who were important to a fail-safe were inherently important to his anomalies. It was a damn inconvenient side effect of the brainwashing.

The loyalty training… it's interesting.

Fury slipped under her skin. She wanted the telepath dead, wanted it almost more than she wanted off the ship.

She managed to turn the hatch wheel another few inches. Sweat trickled down her neck and her jaw ached from gritting her teeth, but finally the wheel loosened. Its hinges squeaked as she let it fall open, revealing a lit corridor below. No sign of smoke. No sign of spacers to witness her entry. Twenty feet to the flight deck's side entrance and she could get to a bird and fly away. The Coalition would be too busy with the Sariceans to worry about her. She'd land on Ephron and disappear.

If it's so easy, why aren't you moving?

The telepath asked a good question. This was her one chance to get off the ship. If she was recaptured, Rykus would make sure she had no further opportunities to escape. Hell, he'd probably execute her on the spot after this. But execution was better than being sent to the institute.

It was better than letting her brothers- and sisters-in-arms die.

"Damn it," she whispered. Then, cursing the sun, the moon, and every celestial object in the Known Universe, she sprinted back to the smoke-filled corridor.

CHAPTER

NINE

"FIND THE SARICEANS' CAPSULE," Bayis ordered his crew.

Rykus stood out of the way and scanned the battle screen that stretched across the front arc of the bridge. The Sariceans couldn't have arrived without a tachyon capsule. The hideous, behemoth-sized containers allowed for interstellar travel. One should have appeared light-years away, in the designated tachyon arrival zone on the outskirts of Ephronian space. Coming out of the time-bend anywhere else was too dangerous. Debris no bigger than a bullet could damage the capsule's fragile *darridean* shell, destroying the ships, the passengers, everything on board. Capsules were too expensive, the *darride* too scarce, to risk.

And the *darride* was one of the reasons there was a conflict with the Sariceans to begin with. They kept attacking *darride*-rich planets.

"Admiral," the comm officer said, "multiple warships are reporting a capsule leaving the TAZ. Enemy ships are engaging our defensive forces."

"And our capsules?" Bayis asked.

"*Aevin's Dream* is fleeing the enemy. Captain Furyk of the *Retribution* is on an intercept course and predicts a seventy percent chance he'll be able to give it enough time to capsule out."

Rykus recognized Furyk's name, knew him to be a demanding and competent officer. The *Dream* would survive. The other capsule, however, wouldn't share the same fate.

Bayis had divided the battle screen into three sections. The first showed the *Aevin's Dream*, the middle the *Obsidian*, and the last, the section to the right, showed Saricean forces pummeling the second capsule, the *Xpedition*. Rykus didn't have to be a member of the Fleet to see that the few Coalition ships in range wouldn't be able to defend the second capsule. Already, fires dotted its surface, extinguished quickly when the vacuum of space swallowed the burning gases.

Bayis issued commands in a steady, authoritative tone. When a hard blow rocked the *Obsidian*, he settled a hand on the console in front of him.

Rykus had no such support near him. He knelt, braced a hand on the floor, and attempted to not fall on his ass. Not easy to do with his muscles cinched tight, but he couldn't force them to relax. There was a damn good reason he hadn't joined Fleet. Sitting behind a console punching buttons while an enemy tried to send you straight to hell wasn't his idea of a good time. He needed to be in the action, his muscles straining, his senses sharp and ready.

When the quake subsided, he rose and clasped his hands behind his back. He kept quiet and, outwardly at least, calm as the *Obsidian* returned fire.

The next vibration felt like all the others until a deep, creaking groan surrounded them. He had no idea where it originated, if the ship's infrastructure was affected or if a vital system had failed, but a change in air pressure caused a sharp pain in his ears. He swallowed to ease the tension just as a new alarm wailed from enviro.

Hagan, who was doing a remarkable job of keeping his mouth shut and staying out of the way, let out a curse.

Rykus blew a breath out between his teeth. If Hagan, who'd once commanded his own ship, was worried, then things weren't looking good.

"Enviro's not responding," a spacer reported, fingers jabbing his keyboard as if the pure force of his will could change that fact. "Vents in sections A and B on deck two and section D on deck three are open."

"Assessing now," one of the ship's cryptology officers said.

"Watch our databanks," Bayis said.

Rykus glanced at the crypty. The Sariceans might be firing on them and the *Obsidian* might be firing back, but half of every battle was fought by two officers sitting at a console. They shouldn't have a problem protecting this ship—that's why the Coalition had lugged it out of the museum. A sentient-class warship, on the other hand, had billions of sensors and datastreams the Sariceans could hijack, implanting worms and false codes. The *Obsidian* had far fewer. A couple hundred thousand at most. Her vital systems wouldn't be as vulnerable as the other Coalition vessels orbiting Ephron.

Another blast rumbled through the ship, and Rykus shifted his weight to the balls of his feet, ready to run and fight even though there was nowhere to go.

"Vents are shut," the crypty reported. "Virus is contained, sir."

"Very good," Bayis said, his posture as relaxed as if he were watching a harmless comet shower. "If you can help our friendlies, Mr. Lieve, do so."

"Aye, aye, sir."

"Sir, exterior amidships shielding breached on portside," a spacer reported. "Hull damaged but holding."

"Evacuate affected sections and seal off in two minutes," Bayis ordered.

"Fires confirmed in med bay. Chance of spreading seventy-two percent."

"Two minutes and seal," he said again in the same firm, unaffected tone.

To hell with this. Rykus was affected, and he wasn't capable of standing back and watching the fight. He wasn't needed on the bridge now anyway. He could help those who were injured.

Or he could find the woman who had to be responsible for this catastrophe. The Sariceans had arrived within twenty minutes of Ash's escape. It couldn't be a coincidence.

The betrayal, undeniable now, wrenched through him.

He spun toward the exit, and when he left the bridge, he wasn't certain if he was storming off to save lives or to take one.

◆ ◆ ◆

ASH MADE IT THROUGH THE HEAT and black smoke in time to see Katie take off her O2 mask and loan it to an injured spacer. It was a damn stupid move. The doctor was already coughing and choking. A few more seconds and she'd be too disoriented to walk, let alone provide help to anyone else.

Keeping her own mask on, Ash grabbed Katie's arm.

"There's an exit in the officer's mess," she shouted into Katie's ear. Then she pulled her down the corridor.

Some of the spacers followed. Two didn't.

Katie choked out their names.

"We have to go," Ash yelled, tightening her grip. She'd throw the doctor over her shoulder and carry her if she had to, but that wouldn't be much faster than their current stumbling pace. Ash was hurt, her last booster was almost out of her system, and she needed to get her ass off the *Obsidian*.

"Move your feet, Doctor!"

Katie stopped struggling, most likely because she couldn't breathe. Ash barely caught her when she buckled over. She bit off a curse, then dragged her the rest of the way.

Three spacers made it to the mess hall with them. They stumbled to the open blast hatch, then dropped through the floor one at a time.

"Go." Ash pushed Katie toward the hole.

"No. The others—"

"They're dead," Ash said. It was the truth. Neither had oxygen masks. The smoke would have taken them by now.

"We can—"

Ash shoved her down the hole. Then she grabbed a bar on the underside of the opening and slid in.

She didn't drop to the floor below. She dangled from the bar with one hand and reached up to close the blast door. If its hydraulics hadn't been functioning, she never would have managed it. But one push triggered the closing mechanism, and the hatch settled back into place. She gave the underside wheel a quarter turn, would have given it more but her muscles gave out. She crashed down hard on her right shoulder.

It took longer than it should have to move. Just as it had taken too long when Jevan and his men had boarded her team's shuttle. Suddenly she was back there, on her hands and knees with a sharp, piercing pain stabbing at her temples.

She'd thought she was hallucinating when she'd looked up and seen Jevan. It would have been pointless to talk to a ghost, so she hadn't said anything. She'd waited for him to disappear. Instead, he'd come closer, and the agony in her mind had increased.

It was increasing now, and unbidden, the algorithms she'd used to encrypt the Sariceans' files appeared in her mind.

With a sharp intake of breath, she pushed the numbers and equations away. When she heard the telepath curse, she relaxed her fists. He hadn't pried the cipher from her mind. Jevan hadn't been able to on the shuttle either.

Jevan was rushed. I am not.

She looked up and to the right. There was nothing there except the wall of the corridor, but it *felt* like the telepath was that direction. That direction and perhaps a deck or two up. She might be able to find him—

He vanished from her mind, taking the stabbing pain with him.

Coward. If she weren't determined to get off the ship, she'd find a corner and hide until he sought her out again. Then *she'd* seek *him* out. She'd track him down, rip him apart, and make him talk.

"You're hurt," a voice said behind her. "I'm a doctor. Let me see…"

The hand was already on her arm, already lifting it to inspect her injuries. Ash still had her O2 mask on, but it didn't matter. The other woman recognized her bruised and swollen wrists.

Katie's eyes widened. She released Ash as if she was a contaminant.

"Lieutenant Ashdyn." The doctor's voice was barely a whisper, but the nearest spacer's head snapped their direction.

The instant he charged, Ash leapt to her feet. She sidestepped, brought her knee up to catch him in the crotch.

He doubled over. She swung her elbow down and delivered a sharp blow to the back of his head that sprawled him face-first on the floor.

"Lieutenant, wait!" Katie called.

Ash ran, dodged a grab by another one of the damn spacers she'd saved, then turned down a side corridor.

This part of the ship wasn't empty. Spacers were running to their fighters. Those who weren't were helping the injured, men and women with cuts and bruises, broken bones and burns.

Ash whipped off her oxygen mask, then joined the rush toward the flight deck.

"Stop her!" someone shouted.

She shoved away a man who grabbed her arm, punched a second one who blocked her path. Then there were too many. Her broken pinky bent beneath her hand when she fell.

She gritted her teeth against the pain, flipped to her back, and let her elbows fly. A quick upkick at a two-hundred-pound monster knocked him backward, then she was scurrying away from the next attacker.

On her feet. Running. She couldn't go directly to the flight deck, but she might be able to make it into maintenance. If she did, one of the birds parked there might fly. It was her best option.

She regulated her breathing as she ran, letting it fall into the quick and even rhythm that kept her focused during ops. She identified every target, every obstacle that came her way, and neutralized them.

Within minutes, she was in maintenance, securing the door with a lockout code that should take at least a few minutes to override. Then she turned to face the bay.

It was a small area, big enough for only three fighters. Two were cranked up on jacks. She approached the third, a Zenith Predator.

She would have whooped if she weren't concerned about drawing attention. Predators were quick and agile, lethal both in orbit and in sub-atmo elevations. Its hull could withstand a heavy barrage of fire and the ship would only be knocked off course by a few degrees. They were sweet, sleek rides and—

She almost stepped on a diagonal thruster.

Hell. The thing was in pieces by the rear wheels. It would cost a minimum of ten minutes to reassemble and install it, with no guarantee the Predator would fly afterward.

She couldn't risk it. She needed a functional bird.

Her gaze scanned the bay, then locked on the closed door to the flight deck. It wouldn't be empty on the other side. She'd have to fight her way to a cockpit.

Grabbing a crowbar off the ground, she sprang into a jog and was halfway across the maintenance bay when the access door opened.

Ash slid to a stop, but it felt like her heart kept going. She could feel it beating outside her chest as her fail-safe—cold, angry, and intimidating as hell—stepped over the threshold.

The room seemed suddenly smaller and the air seemed suddenly stale. Rykus was big and broad, and he completely blocked her route to freedom.

He took a step forward, and the crowbar shook in her hand. She willed her fingers to tighten around it and focused on the pain in her broken pinky. It was an asset now. She could concentrate on it instead of on Rykus's smothering presence.

"You took an oath to protect the Coalition," he said, and his words vibrated through her.

She bit the inside of her cheek, took a step backward when he took another one forward.

"The anomaly program gave you a chance at a new life." His chin angled downward. Any second, he could charge. "It took you away from that hellhole of a planet you were born on. It gave you a family." Another advance from him, another retreat from her. "And you murdered them."

Images of her teammates' lifeless faces exploded into her mind. She wanted so badly to deny Rykus's words.

"And the casualties from today…" His fingers brushed the grip of the gun holstered at his hip. "Hundreds, if not thousands have died. We've lost ships. We've lost a capsule. Ephron is burning."

"I had nothing to do with that."

"They showed up within twenty minutes of your escape." His voice rose and echoed in the maintenance bay. Even though he'd likely never set foot in here before, he owned the place. Everything inside it, the broken birds, the tools, the equipment—Ash—was there because he allowed it to be.

She wet her dry lips. "When would I have had a chance to call them?"

His steps slowed. His aggression faded. Not completely. Really, not even a significant amount, but he still hadn't drawn his gun.

And he still hadn't commanded her.

"You timed your escape to coincide with the attack," he said.

She laughed. It might have sounded a touch hysterical, but then, Rykus's accusation was just as insane. "I'm good, Rip, but I'm not that good."

It was the wrong thing to say. His demeanor changed. His expression, his stance, everything about him screamed that he was rage filled and ready to destroy.

Ash raised her crowbar even though it made a pitiful weapon against a gun.

"*Drop it,*" he commanded. The fury in his voice coursed through her veins.

Shit, shit, shit. She had to break his spell, set him off, suggest they get naked and run bare-assed down the *Obsidian's* central corridor, suggest *something*.

Her back hit a wall—she hadn't realized she was retreating again—and she pressed against it, trying to contain the trembles running through her.

Only a few feet of space separated her from her fail-safe. She willed herself to swing the crowbar.

She dropped it to the floor instead. The instant it hit, he charged.

She tried to slip left. He anticipated the move and threw her to the ground.

She twisted to her back on the way down, threw her fist toward his face. Missed.

He caught her wrist, brought it across her chest to trap her beneath her own arm.

The weight of his body pressed her into the floor. She hooked her legs around his waist in a belated defensive guard, but he easily slipped out of it. Shifting his position, he bent her arm, angling it until her shoulder was close to popping out of socket.

She gritted her teeth against the pain and arched her back. Her free hand pounded on him, but he didn't flinch, didn't budge. He maintained the pressure on her shoulder as he unsnapped and flattened the comm-cuff she'd stolen.

He shoved it into her hand. He didn't say a word. He didn't have to. His gaze demanded she enter the cipher.

She shook beneath him, fighting the compulsion, fighting him. The latter was why her shoulder popped out of place.

Ash screamed.

She bit down on her lip, still shaking, still trying to resist.

"*Stop fighting*," Rykus commanded. There was an odd tension in his voice, but it wasn't enough, and Ash had no strength left to fight the loyalty training.

She looked into her fail-safe's dark eyes. Eyes she feared. Eyes she respected. Eyes she had to obey. Her body convulsed once, and she felt herself break.

TEN

"PLEASE." ASH'S VOICE WAS SO RAW, so striated with emotional pain, that Rykus wasn't sure if the jolt he felt through his heart was her will breaking or his.

She had never uttered that word in his presence before. He was almost certain she'd never used it in her life. It wasn't part of her vocabulary. It would have been seen as a weakness on her home planet, just as it would have been a weakness on Caruth.

But the word was a submission, complete and irrevocable. All her walls were down. She was pleading for his help.

She was pleading for his help, and he was hurting her.

He released the pressure on her arm.

A moment passed. Then another. Then Ash's green eyes opened.

She stared at him.

He stared at her.

It felt as if he'd been sucked into another dimension, one where the loyalty training had flipped the axis of the universe. Instead of her being bound by his wishes, it was the other way around. She held his free will in her hands. He could feel it missing in the center of his chest. His heart beat within in the hollow space, lost, unable to orient itself, but one command, one word from her, could make everything right again.

Her lips parted. No sound came out, though he waited for it, waited for some command he could carry out for her.

Is this what it felt like to be a loyalty-trained anomaly? He wasn't in control. He wasn't thinking reasonably. If he had been, he wouldn't have been this aware of how her body fitted with his. He wouldn't have been able to picture himself lowering his mouth to hers. He could almost taste her. He wanted to taste that beauty mark to the right of her lips.

He allowed himself one weakness. He drew his thumb over the small, dark spot. It was real. As real as the woman lying beneath him. He'd seen Ash naked once before. He'd tried not to focus on her body back then, but he wanted to focus on it now. He wanted to take his time surveying every inch of it.

And he wanted her beneath him, vulnerable to his touch, his presence. Ash was always in control of herself. He wanted to see her shatter…

She *had* shattered. She'd just given him control with one word.

The universe folded in on itself. When it flattened back out, he realized who he was, who she was, and what he'd been imagining. He realized how wrong his fantasy was.

Ash stopped trembling. Her head tilted slightly, and her eyes narrowed with a mix of wariness and confusion. Maybe a little stunned wonder.

He was certain his expression matched hers.

Her gaze darted to the hand that loosely held her wrist. She must have been waiting for it to tighten—*he* was waiting for it to—but his mind had lost control of his body.

He didn't try to stop her when she smoothly and expertly flipped their positions. He didn't try to stop her when she drew his gun and straddled him. And he didn't try to stop her during those three odd, heavy beats of his heart when she sat there, beautiful and frozen and staring down at him.

They were still in the alternate dimension, the one where she possessed him. She'd slipped inside his soul and made it flare and flame and flicker.

Ash, he wanted to say, but he'd lost control of his voice too. He watched her rise, watched her stumble away. He watched her run toward the flight deck, knowing if he didn't stop her, this would be last time he'd ever see her.

He almost called her name then, but two spacers blocked her path.

Rykus couldn't move. Couldn't breathe. He wanted her to escape. He wanted her to remain within his reach.

Ash smashed her fist into the nearest man's face. The second grabbed her arm, the arm connected to her dislocated shoulder.

She didn't scream, didn't cry out. She slammed her head into his.

Another man appeared, blocking her exit. The fury on his face said he knew who she was, what she had done. He helped one of his fallen comrades to his feet, then they both rushed Ash.

Rykus's cadet did the smart thing. She ran.

He rose to his feet. It was like the air had turned to gel, and the thick, viscous liquid slowed his movements.

Ash escaped out the maintenance-bay door, the two spacers trailing in her wake.

His boots took him that direction.

He stepped into the corridor, saw Ash fighting her way past more men. He wanted to go the opposite direction, to extend the distance between him and his anomaly, but he needed more room than the *Obsidian* could provide. He needed galaxies between them. Maybe then he could process what had happened. Maybe then he would understand why he'd let Ash go. Maybe then he'd...

He braced a hand against the wall. The ship's gravity had to be malfunctioning. The corridor spun around while Katie's words spun through his head: *I always thought there was another woman.*

Was Katie right? Was he in love with Ash? And if he was, what did that say about him? He'd grown up in a military family. Rules, regulations, *honor*, they were all in his blood. Hell, the Coalition had pinned a medal on him, branding him a war hero. He didn't deserve the label, but he did his best to live up to it, always conducting himself with decency and integrity. He couldn't allow one woman to tear his life apart. He couldn't be in love with a traitor.

He squeezed his hands into fists.

It couldn't be true.

He lifted his gaze to the end of the corridor, the one Ash had disappeared down.

He wouldn't let it be true.

THE STARS IN HER STOMACH were warm and flickering and unfamiliar. Nerves rarely affected Ash. She didn't focus on the what-ifs or the risks when she was on an op. She focused on her teammates and her mission. She should be in that same mind-set now. She shouldn't be speculating about why her fail-safe had let her go.

That was the only explanation for her escape. Rykus had let her go.

Ash sidestepped a section of collapsed ceiling, then stepped into the ship's central commons. Men and women hurried to their destinations. Some helped injured spacers. Others stared at their comm-cuffs, which were either fastened around their wrists or unlocked and flattened in their palms.

Ash kept her hands by her sides. Rykus's gun, a modified Covar KX90 and an apparent exception to the Fleet's shitty weapons mandate, was a comforting presence beneath her long shirttail. It had serious knockdown power, accuracy that couldn't be beat, and a high-capacity, sixty-round expanding-ammunition magazine. That kind of firepower could buy a person a hell of a lot of time. It could have dropped every one of the unarmed spacers and soldiers who'd tried to stop her escape, and it would be a priceless asset once she reached Ephron's surface. The trick was getting there without killing anyone.

She strode across the commons, her gait casual but not too casual. The Sariceans weren't pelting the ship with torpedoes and plasma blasts anymore, but the crew was not relaxed. If they hadn't been so off-balance from the attack, they would have noticed her ill-fitting uniform and the combat boots that were two sizes too big. Instead, the individuals who glanced her direction had sympathy in their eyes. They saw her smoke-tinged skin, her bruises, her haggard appearance. They didn't see a traitor.

If she hadn't been hurt, exhausted, and in desperate need of a booster, she might have laughed. Her injuries made a perfect disguise. Lucky her.

Ninety seconds after passing through the commons, Ash spotted the portside docking tubes. The nearest three were lit green, indicating small craft were attached. One more minute and she'd be out of there.

She reached the first sealed door, reached up to pry open the security pad, but her hand hung in the air.

Something wasn't right.

Something pressed against her mind.

Something, or someone, was seconds away from exploding from a corridor behind her.

She drew the Covar as she spun toward the shadowy presence. A trio of spacers shouted and backed away, hands held up in submission.

They weren't the threat. The threat was...

The telepath. She couldn't see him, but she felt his quick approach.

Swiveling her aim to the left, she waited for the bastard to turn the corner.

A movement to her right set off her threat instinct. She launched a spin kick at a soldier's head.

Her foot *should* have connected with his chin, but he caught her ankle and gave it a sharp and powerful thrust up. The move took her other leg out from underneath her. She went airborne, then slammed down on her back.

She rolled, barely escaping the booted heel aimed at her face.

A quick jump back to her feet and she lifted her gun, aimed at the overly confident soldier's face—

And he disarmed her in a perfect execution of a Hraurkurian wrist chop.

He wasn't just a soldier; he was an anomaly. Shit.

The only reason Ash's gun didn't end up in his possession was because she anticipated his grab. She knocked his hand away, threw an uppercut that missed, and dodged back.

Distance. It was the only way to survive.

Her legs were long. She was quick. She launched another kick, struck his collarbone, and followed up with a—

Her head snapped back then forward then back again, and belatedly she realized he was landing blows. How many, she didn't know.

A rib cracked. Her vision blackened. She spit blood and tried to counter.

"You kill her and I'll have you counting comets in Norelli Sector."

The blur that was the anomaly glanced toward the man who'd spoken.

Ash didn't think, she dove. So did her opponent, but she was a little closer, a little quicker, and a lot more desperate.

Her hand closed around the grip of the Covar. Twisting to her back, she fired.

The bullet struck the anomaly's chest, hitting with enough force to make his diving body hover in the air a single second before it slammed into the deck.

Ash was already on her feet, already sprinting toward the telepath who'd inadvertently saved her life.

The instant she touched him, the pressure in her head disappeared. She snaked her arm around his neck and dug the Covar into his temple.

"Wait!" a man dressed in a civilian suit shouted. "Don't kill him. Just calm down."

She didn't pull the trigger, not because the civilian told her not to but because she realized whose head she was about to blow off: War Chancellor Grammet Hagan.

A chill colder than the dark side of space crystalized beneath her skin.

These files will destroy the Coalition. That's what Trevast had told her as he died, and that's why she'd fought so hard to keep the cipher to herself. She would not be responsible for destroying the Coalition.

She'd known she would have to take out Jevan, maybe one or two other government officials in order to preserve and protect the Coalition, but not Hagan. Not the Coalition's fucking war chancellor.

Just how far did the telepaths' reach extend?

"Let's talk, Lieutenant," the civilian said. Hagan's aide, most likely. He had the look of a data pusher—pale skin, wide eyes, hands held submissively away from his body.

She took a step toward the nearest docking tube. That's when Rykus stepped into the corridor. He stared down at the anomaly's bloody, motionless body, giving Ash half a second to prepare for his command.

"*Stand—*"

"Mouth shut, Rip. Open it and the war chancellor gets a bullet."

Not a complete bluff. She wanted to send Hagan straight to hell, but she was dead if she did. If she kept him alive, this hastily concocted plan of hers might actually work.

Rykus's chest rose and fell in a familiar, fury-filled pattern. She'd only pissed him off this much a few times on Caruth. She'd pretended not to regret it then. She pretended not to regret it now.

"You'll regret this," Hagan choked out.

Ash shoved her gun harder into his skull. He clawed at her arm. It was locked too tightly against his throat for him to get a good hold, but that might not last.

She took the gun away from his head. The moment it came into his field of vision, he clutched at it. She put a bullet through his palm.

He yelled, tried to double over, but she kept him upright.

Fight me and you're dead. She didn't know if Hagan could hear her thoughts since he was no longer in her head. He didn't seem to. He clutched his bleeding hand to his chest.

Putting her back to the wall, she tightened her stranglehold, then pulled him toward the docking tubes. The spacers and soldiers assigned to the *Obsidian* kept back. They wouldn't put Hagan more at risk unless someone ordered them to.

"Ash—"

"Shut it," she snapped, silencing Rykus. Her hand shook. Her fail-safe didn't give her a command, but his dark eyes were grim as hell, and it took everything in her to keep the weapon pressed against Hagan's head.

Rykus must have seen how close she was to the edge. He went still. It was more terrifying than if he'd let out a roar and charged. The loyalty training sank its talons in deeper.

"Do something," someone ground out. Hagan's assistant again.

Keep moving. Keep moving. Keep moving. She repeated the words like a prayer, hoping distance would break the control Rykus had over her, but her fail-safe stalked forward like a comet on a collision course with a moon.

"I will kill him," she managed to say.

Rykus started to open his mouth again but closed it quickly. The hollow of his cheeks jumped when he clenched his teeth. She could see the tension in his body, practically feel it in her own. He wanted to speak, but couldn't without killing the highest-ranking member of the Coalition's armed forces.

A bitter laugh lodged inside her chest. She knew exactly how frustrating it was to keep silent.

"Kill her, now," Hagan wheezed out. Gutsy bastard. He had to know if she died, so would he. She'd make sure of it.

"The universe knows you hate each other, Rip." Ash made her voice cool yet conversational. "They'll blame you for his death."

Another jaw clench, then Rykus let out a breath. He stopped his approach.

Turning Hagan toward the nearest docking tube, Ash ordered, "Open it." He croaked out a no.

"Open it or I'll shoot a hole through another appendage."

"You won't survive this." he said, but he slammed his uninjured hand against the palm-reader. She could have bypassed the security system, but that would have taken time, time Rykus wouldn't have allowed her, so it was beyond convenient having the war chancellor with her. His palm could open every door on every military ship, station, and complex in the Coalition. She ought to thank him for that.

When the door slid open, Ash backed into the tube, still holding Hagan as a shield. Her eyes remained on Rykus. He hadn't moved, but it felt like his hands were wrapped around her throat. She didn't breathe until the tube door slid shut, cutting off her view.

Free of her fail-safe's hold, she shoved Hagan toward the other end of the tube.

"You're making a mistake, Ashdyn," the chancellor said. Sweat glistened on his face and a red stain grew on the gray uniform beneath his bleeding hand.

"Keep moving." She stalked toward him with her gun raised. "Open the shuttle door."

"Every spacer and soldier in the system is on high alert. More security is capsuling in. You'll never get what the Sariceans promised you. You'll never leave this system."

"I'm an anomaly. I'll figure it out."

"What about Rykus?" Hagan said. "What about every other Caruth-trained anomaly? Kill me and all of you will end up in the institute. The only way to stop that is to give me the cipher. Tell me why you killed your teammates. How you broke the loyalty training."

She aimed at his right kneecap. "Open it."

His left eye twitched, but he placed his uninjured hand on the palm-reader. The shuttle door slid open and she motioned him inside.

Inside a CR2 maintenance shuttle.

Ash fought down a curse. She'd been hoping for a search-and-rescue craft. They had decent shielding, good maneuverability, and a few basic weapons, and if the fight with the Sariceans was as bad as Rykus had made it sound, there should be dozens of SARcraft looking for survivors. This CR2 wasn't much more than a flying bucket. It could barely deflect space dust, and the only offense it could manage was a suicide blow to the nearest flying object. It was built in space and intended for space. Theoretically, it could fly in atmosphere, but it wouldn't be an easy ride.

"Sit." She motioned Hagan toward the three seats in the center of the opposite wall.

"How long have you been working for the Sariceans?" the war chancellor asked, dropping into the middle seat. The shuttle's crew had unloaded most of the hold. She opened one of the remaining crates, found a coil of wire, and tied Hagan's wrists and ankles together, then to the chair.

"Have other anomalies turned traitor?" he demanded.

Sparing a second, she met his eyes. She tried to feel his thoughts, to press her way into his mind. She couldn't be wrong about him. She'd *felt* him approach. The instant she'd grabbed him, he'd fled from her head.

She didn't have time to force a confession; she rushed to the cockpit.

All the shuttle had going for it was that it was here and it was unoccupied. She hacked into the primary interface, bringing the engines online, and futilely checked for any modifications to its shielding or propulsion systems.

No luck.

"This is going to be fun," she muttered. Then she broke the seal with the docking tube. She kept navigation on manual, took the controls, and banked away from the *Obsidian*.

Alarms sounded when she left the old warship's side. She didn't have to look at the status screens to know what was wrong. Debris littered Ephronian space. Crushed and twisted hulls crashed into each other while smaller hunks of broken metal careened through space on dangerous, deadly trajectories. A vessel without decent shielding would be punctured to pieces by the debris. Not even the planet was safe. Bright white explosions lit up its atmosphere, making it look like a lightning storm had engulfed the entire world.

Ash squeezed her teeth together. Not all the space junk would burn up before entry. A significant amount would survive the fall and create a hazard for the planet's citizens.

It was one catastrophic mess, and she was heading straight into it.

Increasing the CR2's speed, Ash checked the situational display. It was even worse than she expected. Life rafts—hundreds of them—dotted the screen. Most of the tiny blue specs would contain life, but that many pods also gave an indication of just how many men and women had died above Ephron.

She gripped the throttle hard. She wanted the Sariceans dead as much as anyone did.

Tapping on the main console, she called up stats for every friendly signal within half an hour of her location. She dismissed the life raft signals, leaving her with several dozen search-and-rescue shuttles, six Coalition warships, and nearly thirty fighters patrolling Ephronian space. None of those would be a problem. They were too far away, and once she put a few kilometers between her and the *Obsidian*, she'd be safe. The fighters weren't close enough to catch up with her, and if the big vessels risked taking a shot, they'd likely injure or kill survivors in the life rafts and the SAR crews now working to bring them to safety.

She could make it to Ephron's surface. Once there, she could disappear and come up with a plan of action. A plan that would preserve and protect the Coalition while clearing her...

She frowned. A bright blue dot on her display broke away from the *Obsidian* and tailed her, no more than a minute behind at present velocity. It was another shuttle, but not a CR2. Her display identified it as a Dugular-class diplomatic transport. No weapons, but it had decent shielding. More problematic than that, it had better acceleration than her CR2, and more than likely, it had one Commander Rhys "Rest in Peace" Rykus behind its controls.

Her communications panel pinged.

"Hail from DDT-12," her shuttle's automated voice announced.

Not going to happen, Rip. He couldn't command her over the comm, but her mind already urged her to back off. If she heard his voice, the discomfort burning through her veins would only get worse.

The comm pinged again. Ash focused beyond her forward viewshield. Instead of blue waters and the browns and greens of Ephron's landmasses, black and gray smeared the skies. Smoke. Thick, heavy, and widespread, it engulfed the biggest continent, centered as near as she could tell over the capital city.

That's where she'd land. The infrastructure would be in shambles. Power would be down. Law enforcement would be occupied saving lives and battling fires. She could disappear, regroup, rest. She just needed a couple of minutes' head start on Rykus.

A third ping. Tearing her gaze from the viewshield, Ash checked the situational display again. She'd hit atmosphere. She needed to slow the CR2, but Rykus was still on her tail. Only forty-eight seconds behind according to the readout. He'd have to slow down too or risk burning up in Ephron's atmosphere.

She waited for him to back off. Instead, he eased more speed from the DDT, shortening the distance between them to twenty seconds.

An alarm sounded on Ash's console, warning her to decrease her speed.

Sweat dripped down her spine. She kept her gaze on the display, watching Rykus close the distance to nineteen seconds.

Eighteen.

Rykus's alarms had to be going off too.

"Slow down, Rip," she whispered.

Fifteen seconds.

The controls shook in her hand, and the CR2's nose pitched up. Emergency safety measures to help slow descent. She overrode them.

Rykus must have done the same. Twelve seconds separated them.

From the rear of the shuttle, Hagan cursed. He spit out threats and ordered her to cease her madness and turn herself in.

A second alarm wailed. She grabbed the console as the whole cockpit vibrated hard. Enviro flashed red, a warning that the air regulators were no longer able to keep up with the heat penetrating the shuttle's skin.

A roaring, ripping sound came from somewhere beneath her, and she was jarred back in her seat. Her ears popped. She needed to pull up if she wanted to have any maneuverability when she descended closer to the surface.

Hell, she was going to have to pull up if she wanted to survive.

So was Rykus. He was a damn fool, pursuing her in atmosphere at these speeds.

"Slow down," she whispered again. The loyalty training clawed at her, each sharp talon telling her she was putting her fail-safe's life at risk.

Distance between them decreased to five seconds. Half her displays sparked and showed static.

The comm pinged again.

Ash slammed her fist down on the green icon. "Back the fuck off, Rip."

CHAPTER

ELEVEN

F INALLY.

"Slow down," Rykus ordered. "Pull up."

"I said *back off*."

"No." He siphoned power from enviro, shifted it to his engines. Ash's fire wake ended just beyond his transport's nose.

"You have a fucking life," Ash bit out. "Go back to it."

His laugh was sharp, caustic. "You shot my XO. You've abducted the war chancellor. I'm not backing off."

"You stay on my tail and you'll be lying in a grave with me."

A wide, white section of skin broke away from Ash's CR2. Rykus jerked his transport to the left, dodging it. "You burn, I burn, Ash."

A part of him—a part he despised—wanted to believe those words mattered to her. He wanted to believe *he* mattered, but he'd been a fool. He'd let her go, let her take his sidearm, let her off the ship, all because his damn emotions had scrambled his gut instinct.

Tabbing through his displays, he scanned for some way to get more power, more speed.

"You're putting Hagan's life at risk," Ash said. "You want that on your conscience?"

Rykus peeled his gaze away from his readouts and focused on her shuttle roaring and vibrating on the other side of his viewshield.

His *cracked* viewshield.

Hell.

He funneled power to his shielding. It cost him speed but kept his transport together. Once he was stabilized, he leaned forward, putting his mouth as close to the comm unit as his restraints would allow. In a low, edged voice, he said, "I'm not letting you go. Get that through your head. You want to commit suicide, you want to kill your fail-safe, then keep your nose down and burn." He thought he heard a strained sound come through the comm, but there was so much static and noise—the roar of heated air and the groaning of a hull under far too much pressure—he couldn't be sure.

When Ash didn't respond, he continued. "I know the loyalty training isn't broken. I know how you've subverted my commands. What I don't know is how long you've plotted your treason. But I will find out, Ash. I'll pry every secret from your mind. You'll tell me everything you don't want me to know. Then you'll spend the rest of your life as a lab rodent on Caruth."

His throat clogged on the last word. Too much damn heat, and something—fuel or gas or the war-strafed planet's noxious smog—leaked into his cockpit and scratched at his lungs. Sweat plastered his uniform to his body. He'd suffocate if he didn't increase power to enviro soon, but so would Ash. She had to be feeling the dry, blistering heat too. She might be running out of air now. She might be in there dying.

She might already be dead.

That thought battered him harder than Ephron's atmosphere. Despite everything, he still cared what happened to her.

"Ash?"

"I'm still kicking, Rip."

Barely. He could picture her hunched over in the CR2's cockpit, sweating, swearing, and searching for options she didn't have.

"This isn't what I wanted. Sir."

Sir. She always punctuated that word with pauses on both ends, but it signaled she was starting to break.

"It's not what I wanted either," he said. "You chose this."

Another piece of Ash's hull separated from the CR2. Red lights flashed across Rykus's displays. He pulled up a damage report, checked it for something he could fix, but he wasn't a mechanic. He wasn't an anomaly. He wasn't even a member of the fucking Fleet.

He reached across the console and tweaked his power settings again.

"Rykus!"

The DDT bucked. His neck popped. He shook his head to clear his vision and saw the crack in his viewshield grow and splinter. Half his displays sparked, then went black, and every warning alarm in his transport wailed.

"Ash," he gritted out. The shuttle vibrated too hard and too loud to hear a response. His restraints tightened, squeezing him into the cushioned seat of his chair. A Mayday sounded from his console. His communications display, scrambled and flickering, but functional, lit up, telling him it was broadcasting his status and location to every emergency beacon in the vicinity.

A brightening yellow circle in the top right corner of the enviro display caught his eye. He cursed, grabbed the arms of his chair and—

The ejection came hard and hell wrenching. It flattened him into his seat as it propelled him beneath the console and into a survival casket.

His vision fled. So did the air in his lungs. He clung to consciousness, the scream of wind and pressure pummeling the small pod.

Automatic settings kicked in, slowing the jettisoned casket. Rykus's vision cleared. His mind returned. Groaning, he reached for the switch that would change the settings to manual. It wouldn't give him much maneuverability. Casket was an apt name for the tiny escape pod. It was created to bring bodies to the ground, dead or alive, not to pursue another craft, but he wouldn't let Ash escape. He'd land on top of her if he could.

Wrapping his hand around the single stick control, he switched the display at eye level to a camera angle that showed hazy ground below. Luck was with him. His DDT burned hot and bright in the middle of purple-leaved trees, an indication he was heading the right direction. He had only twenty, maybe thirty seconds of fuel to burn. Not enough to reverse course or stay in flight for long. He needed to get his bearings and find Ash's crash site.

A quick switch to another camera angle and he knew where he was. He'd spent two years on Ephron recovering from the injury that had nearly cost him his life. The majority of that time, he lived in the capital city, which lay burning to the east. The Tor River was below him, and…

There. Ash's CR2. She'd brought the shuttle down in the river. The hunk of metal had settled lopsided on the bank. It was damaged and smoking, but the crash might be survivable. A few meters more to the north, or a few dozen to the south, and the CR2 would have been destroyed by the strong, towering ever-woods of the Sambori Forest.

Ash might be alive.

No, she *would* be alive. Ash was like all other anomalies. She thought she was indestructible, and as inaccurate as that belief was, it made her partly so. Anomalies survived in situations where any other man or woman wouldn't.

Ash would survive this one.

He burned five seconds of fuel, swerving slightly to the right, then he delayed the release of the casket's parachute. The altimeter counted down the distance to the ground. He waited, waited, waited, until the details of the trees and river became clear on his display. Then he punched a button.

Pain lurched through every limb of his body. His restraints cut into his skin, and he lost his vision again. When it returned, Rykus's weight was in his feet. The parachute had released from the rear of the casket, effectively putting him in a standing position. The display flickered as the pod drifted toward the ground, but when it came back on, he saw he was exactly where he wanted to be, drifting to the ground almost on top of Ash's CR2. He searched it, looking for signs of life, but the only movement was the twitching of leaves and limbs in the breeze and the water lapping against the shuttle's damaged hull.

Had Ash already run? She wouldn't linger around the crash site. Admiral Bayis would send a troop transport down. Of course, with so many fires burning on the planet and so much debris from space, it might take a while for the Coalition to locate the crash site.

He reached for his comm-cuff, intending to expedite the arrival of the troops, but his fingers met bare, chilled skin.

Looking down, he saw a long, angry red scrape stretching from his wrist to elbow. No cuff. Not anywhere in the tiny casket.

He held back a string of choice curse words. They wouldn't make his cuff magically reappear. He didn't have time to contact Bayis anyway. Ash emerged from the wreck. She wasn't alone. She dragged the war chancellor from the CR2, shoved him to the ground, then pointed a gun at Hagan's head.

Ah, hell.

Rykus was still thirty feet above the ground, but he grabbed the emergency strap that would open the casket's canopy and yanked hard.

Ash's scream tore through Rykus. It wasn't a pain-filled sound; it was a sound of anguish. Frustration.

"*Stand down, Ash*," he yelled. He doubted his command would work—hard to get his voice and tone right when he was yelling from twenty-five feet above her head—but maybe it would distract her.

He slipped out of his restraints and stepped to the edge of the casket. Ash looked up. Bright red blood covered the right side of her face. She stared at him as he dropped to twenty feet.

Fifteen feet.

Ten.

Grabbing a bright orange emergency backpack off the ground, she ran.

Damn it.

"Stop!" He jumped, landed, and rolled. The impact sent a sharp pain up through his legs and into his spine, but he launched himself after Ash.

She was only a few feet away from the tree line and freedom.

She was an anomaly. Hurt or not, he wouldn't catch her if she made it that far.

Concentrating on his breathing, he made certain his intonation was perfect and said, "*Sit.*"

Ash fell to her knees. Then to her hands. Slowly, as if she was fighting a multifront battle against every muscle in her body, she turned and sat on her ass.

"I'm. Not. Your. Fucking. Pet." Her rage-filled eyes lifted and met his.

For the first time in his life, he wished she was a slave to his commands. He wished she'd never learned how to wriggle out of his compulsion.

"*Drop the g—*"

Grass and dirt erupted beside him. He threw himself to his stomach, pushed up in time to see Ash rise, his Covar held steady between her hands.

"Say another word, Rip, and I won't miss."

She wasn't aiming the gun at him; she was aiming it at Hagan. The war chancellor was on the ground, curled up into a ball with his bound hands shielding his head. He peeked out from under his arms. "You've lost your fucking mind!"

Slowly, Rykus rose to his feet. He had a duty to keep Hagan safe, but he wasn't going to lose this standoff again.

"*Put down the weapon.*"

Ash's gaze jerked to him. Her hand shook, but his command had been perfect. She set the gun on the ground. When she straightened, her eyes were pinched shut. Her body was tense, her hands in fists, and one tiny vein stood out on her forehead. As strong, resilient, and resourceful as she was, she couldn't fight him. Not anymore.

"Kick it over here," he told her.

She did, harder than was necessary. He picked it up, checked the magazine.

"Toss over the backpack too," he said.

She gripped the bright orange strap, looked like she was about to throw it to him, but her gaze went to the sky.

He heard it a second later, the low, dull roar of approaching sub-atmo engines. He risked a glance over his shoulder and saw three small craft on the horizon.

He squinted as they approached. He wasn't an expert on ship types. The birds definitely belonged to the Coalition, but they didn't look like troop transports.

"Predators," Hagan said. "Flag them down."

"They see us," Rykus said. They were headed straight for their crash site. There was no place for them to land, but at least—

Tiny specs dropped from beneath the craft.

"Are they attacking?" Hagan asked the same instant Ash bit out, "River. Run."

Rykus was already moving. He pulled the chancellor to his feet, then shoved him toward the bank. "Dive. Deep as you can."

He didn't wait to see if Hagan followed his instructions; he leapt into the river after Ash. Cold water closed over his head, his torso, his legs. He kicked his feet, parted the water with his arms, and swam down, down toward the bottom of the river.

The deeper he swam, the darker the muddy water became. His vision was almost completely black when everything suddenly turned orange. His ears popped. The river churned heavy and hot, and a sizzling roar filled his head.

He swam deeper.

Thirty seconds passed.

Forty.

The water heated. Burned. At the surface, it would be boiling.

He kicked again, and his fingertips found mud and rocks. He ignored the strain on his lungs and stayed there, fighting the instinct to return to the surface.

Fifty seconds. Fifty-five.

The fiery orange tint faded and shadows crept in. Not the muddy water this time. Tunnel vision. An indication he wasn't getting enough oxygen.

No shit.

He blew out the stale air and followed the bubbles up.

The water burned like a too-hot sauna. Survivable, but unpleasant as hell. He had no choice but to endure it. He needed air.

He broke the surface, coughing and choking.

"We have to move," he heard Ash say. "They'll come back."

Rykus blinked the scalding water from his eyes and saw her pulling Hagan onto the bank. The chancellor's face was bright red and blistered. He fell to his elbows and knees, wheezing. The trees and ground were charred, but very little fire remained. The Predators had attacked with brimfire, an incendiary that burned hot and fast, eating the oxygen until it quickly snuffed itself out. The stuff was lethal and poisonous. They couldn't linger here.

Rykus swam toward them. He pulled himself out of the water just as Ash turned.

"Status, sir?"

"I'm—" He stopped. Stared. Hagan's hands were unbound now, the wire unknotted at his feet.

Ash had taken the time to help the chancellor. She could have disappeared into the forest. Why the hell was she still there?

He took a step forward and placed his hand on the gun he'd instinctive-ly holstered when he'd run. Water in its barrel might cause its accuracy to be off, but he'd modified it well enough that it would still work. It would still kill.

"Hands on your head," he said.

Her lips pressed together. Her shoulders tensed.

The loyalty training. That had to be the reason she was still there. There was no other explanation for why a traitor would risk her freedom to help others.

"Hands on your—"

Hagan cursed, leapt to his feet, and fled.

Rykus didn't have to search the sky to know why. He met Ash's gaze as the whistle of inbound brimfire filled their ears.

"Kind of hard to run with my hands over my head."

She'd done it before on Caruth. He was tempted to make her do it again, but that despicable, irrational part of his brain that wanted her to be inno-cent kicked in, and instead of shooting her like he should have, he left the Covar holstered.

"*Don't leave my sight,*" he commanded. Then he shoved her after Hagan.

CHAPTER

TWELVE

THE PILOTS MADE A MISTAKE. They attacked south and west of the river. Ash hauled ass to the east, the brimfire burning hot enough to make it feel like her clothes were fusing to her skin. The weight of the soaked emergency pack pulled on her shoulders, but she didn't slow, she didn't look back, she didn't veer off course, not even to make sure her fail-safe was behind her. If Rykus and Hagan didn't keep up, they were dead. Checking on them wouldn't change that.

She sprinted up a steep slope, sweat pouring down her body. Her legs burned from the exertion, her lungs from the heat, but she dug her fingernails into her palms and kept running.

She wanted to never stop. She wanted to go and go and go until her body, and more importantly, her mind, shut down.

She'd been wrong.

She'd been completely, unalterably wrong. The pressure she'd felt back on the *Obsidian* and the voice that had shut up the moment she'd touched the war chancellor wasn't Hagan's. She'd pulled him from the CR2 and pressed her gun into his skull. He'd been furious. He'd called her a disgrace to the anomalies and to her fail-safe, and he'd sworn he'd make sure she spent the next century rotting on a bed in the institute.

And that's when she knew. Hagan wasn't the telepath.

Maybe the telepath didn't exist.

Maybe she'd lost her mind.

Maybe she'd snapped.

It seemed more possible now than it had the previous times she'd considered it.

She jumped over a tree root. There was a way to know for sure. She could ignore Trevast's last order, turn herself in, and give Rykus what he wanted. If she was crazy, the Coalition would comb through the files and find exactly what they expected. She'd be sent to Caruth, to the institute. They'd give her psychological tests, trigger drug-induced hallucinations, dissect her mind and body. It was every anomaly's worst nightmare, but if she'd killed her teammates, she deserved it.

But if she hadn't snapped, if her memories were real and this telepathic stranglehold wasn't some bizarre synapse gone awry, the Coalition would learn the identities of the telepaths. Trevast hadn't said who they were or how many, just that the revelation would lead to suspicions and accusations, paranoia on a universal scale. With so much infighting between the planetary governments already, the Coalition wouldn't survive.

The Coalition *had* to survive.

A hand on her arm jerked her to a stop.

"I said we're resting." Rykus squeezed the pressure point at the crook of her elbow.

The air behind her was cooling, the roar of the brimfire fading, but the indictment in her fail-safe's eyes scalded her as thoroughly as if she'd been caught in the Predators' crosshairs. She lost her balance when she turned toward him, a testament to how exhausted and weak she was. She braced a hand against his chest to stay upright.

And she kept it there.

Rykus's body tensed and his scowl deepened to a depth greater than the Spiral Canyon. She should have retreated or at the very least stopped touching him, but the contact wrecked her mind. His strength, his presence, washed over her, and awareness prickled across her skin.

He looked down at her hand. His jaw clenched, and the muscle beneath her fingers flexed.

Confessions and apologies and regrets tangled in her throat like wires from a power console with one too many upgrades. She couldn't straighten out what she wanted to say, so she swallowed the words and let them kick around her heart. She wished she didn't have to. She wished she could tell him the truth. She wished she could clear her name so he'd never look at her this way again.

She felt his condemnation when he swung the blade of his hand into her arm, knocking her touch away. Before the sting of the chop faded, he'd maneuvered the damp backpack off her shoulders.

"On the ground. Face in the dirt. Ankles crossed."

The loyalty training had her fully hooked, and the only protest she managed on the way to the ground was an overly dramatic sigh.

"I said face in the dirt." He shoved the back of her head down.

Grit and leaves dug into her face. She said nothing and crossed her ankles. It felt like there was a magnet in her chest, one that both pulled her toward and propelled her away from her fail-safe. The more she realized she'd lost control over her actions, the more powerful the magnet became. She was sure it would punch a hole straight through her any second.

"Hands behind your head."

Ash complied, no resistance at all, and hated herself for it. He wasn't even using compulsion. The general influence of the loyalty training was all that was needed to bend her to his will.

The warmth of Rykus's hands closed over her shoulders. They swooped down her back then moved to her sides. Up her ribs, under her arms, then down to her hips and butt.

Perfect opportunity to regain control.

She turned her head a fraction to the left, just enough to avoid a mouthful of dirt, and made her voice husky. "Take your time, Rip. Be as slow and thorough as you want."

His hands patted down her arms as if she hadn't said a word. When he reached her left wrist, he pulled up the sleeve of her stolen uniform, revealing the comm-cuff she'd taken from Hagan when she'd dragged him from the river.

She'd known Rykus would take it the first chance he got. She'd noticed he didn't have his cuff when he'd ordered her to put down her gun and hand him the emergency pack.

Rykus's fingers curled around the device and yanked.

"Ow," she bit out. Even if her wrist hadn't been bruised and tender, that would have hurt. "Why don't you cut my hand off while you're at it?"

"You're lucky you're still breathing."

"So are you," she said into the dirt. "Or did you not realize those Predators could have taken you out too?"

No response to that. Just a heavy silence that even the birds and critters honored. It stretched out over several seconds, and when it became noticeably long, she knew he'd discovered her little trick. "Sorry, Rip."

"What did she do?" Hagan clutched his bloody hand to his chest. He had a dirty strip of cloth wrapped around the bullet hole she'd put in his palm.

"How long?" Rykus demanded. She could picture him squeezing the comm-cuff in his hand, his eyes narrowed, his posture lethal as a sin snake poised to strike.

"Thirty-six hours," she answered. Then, being extra helpful, she added, "Probably thirty-five and a half now."

"Thirty-six hours until what?" Hagan asked.

"She put a lockout code on it." Rykus's voice could have chiseled stone. Yep. Definitely pissed.

"You can't break it?"

"She can't even break it," Rykus said. "Not for thirty-six hours."

She turned her head just enough to see both men.

Hagan's face was red. She didn't think that was entirely due to the brimfire.

"Give me the gun," the chancellor said.

"Why?" Rykus didn't take his gaze off her.

"Because I'm going to shoot her."

Rykus's hand moved toward the holstered Covar. His fingers twitched as if he was actually considering handing the weapon over. Instead, he reached up to his shoulder and pulled off the emergency backpack.

Her stomach dropped faster than the CR2 had through Ephron's atmosphere. She hadn't had a chance to check the pack. It could contain a comm-cuff or another communication device.

She told herself to rise to her feet and run, but her body remained prone on the ground, just as her fail-safe had ordered.

Rykus crouched, unzipped the pack, then searched through it.

Come on, Ash, she told herself. *Get up.*

He set aside a handful of e-rations, a pouch of water, a small med-kit. Everything looked dry and in good condition. The pack had a waterproof liner. Whatever Rykus found in there would function.

Raising her head, she stared at the dense forest. She could disappear into it so easily.

Run, she willed.

"Face. Dirt."

Her head thumped to the ground.

Oh, for the ever-living hell—

"Goddamn spacers." Rykus pulled out a black, hand-sized rectangle. Not a comm-cuff. Just a beacon that would send out a generic signal.

The freefall of her stomach stopped, leveled out.

"Careful, Rip," she said. "Our honorable war chancellor might take offense to that."

"It doesn't work?" Hagan asked.

"It works." His expression remained unreadable, but something in his gaze changed. Intensified. If he didn't stop glaring at the device in his hand, she was fairly certain it would crack. "Along with every emergency beacon from every other crashed shuttle, life raft, and dirtside transmitter." He shoved the beacon into the bag. "It's useless."

"Fleet's always been cheap." Ash meant for her voice to sound cheery but didn't quite achieve it. Damn. It was a sad day when she was too tired to get under her fail-safe's skin.

"Drink." Rykus threw the water pouch to Hagan. "There's a caff-pill and skin glue in here." He threw the med-kit. "Plug that hole in your hand. We're trekking it to Ephron City."

Ash turned her head ever so slightly. "I wouldn't mind a caff—"

"Trekking it?" Hagan said. "It has to be a two-day march."

"Wind's blowing from the west." Rykus held a tightly woven braid of paracord. "The fires will overtake us if we stay here." He used a knife to cut a length of cord, then rose.

Ash looked at the forest ahead again. If she was going to escape, now was the time.

Rykus's boots stopped inches from her face. He stood there, looming like a behemoth-class warship bearing down on a two-seater small craft. He'd always had a talent for making his anomalies feel insignificant. Ash half expected him to shove her head into the dirt again. Instead, his gaze and the weight of his last command pressed her down as effectively as a sub-atmo fighter in a steep climb.

"Why didn't you escape when you had the chance?" His hands closed around her wrists, maneuvering them together over her head.

"Mind being a bit more gentle, Rip?"

He looped and twisted the cord around her swollen and bruised skin, probably in a Caruthian lock-knot, which would be damn hard to break out of. The more she pulled against it, the tighter it would become.

He yanked her into a sitting position. The forest spun. She stared at Rykus's chest until the world settled.

"Answer my question, Ashdyn."

"Ashdyn?" She laughed. "Don't get all formal on me, Rip."

Her gaze rose from his chest to his eyes, and she cut off her laugh. His expression was as dark and cold as space, but there was a hint of heat in his gaze, of galaxies that couldn't be seen with the naked eye. Rykus had a gravitational pull as strong as any sun, and she couldn't resist being pulled in by his flames.

"I should have escaped," she said. "I made a mistake." A huge mistake.

"Wrong answer." He jerked her to her feet.

"What do you want me to say? Sir."

"The truth."

"That is the truth."

Rykus still had himself under control, but she didn't. She was tired, frustrated, and pissed off at herself, at Rykus, at the whole Coalition. She'd bled for them all. She'd given up her free will to become a Caruth-trained anomaly, all so she could protect it. And they believed she was working against it now. Working with the Sariceans.

"Why did you stay?" Rykus demanded again.

She pulled her arm free from his grasp. "I fucking stayed because of you. Sir. Because of the goddamn loyalty training."

Invading her space, he forced her to take a step back. "That training didn't keep you from turning against the Coalition. It didn't keep you from shooting your teammates and the *Obsidian's* crew."

Anger creased his face now. It creased Ash's entire universe.

"Tell me how many people I killed," she demanded. "Tell me!"

He opened his mouth to fling a number in her face but caught himself. The skin around his eyes tightened then relaxed. In a voice much quieter than she'd just used, he said, "Brookins. My XO. You shot him on your way off the *Obsidian.*"

It took her a moment to figure out who he was talking about. She'd shot a total of four people during her escape. Only one of them was likely a fatal wound—the anomaly who'd very nearly prevented her escape.

"Well," Ash said, feeling some of her independence, some of her brazenness return. "If your XO is dead, he wasn't a very good anomaly."

Her fail-safe stared, unmoving, as the wind picked up, carrying the scent of smoke and burning vegetation through the air. Her mental clock clicked to five, six seconds before the rage melted from Rykus's shoulders. Slowly he shook his head.

"Sometimes, Ash… Sometimes I wish I'd never met you."

Ash let a smile spread across her face. "That implies you're sometimes happy you met me."

CHAPTER

THIRTEEN

FOR THE SIXTH TIME THAT HOUR, Rykus watched Ash trip.
She fell to her knees, almost landed face-first on the ground, but she caught herself before she hit. Without a word, she climbed back to her feet and continued on.

She was hurt. She favored her right leg, and the outer edge of her left hand was purple and swollen. A broken bone, perhaps. She should splint it. She should wrap her foot or ankle or whatever was causing her to limp, but anomalies were trained to push through the pain, and Rykus hadn't given them time to rest.

They would have to stop soon. Hagan was struggling with the terrain too. He was uncharacteristically quiet, had been ever since Rykus had argued with Ash. He shouldn't have done that, shouldn't have asked why Ash didn't escape. Her words, her fiery response that she'd stayed because of him, synchronized something in his soul, and no matter how hard he tried, he couldn't knock it out of alignment again.

Rykus stepped over a rotting tree trunk. The dense foliage they trekked through was filled with shadows and slithering critters, not just snakes, but gray-bellied *miranders* that fed on reptiles and, despite being a fraction of their size, the *kibben* monkeys that were endangered on this planet. All the inhabitants of the forest sounded skittish and uneasy. They hadn't yet recovered from the terror of the Sariceans' attack, and the fires burning their homes inched closer and closer.

The latter was why Rykus hadn't called a stop. That and Ash might not have time to rest.

Every few minutes, Ash shivered despite the hot air. It was a sign of with-drawal from the boosters. She shouldn't be experiencing the symptoms yet, but perhaps her injuries and her exhaustion were bringing them on early? A part of him wished he'd let Katie give her a booster on the *Obsidian*, but back then—a mere twelve hours ago—Ash had been sitting in the brig with only a few bruises, most of which were of her own doing. She hadn't been tortured yet. She hadn't fought her way off a Coalition warship. She hadn't crash-landed a CR2 and escaped two attacks of brimfire that were meant to ensure she was dead.

The brimfire that would have ensured *they* were dead.

He glanced at the still-useless comm-cuff wrapped around his left wrist. Thirty-four hours until he could contact Bayis and ask him why he'd sent the Predators. The admiral knew Ash had taken Hagan hostage. He knew Rykus was pursuing the CR2. There were witnesses, and Rykus's transport had broadcasted a Mayday. Bayis should have sent a team of soldiers to re-con the area. Sending the Predators didn't make sense.

But maybe Bayis hadn't sent the Predators. Maybe they'd come from somewhere else. Maybe from someone who wanted Ash dead and to hell with the collateral damage.

Shaking his head, he caught up with Ash and pushed aside all the con-spiracy theories, all the wishful thinking, that kept trying to invade his thoughts. Instead, he made himself focus on the facts: an accused traitor had escaped from the brig of a well-run, fully crewed Coalition warship. How the hell had she done that?

He looked at Ash's wrists. Underneath the cord he'd tied around them, they were still raw and bruised. They were, however, less swollen than they'd been when Katie had treated her.

"The med-gel," he said. Even though he'd kept his voice low and quiet, it sounded loud in the darkening forest.

Stepping over a thick, tangled mass of moss and shrubbery, Ash glanced his way. "Med-gel? Whatever do you mean, Commander?"

Cunning, brilliant vixen.

"I thought I'd thwarted your plan when I didn't remove the restraints."

She slowed until he reached her side. "If it makes you feel any better, it almost didn't work."

He grunted in response, then pushed aside a thorned branch that blocked their path. Ash eyed the skinny limb, then him. When her eyebrows rose, he almost let the branch go. He wasn't being chivalrous. He was just getting the damn thing out of the way.

Ash's mouth quirked into a smile and she continued on. He let the thorns scrape across his hand—punishment for speaking to her—before he followed.

The forest was thinning. They should be nearing Shallow Valley soon. They'd reach Ephron City quicker if they stayed to its north, but at their current pace, the blaze that thickened the air with smoke might overtake them. If they headed straight south and kept the rocky valley to their north, it might slow down the fire enough to allow them time to make it to the city walls.

It might give him and Hagan enough time, at least. Ash's whole body shook as if a blizzard chased her.

"Scyene Desert," Ash said when the shudder subsided.

Rykus focused on the brush underfoot. He didn't respond, but the day she referenced leapt into his mind.

"Did I strip and ask you to spread suntan oil on me?"

He made sure his expression didn't change. Ash had hallucinated during training—all the anomalies did. The last two weeks on Caruth were hell. Rykus and the other instructors kept the cadets up for days without sleep. They ran them through icy water, forced them up snow-sleek mountains, then down into blistering-hot deserts. Toward the end of the training, Ash had fallen behind the men. Rykus went back for her and demanded to know if she was finally quitting. If she wanted to tap out of the program.

"You tried," he said, no inflection in the words. He'd caught the briefest glimpse of her breasts before he'd yanked her combat fatigues back down. "I wasn't carrying suntan oil."

Ash's gaze flew to his. She looked genuinely shocked. "Was that a joke, Commander?"

"No."

"I didn't know Rest in Peace Rykus could joke."

"It wasn't a joke."

"It was funny."

His glare should have shut her up. Instead, Ash's grin widened.

"I swear I saw an ocean." She hopped over a vine-tangled shrub. "Corwin swore he saw whales swimming through the dunes. That's why he tapped out. A fear of whales." She snorted, then glanced at him. "Do you know why Dees tapped out?"

Dees had been the top-ranked anomaly in Ash's class. Fast. Smart. Strong. When he'd punched his ID-sig into the console, Rykus had been surprised. Surprised and pissed. He had a talent for predicting which cadets would give up. He'd thought Dees would make it to the end.

Of course, he hadn't thought Ash would make it through the first week.

"He couldn't stand his own stench." Ash answered her own question. "It was a stupid reason. We all stank like piss and sweat. If he'd lasted three more hours, he would have been in the showers with the rest of us."

The anomalies had no sense of time at the end of the training. Rykus and the other instructors convinced the cadets they still had days to endure. The men who focused too much on the future never made it to the end. They had to focus on the present, the *now*, and not give one thought to what was coming next. Dees hadn't done that.

"Speaking of showers." A sly, teasing tone slipped into Ash's voice.

He knew where she was going with that subject, knew exactly the day she alluded to, and he wasn't going to play her game. "You're suddenly talkative."

"You both are." Hagan shouldered his way between them.

Ash's gaze followed the war chancellor. Rykus's would have too if Ash hadn't looked at Hagan with an abundance of hate. Hate and something else he couldn't identify. This wasn't the first time she'd looked at him that way.

Or the second or third. She'd been throwing those glances over her shoulder during the entire trek.

"Why didn't you shoot him when you had the chance?" Rykus asked, keeping his voice low.

The emotion vanished from Ash's eyes. She looked like she was about to say something, but she pressed her lips together instead.

Ahead, Hagan stopped. He didn't turn, but his voice reached them, hoarse, worn, and holding a fair amount of contempt. "Is that what this is? A conspiracy to execute me?"

"I saved your life, Chancellor," Ash said.

Hagan looked over his shoulder. "A ransom then. And when Commander Rykus ruined your plan, the Predators were sent to cover the failure."

Ash laughed. "Wow. You are full of yourself, aren't you?"

Hagan turned to face her. "The Predators weren't protocol."

Apparently Rykus wasn't the only one who found that suspicious.

"We need to keep moving," Rykus said. "We can explore your conspiracy theories when we make contact with the Coalition, but the fires are getting closer. Shallow Valley shouldn't be far. It might give us a reprieve from the smoke."

He checked the compass on the comm-cuff again—one of the few applications on the device that worked despite the lockout code—then continued southeast.

"You're responsible for her treason."

Rykus stopped. Slowly, he turned, squaring his shoulders to Hagan. "What did you say?"

"She shouldn't be capable of turning against the Coalition. Not unless you made a mistake."

Fury hammered Rykus's gut.

"Either you missed the signs that she was already a traitor," Hagan continued, "or your judgment was impaired and you didn't notice that the loyalty training never took hold. Maybe you didn't want it to take hold."

"I wouldn't repeat that accusation." It was one thing for Rykus to worry he'd made a mistake. It was another for this politician to accuse him of it.

"Were you screwing her, Commander?"

Ash let out a laugh. Rykus looked her way. She lifted a shoulder in an innocent shrug, then leaned against a tree.

"Please," she said. "Continue this testosterone-driven standoff."

Hagan took a step toward him. "Is that why you transferred out of the anomaly program?"

Rykus unslung the emergency pack from his shoulder and let it drop to the ground beside him. He curled a hand into a fist, but as much as he wanted to slam it into Hagan's face, he wouldn't. The war chancellor was the highest-ranked officer in the combined military. Rykus might not respect the man, but he respected the position.

"I transferred out because I don't believe in stripping people of their free will."

"She's betrayed the Coalition. She obviously hasn't been stripped."

Ash let out another snort of laughter. Before she interjected with one of her inappropriate comments, Rykus said, "The compulsion works."

Hagan's blistered face pulled into a scowl. "Then why don't we have the Sariceans' files decrypted?"

"Because she seizes when I use compulsion." The words were out of his mouth before he realized they weren't true. She'd only seized once. She'd followed every command he'd given her since he'd learned how she subverted the compulsion.

"You used compulsion to make her give you her weapon," Hagan said. "You used it to prevent her escape."

Ash's smile disappeared. Her gaze darted left to right and back. And even in the growing shadows of the forest, she looked pale. He hadn't noticed the change in complexion before.

"She only seizes when I ask about her mission," he said, testing the theory as he voiced it.

Hagan looked at him, his brow furrowed. "You're certain about that?"

He faced Ash. She'd become uncannily quiet. Sweat ran down her face, and her respiration rate was rapid and shallow.

"Why would you seize only when I ask about your mission?" he asked.

Ash wet her lips. She glanced to her right, tense as prey ready to explode into a run. Ash rarely showed indecision or fear, but her green eyes betrayed both right then.

Hagan stepped forward. His eyes narrowed, and he leaned toward Ash, squinting at her face. It was an odd thing to do in the first place, but it became odder still when he tilted his head as if he were seeing through her.

Ash went completely still. Her gaze moved from the forest to Hagan, and Rykus suddenly had the feeling he was missing something, a conversation or a conspiracy or a past that hadn't been recorded. The hair on his arms prickled.

"Ash," he said, trying to pull her attention away from the chancellor. "What are you—"

Ash launched herself at Hagan.

ASH'S HANDS WERE BOUND, but Hagan was close, unprepared, and her head collided with his. He staggered backward. She pursued him, rammed her knee into his gut and then into his face when he doubled over.

"Ash," Rykus yelled.

Fucking bastard! she roared in her head. Charging Hagan again, she flattened him to the ground. *It was you.*

"Shoot her!" Hagan yelled.

Rykus grabbed her bound arms. She tried to wrap her legs around the war chancellor, but Rykus was too strong. He body-slammed her to the ground.

Undo the telepathy, she snarled in her mind, futilely lunging for Hagan a third time.

"Telepathy," the bastard choked out. "You're fucking crazy."

Her fail-safe held her down. She stopped fighting him. She was too angry, too relieved, too exhausted. The presence she'd felt back on the *Obsidian had* been Hagan. He'd concealed what he was once she'd taken him hostage, but something had been off about him. She hadn't been able to ignore him. He was like a frayed edge of underarmor. She'd pictured herself grabbing the threads and she'd yanked.

And he'd responded.

She wasn't fucking crazy.

Rykus kept her on the ground, but his grip wasn't bruising, and when she turned her head, he didn't shove her face into the dirt. He wasn't even looking at her.

"What did you say?" Rykus asked Hagan. The question came out slow and quiet.

Hagan dragged his hand across his bleeding forehead. "She's snapped."

"No," Rykus said. "Before that. You said telepathy."

Hagan wiped the blood on his shirt. "Because she said telepathy. She's lost her mind. I don't know how she's functioning like she is. Broken anomalies don't have moments of sanity, but she does. She's different. The doctors—"

"She hasn't said a word about telepathy, Chancellor."

Hagan rolled his eyes. "She just did."

"She didn't."

Hagan's blistered face managed to turn an even brighter shade of red. "Maybe you weren't close enough to hear her, but I was. She attacked me without reason, without provocation."

Rykus didn't say anything. Ash couldn't turn her head enough to clearly see his expression, but he'd heard Hagan. Hagan had said the word telepathy. He'd given Rykus something to think about.

Yes, Rip. Think. Think! Follow that lead.

"What lead?" Hagan demanded.

Ash's gaze snapped to his. The wind stopped blowing. The smoke that hung in the air grew stale.

Tell him the truth.

Hagan frowned. He squeezed his eyes shut. When he reopened them, he stared at her mouth.

Tell him the truth now, she thought to him again.

"Chancellor?" Rykus said.

"I…" He didn't look at Rykus, only at her. "Say that again."

A tightness formed in the center of her chest. Hagan wasn't reacting the way she'd expected. She wasn't wrong about him, but maybe she wasn't one hundred percent right, either.

Tell Rykus I'm not a traitor. Tell him I didn't kill my teammates.

She *felt* Hagan bristle. "I don't believe this."

"Believe what?" Rykus demanded.

"I—" Hagan flinched. Then, he doubled over.

His hands shot to his head. A sound of agony squeezed out between his gritted teeth. His presence suddenly felt hot in Ash's mind. It felt busy. It felt as if all his thoughts were flashing through his eyes. The friction and chaos of their rapid passing burned his mind. And Ash's.

Rykus straightened. "Hagan?"

Could he... Was he... Oh, hell. What if he was a victim the same as she was?

She jerked away from Rykus, then tripped and scrambled to Hagan. She couldn't lose him. If this wasn't some trick or elaborate farce, she needed him. She could *think* to him.

She grabbed his arm. "Hagan."

He shook her off. Cursed. Sweat beaded on his brow, and his chest rose and fell with his breaths.

Rykus grabbed her by the neck. "Are you doing this?"

She ignored the vise putting pressure on her carotid artery, kept her focus on Hagan as he ran his hands over his face, up and down, up and down, up and down.

Hagan, she tried to pull him out of the spiral. *Hagan!*

His hands dropped to his sides. He leaned his back against a tree and his wide, bloodshot eyes stared off into the distance.

He didn't move.

"No," she said, her voice breaking. "No." *You can't die.*

She reached for him again.

Hagan's gaze snapped to her. "I'm not dead."

Rykus's hand tightened on her neck. "What the hell is going on?"

Closing his eyes, Hagan drew in one long breath, then focused on Ash's fail-safe.

"Your anomaly has been telepathically assaulted," the war chancellor said. "And so have I."

CHAPTER

FOURTEEN

RYKUS LOOKED AT ASH. He expected her to laugh, to make some quip or sarcastic remark, but she remained crouched in front of Hagan, her expression mannequin blank. And Hagan didn't correct or clarify his words. He just sat there, apparently waiting for his statement to sink in.

The blood rushing through Rykus's ears almost drowned out the sounds of the forest. Hagan thought he'd believe him? He thought he'd believe telepathy was possible? It was a fiction reserved for movies, literature, and kook sites. Over the centuries, multiple planetary governments had investigated and tested individuals who claimed to be telepathic. They'd all been proved delusional.

So why the hell did Rykus want to believe it?

He looked at his anomaly again. She was as still as a Caruthian deer encircled by predators—until she closed her eyes in a long, spell-breaking blink. When she opened them several seconds later, she finally moved. She closed the distance between her and Hagan, grabbed a handful of his shirt and kissed him.

She kissed him on the mouth. It wasn't a deep kiss, it wasn't sexual or romantic, but it agitated the hell out of Rykus. He locked his jaw shut to keep himself from verbally tearing into her. They weren't on Caruth. She wasn't his cadet. He shouldn't be affected by the behavior of a traitor.

An accused traitor.

Ash sat back. Hagan's expression had changed. He didn't look surprised, upset, or aroused. He looked… sympathetic.

"Someone better start explaining," Rykus ground out.

Ash's hands shook. The quavers were worse now than they'd been the last time he'd noticed them.

"You can't say anything, can you?" Hagan said, directing the question at Ash.

She looked wary. Tense. Her lips parted, but no sound came out.

Leaning forward, Hagan laid a hand on Ash's shoulder. When she didn't respond, didn't blink or focus on him, Hagan humphed.

"How has no one noticed this?" the war chancellor asked.

"Noticed what?" Impatience made Rykus's tone sharp, but he stared at Ash, waiting for her to blink.

"You're anomaly is unresponsive, Commander. Someone's put a lock on her mind. Every time she tries to answer one of your questions, she shuts down."

"She's trained to shut down during interrogations," he said slowly.

When Hagan's gaze shifted from Ash to him, it turned condescending. "I'd say this is a little more complete than that."

The man rose to his knees and then to his feet, his bones popping like a civilian breaking every twig on a nature hike. He wiped at his blistered face again, then stared down at Ash, who was still staring straight ahead.

"Telepathy," Rykus said. This time his tongue tested the word, the theory.

Hagan nodded.

Seeker's God, this was absurd.

"*Ashdyn,*" Rykus commanded. "*Get the hell up.*"

She didn't move.

"She can't hear you."

"Did you two plan this?" he demanded, stepping backward. He couldn't believe this. He *couldn't*. "I expect something like this from her, but not from the Coalition's goddamn war chancellor."

"Listen to yourself. You think I arranged for her to escape? To conveniently abduct me? To cut us off from all communication with the Coalition?"

"It makes more sense than what you're suggesting." His heart was beating too quickly, too hard. He wasn't in combat. He shouldn't feel like he was walking into an ambush.

"You were selected to be an instructor on Caruth." Hagan's voice morphed into the cold, cavalier tone he'd used during the anomaly hearings years ago. "It was a job reserved for the best military personnel in the Coalition. I'm surprised someone with your résumé is so slow on understanding the situation."

"I understand what you're saying. I just don't believe—"

"She says you didn't train a traitor."

Some unseeable, unidentifiable force ripped through Rykus. Ash hadn't moved, but her posture was different, and while her expression remained neutral, it wasn't as blank as it had been. She seemed to be seeing now.

Was it really possible she hadn't been seeing before?

Her green eyes slowly rose and met his. He felt like a paper tachyon capsule. If he moved any direction, he'd crumple. He'd been searching for a way to explain her behavior. Treason had never made sense. A mental breakdown hadn't fit either. A telepathic rewiring of her mind, as ludicrous as it sounded, could explain the inconsistencies. And it wasn't that far-fetched, was it? The Coalition had brainwashed her with science.

But science was accepted. Science could be proved.

"I need evidence." He had to force the words from his throat. "Show me... tell me..." He swallowed to work moisture into his mouth. "Tell me something only you would know."

Ash's expression shifted from serious to slightly amused. She looked at Hagan.

Hagan's brow wrinkled. "The night before D-day. She says she—"

Rykus held up his hand. "That's enough."

Adrenaline sped through his veins, quick as a bullet chasing its target. His vision sharpened. His breathing deepened. No one else knew about the night before Drop Day. He'd given his cadets leave, time off so they could think about the consequences of completing their training, and time for him to come to a final conclusion about who should be dropped from the program. No one should have been in the barracks that night. The fact that Ash had returned early meant trouble, and idiot that he was, Rykus had gone to investigate.

He closed his eyes, willing himself to block out the memory, but he could still hear the squeak of the shower. He hadn't wanted to turn, hadn't wanted to see her standing there, her back to him, her lean, sculpted body drinking in the water's heat. He'd started to leave, but then he'd seen the flesh-stitcher shaking in her hand and a gush of red slithered over her left hip. She shuddered, the stitcher fell, her knees buckled…

And he'd caught her. How the hell he ended up in the shower, immersed in its steamy heat, he didn't know, but he was there before she hit the tile, his arms wrapped around her body. God, she'd felt divine.

He opened his eyes, saw the teasing brightness in Ash's gaze. Did she remember that night as clearly as he did? Nothing had happened, but he hadn't been able to get the sight of her out of his mind since then.

"You aren't working with the Sariceans," he said. Those were the only safe words he could grab hold of. Ash had been set up. All the evidence— the evidence that he'd *known* was too blatant, too convenient to be true— had been fabricated. She hadn't fooled him, hadn't turned against her team and the Coalition. She was the victim. She needed his help, not his condemnation or his…

"Why the hell did you try to push me away?" he demanded.

Ash's half smile confirmed his suspicion. She *had* been trying to get rid of him.

She drew in a breath like she wanted to say something. Her lips parted, but then she pressed them together and looked away.

He looked at Hagan. "Ask her why."

Hagan kept his gaze on Ash. "She isn't deaf, Commander."

"Then what did she say?"

His gaze flicked Rykus's direction. "Perhaps she dislikes your company."

Ash laughed. Rykus tuned to give her a glare, but there was an odd note in the way her laugh ended, and when he focused on her, she didn't focus on him.

Another blackout.

His right hand clenched into a fist. He wanted to destroy something.

Or someone.

"Who did this to you?" he asked, his voice barely a whisper.

"My assistant. Stratham," Hagan answered, even though Rykus hadn't directed the question at him.

"He's been with me the past four years," Hagan continued. "He knows everything I know."

His gaze shot to the war chancellor. "Everything?"

Hagan gave him a grim nod. "He reports to someone else. I don't know who."

"He silenced you like he has Ash?"

"No. He didn't..." Hagan's brow wrinkled, and he rubbed at it like he was trying to rub away a headache. "I believe Lieutenant Ashdyn has been aware of what's been done to her. I wasn't, not until she ripped off the veil Stratham threw over my memories. This isn't the first time I've learned what he is. He... partitioned my mind. When I come across evidence of what he is or what he's done, he wipes my memory."

"You remember now?"

"I remember what I've discovered," Hagan said. "He and whoever he represents are trying to take over the Coalition."

Rykus eyed Hagan as he knelt in front of his anomaly. "They're not the Sariceans?"

"I..." Hagan's mouth thinned. "I don't think so. Not entirely, at least."

Rykus turned his attention to his anomaly. "Ash?"

She didn't respond, and the skin around her mouth was white. He placed his hand on her shoulder. Several seconds passed before she swayed slightly under the weight of his touch.

"She wasn't like this on the *Obsidian*," he said. "I would have noticed."

Ash blinked. She focused on him, squeezed her eyes shut again, then looked away.

"She says the blackouts are getting worse," Hagan told him. "Longer and more debilitating."

The breath she drew in turned into a cough, but even after she cleared her throat, her shoulders shook. Her whole body shook.

He wanted to pull her into his arms and hold her until she stopped trembling. But that would be wholly inappropriate, so he just tightened his grip on her shoulder and quietly asked, "You going to make it, Ash?"

She raised her eyes back to his, gave him a little smile. "Of course I will."

Her tone was light, but he heard the tension in it, the slight hesitation, the fear. She would never admit to the latter. No anomaly would. They lived by the motto *No fear. No failure.* She wouldn't quit until she was dead.

The underbrush crunched behind him. Hagan moving nearer.

"What happened on your last mission, Lieutenant?" the chancellor asked.

Ash's gaze seemed to fade. Rykus thought she might have blacked out again, but then he saw the fire in her eyes. Her nostrils flared and she wet her lips.

"I need to move." She got her feet under her then awkwardly stood. Awkwardly because her hands were still bound.

Rykus drew his knife from his boot and straightened. Gently, he grabbed hold of her right arm, just above her wrist. Carefully, he cut her free.

She let out a low, almost silent moan and flexed her left wrist. She kept her right one still though. It remained in Rykus's hand. He didn't let it go. She didn't pull it away.

Seeker's God, he wanted her. He couldn't stop his thumb from sliding across her skin. Her arm looked small in his hand, undeniably soft and feminine. How was it possible for someone to be both fragile and unbreakable?

Her hands shook again. He wrapped his around both of them.

She tilted her head up to meet his eyes. A hot wind blew strands of hair into her face. He resisted the urge to tuck them behind her ear. It would only have been an excuse to slide his fingers down that half-hidden lock of braided hair. He wanted to say so many things. He wanted to apologize for the bastard he'd been—the bastard he'd always been—and for not believing in her. He wanted to tell her she was safe now, she no longer had to fight, he'd take care of everything. But those confessions and promises were too revealing.

Instead, he leaned close to her ear and said, "You're absolved, Ash."

Her entire body stiffened. Not the reaction he'd expected, but it only lasted a few seconds. The tremble that went through her this time wasn't like the tremble in her hands. It went deeper than that, like those words—those words from *him*—were all she needed to hear to be free.

Goddamn loyalty training.

Hagan cleared his throat. Whether that was due to the smoke or to the fact that he and Ash stood almost forehead-to-forehead, Rykus didn't know. But he took a step back. He hadn't intended to get that close. He hadn't expected Ash to let him. She kept people at a distance with her flirtatious comments, her innuendos. It was a form of self-defense. But where were her provocative smiles now? Why wasn't she making some remark about how close his mouth had been to hers?

The air clawed his throat. He used a cough as an excuse to put more distance between them, then said, "Let's head out."

RYKUS TRAILED BEHIND ASH AND HAGAN. He'd been kicked out of their conversation because he hadn't stopped his "goddamn interrupting." Hagan was the same short-tempered, condescending politician he'd always been, and Rykus had been close to powering him down a notch. He'd stepped into the war chancellor's personal space and had opened his mouth to tell him exactly what he could do with himself, but Ash's stillness had caught his attention. The only part of her that had moved was her lower lip, which she pulled between her teeth.

She *needed* to talk. She'd had to hold back all hints of the truth for over two weeks, and it had been killing her as surely and slowly as the days spent without a booster. Rykus couldn't stand in the way of her liberation, so he'd swallowed his words, and difficult as it had been, he'd retreated from the verbal fight with Hagan.

It wasn't easy to stand down. It wasn't easy to walk behind Ash, watching her stumble and sweat and shake. He wanted to hear her voice. If it contained even a hint of her lighthearted, teasing sarcasm, he'd know she still had some time, but all he heard was Hagan's side of the conversation, and that was like listening to a bad translation of an alien language. It grated on Rykus's nerves as much as Hagan's tone did. With Ash, he wasn't condescending. He wasn't judging or acerbic. He was understanding and sympathetic.

Or he had been. Now he stopped Ash with a firm hand on her shoulder.

"We need to know what he saw," Hagan told her.

Ash's chin jutted out in that stubborn, I-can-take-anything-you-throw-at-me way she had.

"Know what who saw?" Rykus asked.

Hagan's expression immediately lost all hints of compassion. He folded his arms when he turned, placing himself slightly in front of Ash as if he were a wall sheltering a sensitive military complex. Hagan saw her as an asset, not as a person. Not as a woman. Rykus wanted to crush the wall the chancellor was attempting to build.

"Her team lead," Hagan said. "Trevast reviewed the Sariceans' files to make sure they contained the shipyard schematics. That's when he found evidence that telepaths exist and that they had infiltrated the Coalition. I think he saw a list. I need to see it, but she"—he jerked his head Ash's direction—"refuses to decrypt the files."

"Maybe she doesn't trust you."

Hagan showed his teeth. "That means she doesn't trust you either, Commander. She could have given you the cipher at any time."

He snorted out a laugh. "If that were true, we wouldn't be out here cut off from communication and trekking it to Ephron City."

"It is true," Hagan said. "And if she had given up the cipher on the *Obsidian*, the Saricean's files would be in an intelligence committee whose members were handpicked by me. Or rather, by my assistant."

Rykus stared at Hagan, a locking bolt sliding into place in his mind. If Hagan's words were true, if Ash could have given him the key but chose not to because she was determined to keep the files out of the telepaths' hands, it explained why she'd tried to push him away.

Ash didn't look at him. She focused on the dirt at her feet. If Hagan was lying, she would signal him somehow, wouldn't she? Glare at the war chancellor or give some other indication that his claim wasn't true?

Or had she tried to do that and was now caught in another blackout?

"Ash?"

She glanced up. Not a blackout then. And her expression had an edge to it, as if she was silently daring him to question her decision.

Her decision to not give him the cipher.

"I used compulsion," he said, trying to remember exactly when and what he'd commanded her to tell him. He'd asked specifically about the cipher only once, the time when she'd broken down. That's when she'd said please, and his universe had been knocked askew.

Ash had fought the loyalty training, fought him, to keep the Sariceans' files out of the wrong people's hands.

No wonder this woman amazed him.

"I need to see the files," Hagan said.

"What do the... telepaths want from the files?" It was difficult to say the word *telepath* out loud. That meant he believed they were real, and he still half expected soldiers to step out of the trees, laughing because he'd fallen for a hoax.

Hagan slipped a finger under his collar, pulling the dirty fabric away from his blistered neck. "It was something worth risking discovery for. More than just those shipyard schematics you were after."

When he didn't continue, Rykus asked, "What was it?"

"I'm not sure. There's been some speculation the Sariceans have developed a new technology, a weapon or defense that could give them an advantage in armed conflicts."

"They've learned how to exploit weaknesses in our sentient-class ships," Rykus said. "They already have an advantage."

"Our crypties are addressing those issues. No." Hagan shook his head. "This is something different. I think Stratham knew what it was, but I don't. That's why you had orders to capture the Saricean vessel in addition to blowing up the shipyard. We think they're working on a prototype."

"Ash doesn't know what it is?" He directed the question at Hagan but kept his gaze on his anomaly.

"No," Hagan said. "She didn't get a look at the files. She just re-encrypted them. But I'd bet my home world there's reference to the technology in the data she stole. We need it decrypted."

Ash fidgeted. She didn't want to give the key to Hagan. That had to mean she didn't one hundred percent trust him. That was fine by Rykus. He didn't one hundred percent trust the man either.

"The key won't do you any good here," Rykus said. "We'll decide what to do when we reach Ephron City."

Some emotion flickered across Ash's face. She kicked at a stone, then started walking.

"They underestimated her," Hagan said, watching Ash depart.

"The telepaths?"

Hagan nodded. "I guarantee they don't know there's a list."

Rykus raised an eyebrow his direction.

"They wouldn't have risked letting her live," Hagan said. "They're extremely careful with the knowledge of their existence. It's easier to manipulate a mind when no one knows your abilities are real."

Rykus grunted in response. Then he followed Ash.

"Any chance we can take a break?" Hagan called after him.

"We'll rest when we reach Shallow Valley."

He lost sight of Ash in the purple foliage. Only for a few seconds, but when he spotted her again, she was slouched against a crooked, wizened tree, her shoulder pressing against it like they were holding each other up. Her eyes were pinched shut, and her dark hair clung to her sweat-glistened face.

Rykus glanced at the useless comm-cuff strapped around his wrist. Twenty-five and a half hours until it was fully operational. Too long. He was going to watch Ash die.

A sensation of pure helplessness charged into him.

"That lockout code is biting me in the ass." Ash pushed away from the tree. She still looked tired, the crescents under her eyes darker than a few hours ago. She was paler too, and she kept her hands tucked under her elbows, trying to conceal how much they were shaking.

"I always warned you not to use them," he said. Then he stopped breathing.

He thought he'd seen all of Ash's smiles: the seductive ones she used to lure people closer, the flirtatious ones she used to keep people away, and the menacing ones she delivered right before she kicked someone's ass. But he'd never seen this smile before. Even though it was set in a face that was smoke-smudged and exhausted, he felt its glow. It was real. It was light. It was fucking beautiful.

He would not let this woman die.

"You do have a sense of humor," she said.

He didn't acknowledge her words, just stepped closer and said, "You're going to make it to Ephron City."

She met his eyes, her smile fading. "Is that a command?"

"No fear. No failure."

Her mouth narrowed into a thin, determined line. "No fear. No failure."

CHAPTER

FIFTEEN

H AGAN'S INCESSANT QUESTIONING almost made Ash wish she could close the gateway she'd opened into his mind.

She'd already told him every detail she remembered—details it hurt to remember—about the boarding of her shuttle and the murders of her teammates. He'd quizzed her over and over again on Trevast's actions, what he'd said, what he'd done, how he'd reacted to what he saw in the files. Trevast hadn't said anything about a new piece of technology. He'd been completely focused on the fact that telepaths existed, and he was convinced they'd infiltrated the Coalition's government. The significance of that information had stayed with him in his final moments, despite the nonsensical reference to his and Ash's argument over fashion.

And Ash had told Hagan everything she knew about Jevan too. It didn't matter how many different ways Hagan phrased his questions; she couldn't tell him what she didn't know.

She squeezed her hands into fists. It felt like her fingers were made of ice. She couldn't even feel her broken pinky anymore. How could she be this cold when she was constantly wiping sweat from her eyes? The last time she'd been this soaked with perspiration had been when Rykus ran her and his other anomalies through Caruth's Janul Desert. She'd almost tapped out during that stretch of their final evaluation. She'd been so dehydrated she couldn't swallow. She could barely swallow now. The smoke poisoned the air, making her throat itch.

They were still hours away from Ephron City. Would she make it? Or would she drop dead before they...?

She shut down that line of thought.

Doubt kills. That was another saying from Caruth. The only way to make it through the training was to believe you'd make it. The second you let doubt in was the same second your mental armor shattered. No one survived without that. Ash hadn't tapped out three years ago. She wouldn't tap out now.

She focused on her next step, her next breath.

I will personally review the Sariceans' files, Hagan said.

She glanced at the war chancellor. There'd been a two-minute reprieve from his questions, but not because he'd come up with a different angle of attack. He'd used that time to come to a decision.

She didn't say *I'm not decrypting the files for you.* And he didn't say *I'll make Rykus command you to decrypt them,* but the conversation hung there between them. He was the war chancellor, the highest-ranked officer in the combined military. He'd get what he wanted.

"Is there a problem?" Rykus asked, stopping behind them.

"There won't be," Hagan said. "Right, Lieutenant?"

Ash looked at her fail-safe. Would Rykus order her to decrypt the files? He was a well-respected, well-known hero in the Fighting Corps. He'd been chosen to train and control anomalies because of that reputation and because he always followed the rules. That kind of man wouldn't violate a direct order.

But she'd glimpsed a different man, a different Rykus a few hours ago. She didn't see any sign of that person in the looming, larger-than-life officer staring at her now. She wished she could. She wished she could feel his presence like she could feel Hagan's.

She tried again to find a frayed edge in Rykus's conscience. She wanted to know what he was thinking, why he'd sounded so relieved when he'd said, "You're absolved." A man who whispered those words with such a raw conviction… that kind of man might not use compulsion against an anomaly's will.

"Ash?"

"There's no problem." There wasn't one yet. She focused on the path again. Hagan turned too, leading the way. He didn't go far before he suddenly stopped. It took Ash's sluggish brain two more steps to command her feet to fasten themselves to the ground too.

The forest ended. The leaf-covered dirt beneath their feet changed to rusty-orange rock, and no more than ten feet ahead, that rock plummeted down.

Rykus stopped beside her.

"Shallow Valley?" She looked at him, eyebrows raised. "This is a deep fucking canyon, Rip."

He stared at the valley as if he was personally affronted by the steep drop off. "It's shallow closer to Ephron."

She laughed. It was a short, tired sound. When Rykus turned a concerned look on her, she forced her chin up, her shoulders back. She was fine. No one needed to worry about her.

Tossing the emergency pack on the ground, Rykus said, "We'll rest here."

Hagan dropped down. Ash waited a good handful of seconds before she gave in to gravity. She didn't need to sit. In fact, it probably would be better not to rest at all. Moving kept her muscles loose and her mind working. Sitting… Hell, her body was already protesting the thought of moving again. Sitting wasn't a good idea.

Rykus opened the emergency pack, tossed a ration bar to Hagan and another one to her. Hagan tore into his, but Ash watched Rykus close the pack. She hadn't inventoried its contents. If it was a Fleet standard-issue, single-survivor pack it would have five bars. They'd all eaten one once before. Do the math, and that left them one bar short this meal.

She tossed hers back.

It hit Rykus in the chest, and even though he hadn't seen her throw the bar, he caught it before it fell.

His expression shifted from confused to annoyed. "You're eating."

He tossed it back.

And she chucked it again.

"Ash—"

"I'm an anomaly. I can—"

"You're not goddamn immortal, Ash. You've been through hell and you're injured."

"You require more calories—"

"Seeker's God," Rykus muttered. "Out of all the times you fight the loyalty training, can't you make yourself fight it now? Your fail-safe doesn't need you to take care of him."

When he launched the bar at her head, she caught it. She fisted it in her hand hard enough to make small indentions in the dense, tasteless protein. Was that why she wanted to throw it back? Her mind was so clouded she wasn't sure. She tried to take Rykus out of the equation. If he weren't there, would she eat?

If he weren't there, there wouldn't be an issue because there'd be an extra bar.

Her head hurt. She didn't throw the ration bar back, but she didn't open it either.

"You may have been right about the loyalty training," Hagan said, chewing.

Rykus looked at him like he'd look at a trip wire across his path. "I might have been?"

"It alters the way they reason."

"I believe I was clear on that point three years ago."

Ash felt the mental swoosh of Hagan's annoyance but didn't see any sign of it on his face.

"You couldn't give me concrete examples of the changes then," Hagan said. "I thought you were overreacting."

"I wasn't chosen for the position because I overreact."

Another flare of annoyance, but Hagan's tone remained calm and thoughtful when he said, "True. I was under a lot of pressure from certain members of the senate. The size of the Fleet and Fighting Corps made them nervous. Some senators were threatening to leave. The Anomaly Program was a way to have a smaller Fighting Corps and—"

"'One anomaly is worth ten soldiers,'" Ash quoted. Then she smiled. "I watched the hearings, Chancellor." She'd watched Rykus. "It was a great show, and yet despite all your work, the Fighting Corps has still expanded."

"The Sariceans hadn't taken over the Kelin Mines then," Hagan said. "That was a direct threat to the well-being and prosperity of the Coalition worlds. We needed manpower to retake what was ours. We have an obligation to protect the citizens within our territories." His gaze speared Ash. "*You* have an obligation to protect them."

She was protecting them by preserving the Coalition. Why Hagan couldn't see that, she didn't know. Perhaps he didn't want to see it. He didn't want to see the cracks in the alliance he had so much influence in. Like Hagan, most planetary leaders saw the benefit of being part of the Coalition, but some didn't. Some, like Rykus's home world, shied away from giving up any power to a central authority, no matter how loosely that authority governed them. They looked for abuses of power and reasons to convince their people they needed to secede. That's why she couldn't give up the cipher. Even if Jevan and Hagan's assistant were the only two telepaths in the Coalition, the knowledge of their existence would be enough to make a number of worlds withdraw.

It will destroy the Coalition, she told Hagan.

"Then so be it," he snarled. The vehemence took her by surprise. So did the sound of a twig breaking from the edge of the forest.

"Cover!" Rykus shouted, but Ash was already moving. Bark exploded off the trees to her left as she rammed into Hagan.

"Down!" she yelled, flinging them both toward the valley.

Ash kicked and grabbed as she slid down the steep incline.

She found a good handhold, flipped to her stomach. "Rykus!"

"Here." His calm, steady voice came from her right. He was flattened against the slope too, his gun—their only weapon—drawn and ready.

He focused behind her. "Stay down."

Turning to her right, she saw Hagan working his way up the rocky slope. She grabbed a fistful of his uniform. "You want your head blown off?"

"They're Coalition soldiers," the chancellor said.

"They shot at us."

"At *you*, Lieutenant. As far as they know, I'm your hostage. I'll talk to them. I'll make sure you aren't harmed, and *when* you decrypt the files, I'll clear your name."

Her hand shook, but she didn't release his uniform. Her instincts screamed this was a bad idea.

"Take one more step and I'll blow the war chancellor's head off," Ash yelled. She hadn't heard anyone move, but the soldiers weren't firing, and she needed time to think.

"She's lying," Hagan called out. "She's unarmed. I'm War Chancellor Grammet Hagan. I'm coming up."

"Hands over your head," someone yelled back. "Move slowly."

Hagan tugged his uniform free and climbed.

"You need a booster, Ash," Rykus said.

Her nostrils flared. Her fail-safe was with Hagan on this. He wanted her to be taken back into custody.

She looked down at the valley—no, the Deep Fucking Canyon—below. She might be able to find a survivable way down, but damn it. She needed Hagan.

Craning her neck, she looked up in time to see the chancellor pull himself to the top of the cliff. He made it to the flat ground, rose to his knees, arms held out to either side.

"Are you injured?" a soldier above asked.

"Lieutenant Ashdyn is not to be harmed," Hagan said. "I've spoken with her. We've come to an agreement. She'll—"

Bang.

Adrenaline surged through Ash's body, slowing down time and making the *woosh-woosh* of her heart sound loud in her ears. Her hands tightened on the rocks embedded in the canyon, and she watched Hagan's brain tissue explode out the back of his head.

She heard herself scream "no," just like she'd screamed no when Jevan's bullet had slammed into Trevast's skull. The same agony of disbelief ripped through her, leaving behind a useless, hollow shell. She watched Trevast's blood splatter, watched his body fall backward, his head crack on the deck.

Then Hagan's corpse fell through the flashback, landing between her and Rykus. It slid half a meter down the cliff before it hit a rock. Momentum carried his feet over his damaged head, and he rolled down the precipice, end over end, in a cloud of rocks and pebbles.

Screaming, she lunged for the top of the canyon, determined to kill the son of a bitch who'd murdered the one person she could talk to.

"Ash!" Rykus grabbed her arm.

"They killed him." She reached a hand to a stone at ground level. Bullets sprayed the dirt.

"Get down!"

She reached up again, mad with rage and loss and helplessness.

Rykus jerked her back hard. They slid down the ravine, stopping only when her fail-safe threw his body on top of hers, pressing her into the rocky cliff face.

"Listen, Ash! Think! We have one weapon. They have dozens. We have to run. We have to escape." He shook her until she looked him in the eyes. "*You* have to survive."

Fury, determination, and something else, something she couldn't recognize, burned in his brown eyes. He centered her, brought her sanity back, and despite the hopelessness running through her, she gave in to his pull.

Drawing in one long breath, Ash let all her fears and frustrations go, and she focused on the present, focused on survival. "Race you to the bottom, Rip."

IN RETROSPECT, THROWING THEMSELVES down the canyon was as suicidal as climbing back over the ridge. Ash tried to hang on to Rykus, to keep him close and safe, but an outcropping of rock hit her elbow, flinging her arm in the air. She lost sight of him in the cloud of dust and debris.

A cloud that saved her life. Bullets pelted the ground around her, but the soldiers couldn't have seen her. She was too obscured in the haze, and she was falling fast.

Too fast. She slid on her back in a rain of rocks and pebbles, arms and legs scrambling for some way to control her descent. Dry, thorned shrubs tore at her clothes and skin.

The bullets from above became distant thunder in the background compared to the cacophony of her fall. Her shoulder smacked against a sharp, jutting rock, and she went airborne.

She didn't know how long she hung there, didn't know which way was up or down. A millennium passed before the canyon gave her an answer, smashing her face-first into the cliff. The ground bruised and cut her, but she slowed. A few more flails of her arms and legs and she finally came to a stop on a relatively level slab.

"Rykus." She strained to get his name out. Her throat was filled with dirt. She tried to spit, to clear it out of her system, but she had no moisture in her mouth. Rubbing at the grit in her eyes, she searched for her fail-safe.

If he hadn't been wearing the useless emergency pack, she would have missed him in the dust cloud. But the flash of orange in her peripheral vision caught her attention, and she lunged, grabbing the pack.

Momentum tripled his weight. Ash almost lost her grip, but Rykus caught himself just before skipping over the edge of the slab.

Flipping to his stomach, he aimed his Covar up the cliff face. The soldiers were still shooting. Rykus returned fire in quick but careful bursts. Ash watched, feeling completely useless. All she could do was lie there and watch.

Watch as Rykus's ammunition ran out.

Watch as a bullet struck his shoulder.

Watch as a man who was supposed to be invincible bled.

Instinct and training and a deep, almost incapacitating panic cracked the ice enclosing her. She threw her body on top of his.

"Fall back!" Rykus shoved her away. "Fall back!"

Fall back? There wasn't anywhere to fall back to but down.

"Go." He pushed her over the precipice.

Her chin hit first. Pain radiated down her spine when her neck snapped back, then she was airborne again, an impossible-to-stop human avalanche.

Her shoulder hit next, skipping off the rocky ground. She landed on her opposite shoulder and rolled.

She rolled for eons, the ground ripping at her clothes and flesh. Snatches of gray sky and brown earth tumbled through her vision, over and over. Her lungs filled with dirt and dust, her mouth with dirt and blood.

Finally the world went blessedly black.

CHAPTER

SIXTEEN

PEBBLES CRUNCHED NEAR ASH'S HEAD. It was a suspiciously soft, harmless sound, but it was a sound that jerked her back to consciousness.

She caught a reaching hand.

"It's me." Rykus sounded like an engine in need of oil. She could barely make out his face through the grit in her eyes.

The dirt was everywhere. Her mouth. Her nose. Her ears. She could feel it rattling around in her lungs.

Rykus coughed. "Status?"

Releasing his hand, she stared up at the haze above them. They should both be dead. If she wasn't an anomaly, if Rykus wasn't such an invincible, unconquerable soldier, they would be.

"Status," Rykus barked again, a deeper rumble in his voice. He was her cold, emotionless fail-safe again. That worked for her. She didn't know what to do with the other Rykus, the one she'd glimpsed earlier. The one who'd leaned his forehead against hers as if the universe had righted itself when he learned of her innocence.

"My neck isn't broken. My back is functional. Legs functional." She tried to swallow, but it was impossible with the grit coating her throat. "Your status?"

"Functional."

"You were shot." Her words came out controlled and careful, but she turned her head slightly to look at him, afraid of what she might see.

"Left shoulder," he said. "The bullet didn't pass through the *bruidium*."

She eyed the shoulder. The hole in his uniform was dark and wet, but the damage seemed contained to a relatively small area.

Relaxing, she said, "*Bruidium?* That's what they used to reconstruct your shoulder? The Coalition does think highly of you, doesn't it?" The compound was rare, exotic, and expensive enough to fund an entire platoon of special forces soldiers for a standard month.

"The dirt's stopped the bleeding," he said, ignoring, as usual, the reference to his past.

"You didn't hold on to the emergency pack." He wasn't going to bleed out, but infection could become a problem.

"I was busy trying not to break my neck."

A smile bent her lips. "You're funny."

She wasn't certain, but it seemed like her comment made his expression grow more serious.

"There's a river that runs through the center of the valley—"

"DFC," she interjected, staring at the cliff face towering high above them. The upper ledge was obscured by the dust cloud their avalanche had caused. "Deep. Fucking. Canyon. Sir."

A pause. Then, "Canyon. We can get the sand out of our joints there."

"Then what?" She couldn't help the frustration that leaked into her voice. She wasn't defeated, but she'd been knocked down so many times it was difficult to tell which way was up. Hagan's murder, so soon after she'd unloaded everything, had throttled her.

"Then we keep moving until we find help."

"Our 'help' just assassinated the Coalition's highest-ranked military officer."

"I know." Those two words contained enough force to cause a galaxy to expand. "But they weren't my men. They weren't from the *Obsidian*."

"Oh, you know every soldier on the ship?"

"I know the officers."

She sniffed. "Of course you do."

"I trust Admiral Bayis."

"I don't."

A scowl creased Rykus's face. "Do you have evidence the telepaths have infiltrated the *Obsidian*?"

Still lying on her back, she closed her eyes. If she thought she could get away with it, she would have asked Rykus if he was trying to make her black out. His question was so obviously *un*answerable.

Don't react. Don't. React.

Opening her eyes, she saw a barely there grimace on Rykus's face.

"All right," he said slowly. "Let's try this. One blink for yes. Two for no. Have telepaths infiltrated the *Obsidian*?"

The darkness blindsided her. A roar filled her ears, and the world dropped out from underneath her. A chill swept over her skin and she shook. She shook despite the fact that she awoke wrapped in Rykus's arms.

Damn it. She hadn't even tried to blink—she'd tried to roll her eyes—but it hadn't mattered. There'd been enough intention in the action to trigger the blackout.

"I'm sorry," Rykus said when she focused on him. "I wanted to... Damn. I'm sorry, Ash."

He looked almost as frustrated as she felt.

"We'll figure it out," he assured her. His hand touched her face. It was the lightest brush of fingertips over the curve of her jaw—it might even have been an accident—but Ash's stomach fluttered.

It *fluttered*.

No part of her body had ever done that before. She wasn't capable of such a soft, vulnerable feeling. But Rykus's arms were strong. They were warm. And they held her as if she wasn't just an anomaly but a human.

A woman.

She jerked away. The pain running through her body sharpened, and she focused on it. Damn near embraced it. Her heart beat as quickly as it had when they'd been under fire. She stared at Rykus's expertly blank face.

His dirty, scuffed face. The grime only made him look tougher, stronger. Sexier.

Ah, hell. Ash closed her eyes. She'd always thought Rykus was attractive, but she'd met hundreds of good-looking men. She could have her pick of any one of them, and often had, but they didn't have Rykus's presence. They didn't have his moral strength.

They didn't have the ability to make her *flutter*.

"They'll be looking for our bodies," she said, making sure the steel in her voice disguised how much she hurt. She wouldn't show weakness around him. She sure as hell wouldn't show vulnerability.

"Yes." Rykus rose. He offered to help her up, but she bypassed his outstretched hand and climbed to her feet on her own.

"Can you run?" he asked.

She met his gaze and her raised eyebrow said, *I'm an anomaly. Of course I can run.*

Two minutes later though, she was cursing that eyebrow. It was a miracle neither of them had broken a leg in the fall, but Ash's ankle was at least sprained. She blocked out the pain and ignored her broken ribs, her cuts and bruises, and her throbbing pinky. And she ignored the sick, shaky feeling that ran through her body, the feeling that told her she was close to falling apart. They needed to put distance between them and the soldiers who had attacked, so she couldn't stop. She couldn't rest. She could only ignore the pain and weakness and fear and continue.

It took them twenty long minutes to reach the river. Most of that time was spent jogging through the purple-leaved trees that filled the bottom of the DFC. They provided good cover, but hopping over roots and ducking beneath their low limbs drained even more of her energy. When she stopped beside the river, she meant to slowly lower herself to the ground. Instead, her legs gave out and the motion turned into a semi-controlled fall. The only reason she didn't land face-first in the water was because she caught herself at the last moment. The rocky bottom bruised her palms, and the chilly water sloshed up to her elbows.

She didn't care. Scooping water into her mouth, she tried to rinse out the desert that coated her tongue.

Beside her, Rykus did the same, drinking and spitting and coughing. He dunked his head into the stream and ran his hand through his short hair.

Ash's hair was past her shoulders, dirty and tangled. A quick dunk wouldn't work for her, so she settled for shaking out the arms and legs of her stolen uniform.

Rykus tried to shake out his clothes too. A beach was forming underneath them, but still Ash felt the rocks and grit everywhere.

Screw it.

She stood up and stripped.

In her peripheral vision, Rykus froze. She felt his gaze as she unfastened the last button on the shirt, threw it aside, then shimmied the pants down over her hips.

Rykus didn't say a word when she stepped into the cold stream. Neither did she, but she couldn't keep a small grin off her lips as she moved deeper into the water. She might be black and blue and covered in blood and dirt, but she had a lean, toned figure, and Rykus was a man.

An untouchable man, she reminded herself.

The stream was only waist-deep in the middle. She crouched until the water lapped at the top of her shoulders, and then she began scrubbing.

Seconds later, she heard Rykus wade into the stream.

It was hard not to turn around to see if he'd stripped too. She'd seen him almost naked before, shirtless and wearing only a tight pair of black briefs. She was the only woman in her class of anomalies—the only woman ever to complete the training—and he was built like a Zenith Predator, all hard, defined muscles and smooth, lethal movements.

Almost-naked wasn't the same as naked though, and she wouldn't mind seeing him again.

But it would be a bad idea. An epically bad idea.

Sucking in a deep breath, she dunked herself.

Underwater, she ran her fingers through her hair, pulling out twigs and grass and a surprisingly large rock. She rubbed her face and neck, then she stayed there, submerged and unmoving, letting the shallow river rinse the sweat and grime from her body. She hadn't had a shower in weeks, not since she was first taken into custody, and despite the exhaustion in her limbs and the chilly water, it felt good to be clean again.

She rose when her lungs first began to feel the strain of holding her breath. She heard Rykus behind her, felt him move closer. Once again, she had to fight not to turn.

Her hair moved. He lifted it to find the small braid that rested underneath it all. His breath was warm on her shoulder. He let the braid slide lightly through his fingers.

"Why do you wear this?" he asked. He was close. If she leaned back just a fraction, she'd press against him. She'd feel him. She'd learn whether the cold water affected a certain part of his anatomy or whether she did.

And he'd probably tear into her, going off about her insolence and recklessness in a combat situation.

Probably.

"You ordered me to," she said, keeping her tone light and flirtatious to hide just how much she wanted him to move closer. It was a ridiculous need. She was under his control, and he had a code of ethics. Even if he wanted her—and she acknowledged that her emotions and thoughts were so screwed up that he might not—he wouldn't cross that line with her.

He didn't respond to that, not even with a noncommittal grunt. Instead, he turned and splashed out of the stream.

Ash couldn't help it. She glanced over her shoulder and took in his perfectly sculpted back and ass. He had strong, wide shoulders. His left shoulder was scarred from the injury that had almost taken his life a decade ago, and bruises and scrapes decorated his skin.

Bruises and scrapes and a bullet wound she couldn't see from this angle.

Bruises and scrapes and a wound that was her fault.

A strong, almost debilitating wave of guilt moved through her. He was her fail-safe. The programming that made her obey him also urged her to protect him, and even though she told herself the feelings—the worship, the want—were the results of the loyalty training, it didn't make them go away. It didn't make them any less potent.

Rykus shook out his clothes and dressed with his back to her. She waded out of the water and did the same. The stolen uniform was still stained and dirty, but she didn't have time to rinse it out and let it dry. Even if the soldiers who'd killed Hagan didn't come searching for their bodies, Ash didn't know how much longer she'd last. She'd never felt so weak before, not even as a starved and beaten child on the streets of Glory.

Rykus waited while she dressed, his back to her.

"I'm ready," she said, fastening the last button.

He nodded once, then led the way east without even a glance in her direction. She ignored the stab of disappointment, told herself it was a good thing he hadn't looked at her. If he had, he would have seen how much her hands were shaking. He would have seen how hard Ephron's gravity pressed on her shoulders.

Drawing in a breath, she gave herself a few seconds to get her body and mind into a combat state, then she soldiered after him.

CHAPTER

SEVENTEEN

T HE SOUND OF FALLING ROCK echoed off the walls of the DFC. Rykus stopped in the thin forest at the bottom of the canyon and glanced behind him. Ash had stopped moving as well. He motioned her to stay where she was; then he eased to the edge of the tree line.

The cliff—and Ash was right, this was a canyon, not a valley—stretched toward the smoke-smeared sky. It wasn't as steep as it had been before, but it was still a rocky, sharp incline. Since he and Ash had started walking, they'd heard a dozen small avalanches. If the soldiers decided to pursue them, they would have a warning.

And if he and Ash decided to scale the DFC back to the top, the soldiers would have that warning.

He leaned his shoulder against a tree and slowly scanned the cliff. No movement. At least none that he could see.

"I wonder if they think you're dead," Ash mused behind him.

It was a nice, almost believable fiction. The Coalition's resources were stretched thin, millions of people were hurt and homeless. The pursuit force could have been reassigned to search-and-rescue operations.

"It would be ironic, wouldn't it?" Ash continued. "The pursuit force declares you dead. You show up again later, maybe at your second funeral."

After one last scan of the wall, he moved back into the deeper shadows of the forest. "They don't think we're dead."

"This funeral might be even more spectacular than the first," she continued. "The mourning would last for weeks. They'd name a capsule after you. Or a planet, that would be—"

"Ash."

She stopped, eyebrows raised as if asking an innocent question. When his expression didn't change, her shoulders slouched. "How long until the ambush?"

He wanted to say something that would bring back her light, teasing tone, but Ash knew the reality of their situation, and she'd never needed to have the truth coated with lies.

"I don't know."

She turned her head to the right, the direction they'd been heading. "We should separate."

The suggestion felt like a punch to the chest.

"That won't accomplish anything," he said.

"I'll throw the pursuit force off your trail."

"We're staying together."

"It would be better—"

"No." He took a step toward her. "We'll keep a look out for the ambush. If a stone or a blade of grass is out of place, we'll retreat and reroute. We'll stay together, and we'll keep moving until we reach the city."

"I won't make it to—" She snapped her mouth shut.

He kept a grimace from his face, but inside his heart flinched. She wouldn't make it to Ephron City. That's what he feared.

He reached for her, but she turned and walked away.

Rykus's hand fell to his side. Ash's armor was cracking. She was doubting her abilities, doubting herself. If she kept doing that, she wouldn't make it.

He jogged to catch up with her. "A new sentient-class ship."

She threw a frown his way.

"That's what I want dedicated to me at my next funeral."

A smile shattered her grim expression. Something loosened in his chest. With a hand on her lower back, he kept her moving forward. He'd do whatever it took to keep her morale up, her thoughts focused on their goals, not on their obstacles.

"That would be one hell of a ship," she said. Then, after a long pause, she added, "I think I'd like to study it."

That was the type of ambiguous, almost innocent comment that had gotten Ash into trouble so often during her training. He put on a tough, unamused glower now.

Her smile grew, just as he'd known it would.

He took his hand off her back but stayed close. Whenever her steps slowed or faltered, he spoke to her quietly. They exchanged memories of Caruth, of their time in the Fighting Corps, of random missions that had nothing to do with telepaths, teammates, or treason.

Another hour passed. Twenty more until the lockout code on his commcuff expired. Maybe they could find a place to hide and wait. Ash was looking better. She might have more time left than they thought. It had only been a little over three weeks since her last booster. Most anomalies didn't experience severe withdrawal symptoms until four or five weeks had passed. They might be worrying about nothing.

Or they might be worrying about something.

He peered through the trees at the cliff again. It was less than a hundred meters high here. Still a long, loud climb. Hard to tell if that would be more risky than walking into an ambush. If he had a choice, he'd…

He squinted at the cliff. A narrow, dark shadow stretched from top to bottom.

Ash was watching him. He motioned her to follow, then stopped before they reached the edge of the thin forest. A few paces away, the tall shadow became a crevice.

"Can you climb?" he asked.

She stared at the fissure. It was damp from a recent rain. No guarantee it would be scalable all the way up, and no guarantee Ash could handle it.

Her eyes went to the top, scanning the brim of the DFC. Jaw set, she nodded in a way that told him yes, she was choosing this option.

Together they sprinted from the trees to the shadow at the base of the wall. They both fit inside the crevice with room to spare for a third person. Rykus spotted a number of possible handholds, and several meters above their heads, the crevice narrowed. They'd each be able to brace their feet and back against the two walls and shimmy up. It wouldn't be easy though.

The barrier he'd erected between his mind and his bruised and battered body cracked. His shoulder ached, his back and ribs. Ash was in worse shape than he was. This might not be the best idea.

"You sure you want to do this?" he asked.

"Yeah." She found a small crack in the wall above her head, then pulled herself up.

Or tried to. Her hand slipped, and she fell back to the ground with a curse.

He watched her hands shake. The left one was swollen from her pinky to her still raw and injured wrist. Damn it, she wasn't going to be able to do this.

"We'll keep going," he told her.

She shot him a cutting glare. "Until we hit the ambush? No. I've got this."

"It's a long way up."

She wiped her palms on her pants and reached up again. Again, she fell.

"Ash—"

"I'm not going to be brought down because of a broken pinky," she said. "Trevast and the guys would…"

She stared at the wall, and even in the crevice's shadows, he saw her go pale.

The raw pain in her expression damaged something inside him. He wanted to take her into his arms, heal her wounds, but the only thing that could make those more bearable was time. He'd lost people before. He'd lost friends who would have given him hell for not being able to climb the crevice.

"Ash."

She met his eyes. Hers were wide and glassy. They weren't seeing him; they were seeing the men she'd been accused of killing.

"Excuse me a moment," she said. Then she stumbled back to the trees.

❖ • ❖

THE FLASH grenade.

Jevan's smile.

Other faces. Other sounds.

The cipher.

Ash held her head and rocked. Her teammates' blood soaked the knees of her combat fatigues.

What had happened? Where had she failed?

The flash grenade.

Jevan's smile.

The faces. The sounds. The cipher.

Kris's plea.

Bullets.

The flash grenade.

More bullets.

Trevast.

Shit. He was dead. They were all dead. It should have been her. She was the one who'd fucked up. She was the one who'd let Jevan into her bed, into her mind. They were dead because of her.

She wasn't getting enough oxygen. Her heart was beating too fast. It was going to kill her. It should have killed her then, but the… the…

The flash grenade.

The flash grenade. The flash grenade. The flash grenade.

"Look at me, Ash."

The command wrenched her eyes open. Her fail-safe gripped her forearms. Her hands were still at her temples. She was hunched over on the ground. Her knees were wet from the forest floor, not from her teammates' blood.

Her teammates…

"No," Rykus said. "Stay with me, damn it. It wasn't your fault."

It was. If she hadn't been such a fool…

Her throat swelled. She was going to pass out. She needed to pass out in private.

"Get away from me, Rip."

"No."

She jerked an arm free and swung at him. He dodged and came around behind her, hooking his arm around her neck and shoulder. He pulled her back against his chest.

She couldn't fight him. She was too busy trying to gasp in enough oxygen to stay conscious.

"Breathe, honey. Breathe."

She rocked back and forth, back and forth. She'd been holding Trevast and rocking when the Coalition soldiers rushed in. They'd peeled her away from her team lead. They'd taken her away from her brothers.

"Ash." He turned her toward him, almost cradling her. With a gentle pressure on her jaw, he lifted her face toward his. "Focus, Ash."

She tried, but his gaze was only a temporary haven. The panic, the damn weakness, crept over her again.

Rykus tensed, and there was a deep desperation in his gaze. It didn't make sense. But very little made sense to Ash. She was lost, falling, and—

And Rykus kissed her.

The shock of his lips anchored her as efficiently as gravity anchored a ship.

She didn't stop hurting. The pain of failing her brothers went back into containment, but the permanence of their loss, the unfairness of it, lingered even as every one of Ash's nerve endings flared to life. Something coursed through her. She wanted to move closer, explore the feeling, the sensation, further, but this was Rip. Her fail-safe. She couldn't have him. Couldn't want him. Couldn't need him.

She started to shake.

Rykus kissed her harder.

She put a hand on his shoulder, intending to push him away, but he took hold of her arms.

She fought back with her teeth, made him grunt when she bit his lower lip, but as soon as she tasted blood, she softened the violence with a stroke of her tongue. Then another. And another.

She wasn't sure if she shook this time or if it was him, but she was certain the universe moved. She felt the great ache of it deep in her core. His next kiss sent a shiver through her, but then he put an inch of space between their lips.

"You back with me, Ash?"

"Yes," she breathed. He didn't take the yes as she intended it, as an acceptance, a desire, a plea. When she leaned forward, he kept them apart.

"You're hurt," he said, his arms locked on hers. "The soldiers... The loyalty training."

She didn't know if his words were a reminder for her or for him, but he wasn't moving away, and she needed this.

She slipped under his guard and used a Balazian throw-hold to swing him to the ground.

He countered the move easily, using his weight and superior strength to end up on top. "Ash..."

"I need you." She reached between them, unbuckled his belt, his pants. Every muscle in his body was cinched tight. She grabbed his waistband, tried to jerk it down.

His arms bracketed her body, and he gazed down at her, still straining against what he knew was right and wrong.

Giving up temporarily on his pants, she grabbed the hem of her shirt instead and pulled it over her head.

His lips parted as his gaze dropped to her breasts. An unfair attack, yes, but he'd trained his anomalies to fight dirty.

His eyes shuttered in something that was either a grimace of regret or of surrender.

She reached up, rested her hand on his shoulder, and waited for him to meet her gaze.

"I want you, Rip."

He just shook his head on the way to capture a breast in his mouth. The warmth of him closed around her, and heat flared through her body.

She reached down to pull up the back of his shirt, letting her nails scrape along his skin as his fingertips brushed over the bruises on her ribcage. She felt his teeth, willed him to send a sharp twinge of pain into her aching breast, but he suckled instead, only separating from her long enough to let her pull his shirt over his head.

"Pants," she whispered when his tongue swirled around her again.

He gave her breast one last kiss, then went for her stolen uniform, shimmying the pants down her hips. She gave in to the temptation to touch him, sliding her hands over the planes of his chest. He was a chiseled creation, hard everywhere a man should be hard. She wanted to trace his muscles with her tongue, taste the salt of his skin. She wanted this man inside her.

And he wanted her. She saw it in the way his gaze raked down her body. It was so intense it terrified her. It terrified her because she saw something other than lust in his eyes. Lust, she could comprehend. Lust, she could quench. This other emotion, this thing that bordered on an entirely different and incomprehensible *L*-word, she had no idea how to deal with that. And she didn't trust herself with it.

He must have sensed something in her. His hand went still on the waistband of his pants. In her peripheral vision, she saw the corded muscles tremble in the arm bearing his weight. Not from exertion—he was too strong for that—but with a different kind of strain. He would stop if she gave him a sign.

She wouldn't. She needed to stay lost in this oblivion.

Grabbing the back of his neck, she pulled him back down and kissed him until neither one of them was capable of complicated thoughts.

She helped him strip off his pants, gripped him as soon as he sprang free. She reveled in the way he groaned against her mouth, the way he jumped against her palm. Her fail-safe was no longer in control of her. She commanded his body more than he'd ever commanded her mind.

"Ash," he murmured.

She shifted her hips, slid him across her entrance, back and forth, back and forth, until she felt him shake. She wanted him to plunge into her, take her hard and fast and desperate.

He placed the lightest kiss on a bruise on her shoulder.

She bucked her hips, signaling it was time. She wanted violence and mayhem. She wanted him to fuck her senseless so she wouldn't care about the past, the present, or the consequences of what they were doing.

He kissed her with a sensuous slowness, then eased inside, a glide of friction that was more torturous than any injury she had. He didn't want to hurt her. He was being *careful* with her.

The shock of that discovery, of what it might mean, sent a swirling, scorching heat through her body. He was strong and safe and...

She shut down those thoughts, unwilling to deal with where they would lead. This could only be a physical pairing between them. Nothing more.

Rykus's next kiss turned unbearably tender. Before it further damaged her mental armor, she broke it off with a hiss.

"Don't be gentle, Rip."

◆ · ◆

DON'T BE gentle, Rip.

He nearly lost it right then. He froze, halfway inside her, willing her not to move, not to breathe. It would be over if she did.

"I don't want to hurt you," he whispered. She was beautiful, breathtaking, brave. He had no idea when he'd fallen for her. Maybe if it hadn't been so unthinkable, so wrong, he would have realized it sooner.

Her green eyes stared up at him, still demanding he be rough and unrelenting.

"I *won't* hurt you." Before she could protest again, he moved, sliding in then out, watching her face react. Just enough light leaked through the smoky sky to make the shadows from the leaves above them dance across her skin. The dark design blended with her bruises, bruises he wanted to kiss away.

Her fingers dug into the muscles of his back. He loved her touch, the feel of her beneath him, the way she made the atmosphere around them vibrate with her passion. He sank in deep, murmured her name, then slid out and in again. And again, faster each time.

Ash's lips parted in a barely audible moan as she met his thrusts. The sensations built—the need, the desire. He saw the edge of the universe in her eyes. She tried to contain its power. So did he. They were both on the brink of giving the other what they wanted. If he lost control, he'd give in to her need for a hard, fierce fusion. If she lost control, she'd give in to his need for a deep, soul-touching connection.

Heat and pleasure escalated. When she trembled, he almost broke apart.

They separated quickly, almost desperately, rising to their knees, then to their feet, hands and mouths still touching, still kissing. A few unbearable seconds passed, then she was in his arms again, her legs wrapped around his waist.

One leg slipped off his hip, throwing him off-balance. He stumbled until he found a tree, then pressed her against it. A low limb grew just above her head. He grabbed it and used it to keep his footing as he found her entrance again. Her body bucked each time he thrust inside her. He gripped the firm muscles of her ass, lifting and dropping her onto him. She was hot and moist, and the friction nearly made his knees buckle.

He saw the pleasure building in the way her eyes hooded, saw it in her shallow breaths, and felt it when she clenched around him. He was close to his own release, but he didn't want it yet. He wanted more of her. And he wanted to watch her come undone.

He lowered her back to the forest floor. Then he gave in. He gave her what she'd asked for. He fisted her hair in his hand and slammed into her, again and again, watching her face as the pleasure built.

She tilted her head back, exposing her throat as she let out a loud, arousing cry.

Holy shit! He cut off her scream with a hand over her mouth, but still she came, rocking into him again and again and again. The rapture rolling through her rolled through him, and he groaned.

No way to hold off when she orgasmed like that. He released inside her, caught in her comet trail of ecstasy. It banked through him, hot and stabbing and addictive.

When the spasms at last subsided, he took her in his arms, rolling to his back so she didn't remain pressed against the cold, hard ground. He slid his cheek alongside hers, buried his face in her dark, tangled hair. The smoke that permeated the atmosphere lingered in the long locks. It was the scent of what they'd endured, the scent of what they might be able to endure together, and beneath it was the unmistakable fragrance of her.

He wanted to make love to her again; not out here, sweat-covered and dirty, but somewhere opulent. Somewhere that matched her strength and her beauty. Mikassia, perhaps. On a balcony beneath the purpled sunrise. Somewhere they could take their time. Somewhere they wouldn't have to worry about who might be close enough to overhear them.

That last thought made him grimace. They deserved to be caught. What they'd just done—what they were currently doing, lying there naked in each other's arms—was dangerous and careless and irresponsible.

And he couldn't stop, couldn't bring himself to put an end to this, because he knew once they moved, once they dressed themselves and climbed that wall, all the reasons they shouldn't have tasted each other would crash down on them more quickly than they'd crashed down the DFC.

He had the impression that Ash sensed his thoughts. She stiffened slightly, and the hand that was resting on his chest curled tentatively, like it was no longer certain it had the right to touch him.

You have every right, he wanted to say. It was he who didn't. He was the one who should have been strong enough to say no.

"Ash—"

"That was a nice diversion, Rip," she said as she quickly slipped out of his arms.

Her words knocked the air out of his lungs. A nice diversion?

The tilted smile she gave him now and every move she made as she dressed told him this was nothing more than a casual affair. Something she'd done time and again. It had no meaning.

He balled his hands into fists. He didn't want to be another man on her list. He wanted to be her weakness.

She was fully dressed before Rykus had his pants on. He watched her head back to the crevice while he buckled them. Pulling his shirt on over his head, he told himself it was best that she didn't care. Even if they survived this, even if they cleared her name and resumed their lives, they couldn't be together. The Coalition would never allow it.

And *he* could never allow it.

CHAPTER

EIGHTEEN

A SH ROLLED ONTO THE top of the DFC.

She'd done it. She'd scaled the damn crevice. It hadn't defeated her. The pursuit force hadn't recaptured her. The withdrawal hadn't taken her mind or her life. If she could make it to the city, she had a chance.

She stared up at the darkening sky, consciously regulating her breathing while she listened to the soft scrape of Rykus's ascent. She still tasted him on her lips. She still felt the heat of his touch. Being with him had been…

She closed her eyes, unwilling to place too much significance on what had happened between them.

Flipping to her stomach, she forced her tired and sore arms to push herself off the ground.

As soon as she sat up, her gaze went to the east. Ephron City was finally visible beyond the treetops and a big, dark lake. Even from this distance, it was obvious the Sariceans had completely devastated the place. The attack had toppled the spires of the military industrial complex, and the fires that were still burning turned the thick haze hanging over the city a bright, angry orange. The entire region looked like it had been crushed by a capsule that had exited the time-bend off course.

She was still numbed by the sight when Rykus reached the top of the wall. Like Ash, he turned toward the city, then went still.

She saw rage in the way he clenched his jaw. She understood it. The death toll in Ephron City alone would reach the millions. They'd never find all the bodies. And the damage to the planet's infrastructure would take years, maybe decades to recover.

"The Coalition needs to see what's in the Sariceans' files," Rykus said without looking at her.

She wanted to decrypt the damn files, but she knew the inevitable outcome. Trevast and Hagan had known it too. Hagan might have decided he didn't give a damn if the entire KU learned about the existence of telepaths, but Ash did. She'd sworn an oath to protect and preserve the Coalition. She couldn't let it fall apart.

"You told Hagan you wouldn't decrypt them." A question invaded Rykus's statement, and he looked her way.

When she met his gaze, heat flared through her stomach. It was mixed with another feeling, a feeling that might have been... awkwardness? She never felt awkward after sex. But then, she'd never lost control during it. She'd never *wanted* to lose control.

She focused on the city again.

"The files will clear your name," Rykus continued. "And they'll help us strike back against the people who did this. Keeping the information inaccessible makes no sense."

She didn't plan to keep the information inaccessible forever, just long enough to see what Trevast had found. Once she located Jevan and his copy of the files, she'd know more about what she and the Coalition were facing and who she could trust to help her take care of the threat.

How much of that could she tell Rykus? Something in her thoughts made the hair on the back of her neck prickle. Say the wrong thing and she'd black out. But she needed Rykus on her side, needed his help, needed...

No, she didn't *need* him. She wanted him.

"Why won't you trust me?" Rykus asked, misinterpreting her hesitation. "I'm trying to save your life. It would help if you tried to save it..."

He stared at her. She could see the thoughts moving through his head one at a time, like an antique revolver with one round in the cylinder. His thoughts clicked and clicked and clicked until he found the loaded chamber.

"Goddamn it." His whisper was so low she barely heard it.

Her eyebrows went up, waiting.

"You're determined to preserve and protect the Coalition."

"That was my oath, Rip." A warning pressed against her upper spine. A cold sweat dampened her skin. She needed to change the subject.

"No, it's..." He dragged a hand over his face. "It's more than that. It's the loyalty training. It brainwashed you into putting the Coalition first, your life last. That's why you don't want to decrypt the files. You think worlds will secede when they learn that telepaths infiltrated the government."

Apprehension stabbed through her stomach. Rykus had identified precisely the reason why she wouldn't decrypt the files, but he'd twisted her motivation. She wasn't doing this because she'd been brainwashed. She believed in the Coalition's mission to bring freedom, protection, and dignity to the citizens of each of its member worlds. She'd benefited from that mission. The Coalition had saved her soul when it dragged her away from Glory. It had saved billions of others over its short history, but more people needed help. More people were enslaved, starving, and hopeless.

"You're wrong," she said. Turning, she restarted the trek toward the city.

Rykus caught up. "I'm not wrong."

"I'm not decrypting the files."

"You don't know what's on them. It's possible Stratham is the only telepath who's infiltrated the Coalition. We can—"

Ash stopped walking. She stared at her fail-safe.

Rykus didn't know about Jevan. How the hell was that possible? Had Hagan never said his name out loud? She tried to remember if he had. They'd talked about him for hours. Ash had answered every question Hagan threw her way, over and over again, but she couldn't recall if he'd ever turned to Rykus and said Jevan's name.

He must not have.

Rykus frowned, then slowly said, "Stratham isn't the only telepath?"

His last word echoed in her mind as her consciousness dropped out from under her. She spun in the dark like a spacer who'd broken the tether to his ship. When she became aware again, her stomach cramped and the ground beneath her feet felt unsteady.

"I'm sorry I didn't notice before." Rykus was standing a few paces away, arms crossed over his chest, a sober expression on his face.

She closed her eyes. Rykus had mentioned telepaths. All Ash had done was stop walking. She hadn't tried to nod or speak or otherwise answer his question. The situation was still too far out of her control.

"Ash."

Her eyes snapped back open. Rykus's tone had held a warning. It wasn't directed at her.

The only thing that moved was Rykus's right hand. It rose to his gun, a gun he'd somehow managed to hold on to despite their fall down the DFC, the climb back up, and everything in between.

Ash's mind cleared. Her senses sharpened. It was too quiet. With gray smoke darkening the sky and the trees and boulders scattered along the canyon's rim, there were plenty of shadows to hide in, plenty of strategic places where her enemy could be placing his crosshairs on her. Or on her fail-safe.

Her eyes strained to pick up some movement; her ears strained to hear some sound. When Rykus turned his head slightly to look to their left, she turned hers slightly and looked to their right.

She almost missed the rifle. If the wind hadn't shifted enough to let a faint beam of evening sunlight penetrate the haze, she wouldn't have noticed it at all.

"Always knew you were trouble, sweetheart," a male voice drawled. A silhouette separated from the shadows. And a smile spread across Ash's face.

◆ ◆ ◆

SWEETHEART.

Rykus recognized the voice, and even while the tension in his muscles began to relax, a different tension—an irritation—coiled in his stomach.

He turned, and Jon Kalver, an anomaly who'd been one of Ash's classmates back on Caruth, lowered his rifle, a sweet-looking Kinetic A88. "You look like you've been smashed by a meteorite."

"I'm glad to see you too," Ash said.

The way her face lit up with a genuine grin grated against Rykus's nerves. He was happy as hell to see Kalver too, but if Rykus had had his pick of any anomaly who might have been stationed on Ephron, Jon Kalver would have been the last man he chose.

But he undoubtedly would have been the first anomaly on Ash's list. The two had been close during training. And the two had been trouble.

"How did you find us?" Ash asked. She might be battered and bruised, but she stood tall, shoulders back, chin thrust out like she could take on a whole army of anomalies. She had never allowed herself to show weakness, especially in front of her classmates.

Kalver slung the rifle over his shoulder. "The whole planet heard you rollin' down that cliff a few hours ago. I'm surprised you're still in one piece."

"I'm surprised you paid attention to a little avalanche when the rest of the world is burning."

"Picked up a Mayday a while ago." Straightening into something close to attention, Kalver met Rykus's gaze. "Sir."

"Kalver," Rykus said, acknowledging him with a nod.

"You're being tracked, sir." Kalver's drawl disappeared. "A small pursuit force is sweeping the canyon below. Six soldiers are two klicks to the north and closing. More units are on the way."

"What's our best route to the city?" Rykus's focus sharpened. He had data to analyze, a plan to construct.

"Heading east is the most direct route, but you'll be trekking alongside the canyon most of the way, and the nearest unit could become a problem."

Rykus ground his teeth together. Kalver hadn't asked why he and Ash were being hunted by their own forces. He hadn't asked why Ash was wearing combat fatigues that were too big and had another soldier's name sewn into the material. He hadn't asked any questions at all; he'd just provided information that would help them evade contact with Coalition soldiers.

Reason number 389 why the loyalty training was dangerous. If Hagan had been alive, Rykus would have pointed it out.

"What's your recommendation?" Rykus asked.

"It's a two-hour run to Ephron City. Longer with both of you injured. If the opposition force has men to spare, and they want you badly enough, sir, they'll have observers at every point of entry. I'd recommend heading for an outpost instead of the city. There are two nearby." He pulled his comm-cuff off his wrist and snapped it straight. "They'll have guards, but I should be able to neutralize the threat without killing…"

Rykus and Ash both stared at the comm-cuff in his hand. The *functional* comm-cuff.

"I need to borrow that," Rykus said.

Kalver held it out, but Ash cut between them, making a grab for it.

Rykus yanked her back. "We need help, Ash. *You* need help."

Pulling her arm free, she lifted her chin to meet his gaze. "No."

Defiance simmered in her eyes.

"I know the truth, Ash. You don't have to be afraid."

Her nostrils flared on his last word. Her chest rose when she drew in a breath, and her lips pressed together as if she was holding back words.

She probably was.

"We'll encrypt the transmission," he assured her. "I'll contact Admiral Bayis directly."

"Admiral Bayis sent a Predator to kill us."

"We don't know that."

"We don't *not* know it."

"Ash—" He cut himself off when he heard the growl in his voice. If he pushed, if he intimidated, she'd do everything she could to do the opposite of what he wanted. He needed to coax her into seeing things his way.

Taking a small step toward her, he softened his words. "You can't do this on your own. This is bigger than you. It's bigger than us."

Ash's posture screamed that she was on the verge of fight or flight. In most people, that instinct was triggered by fear. In anomalies—in Ash—it was triggered by the overwhelming desire to accomplish her mission. But the loyalty training had screwed with her logic. It made a threat of something that wasn't likely to happen. The Coalition had weathered dozens of storms in its history. It would survive whatever was revealed in the files.

Her eyes darted toward Kalver. The other anomaly stood there listening to their words and watching their body language. Rykus wanted to move closer to Ash, place a reassuring touch on her shoulder, but he already felt he was revealing too much.

"You won't survive without help," he said, forcing himself to keep a distance between them. Then he lowered his voice and added the words that he knew would reach her. "You won't avenge them without help."

Her eyes turned glassy. He was an ass for using her teammates against her, but she needed to see reason.

"I encrypt the transmission," she finally said.

He hesitated. Ash had an arsenal of encryptions she could put on the transmission, but so did Kalver, and Kalver wouldn't defy him and put a lockout code on the cuff. Ash could do that in seconds, and they'd be back to where they were now, on the run and cut off from help and information.

But if he didn't allow her the chance to encrypt it, she would run. She wouldn't get far, but he'd lose any chance of her trust, any chance of her cooperation. She'd fight him every step of the way, and the only way he would get her help would be by force.

He filled his lungs with air, then exhaled. The fall down the DFC must have damaged his brain, because he was going to take the chance. He nodded to Kalver, and the other man handed Ash his comm-cuff.

The suspicion in Ash's eyes transformed into surprise. She regained control of her expression quickly, then took the comm-cuff without looking away from Rykus. She was expecting a trick or a trap.

Folding his arms, he leaned against a tree, outwardly calm and unworried.

Ash's mouth tightened. Then she lowered her head and tapped commands into the cuff. When she finished, she tossed it to him. He caught it, then leisurely looked at the screen. The symbol in the upper left corner indicated it was encrypted and ready to send a transmission.

"Two minutes," Ash said.

"No problem," he replied smoothly, but he had to force his grip on the cuff to relax. Two minutes to convince the admiral that Ash was innocent and telepaths existed. No problem at all.

He tapped in Bayis's personal ID code.

Twenty goddamn seconds passed, seconds that counted. He could see them ticking by in Ash's head.

The cuff chimed when the security parameters were accepted, and Admiral Bayis's face filled the screen. "Commander."

"We have one minute," Rykus said. "I'm with Lieutenant Ashdyn—"

"War Chancellor Hagan," Bayis cut him off. "What happened?"

The interruption took him off guard. "He survived the crash. Ash—"

"I'm being told he needs a body bag."

He felt Ash's gaze. He didn't look away from the cuff. News of Hagan's death had reached Bayis capsule-quick, but that didn't mean the admiral was compromised. "I want to know why Predators attacked us."

Bayis's right eye twitched. "Predators?"

"Within minutes of coming to ground, two birds attacked the crash site. Hagan was with us. He was injured but in good condition. We—"

"The Predators were sent to eliminate Saricean survivors. Three of their Black Wings kissed the dirt."

"*We* were attacked," Rykus said, conscious of the time ticking by. "Check our crash site." The fact that Bayis hadn't done so already indicated how chaotic things were.

Rykus was about to add another level of chaos.

"After we left the site, Ash was able to communicate with Hagan. Sir… Admiral, she communicated with Hagan telepathically. She didn't murder her teammates. She didn't betray the Coalition. She hasn't been able to deny the charges brought against her because she can't speak out loud about her mission or what was done to her. And until he communicated with Ashdyn, Hagan hadn't known he'd been telepathically influenced as well."

As soon as the words left his mouth, he heard how ridiculous, how impossible, they sounded. The lack of reaction from Bayis signaled it too, and Rykus suppressed a curse. With Hagan dead, Ash still telepathically handicapped, and the Sariceans' files encrypted, he had zero evidence to support his claim. Zero.

"Is your judgment impaired, Commander?" Bayis's question wasn't laced in sarcasm or disdain. It was a search for an explanation, for a reason why his friend would so desperately grasp at the stars.

"I didn't create this explanation," he said. "War Chancellor Hagan did."

"You've always had issues with him. You've had public arguments. You have a motive for killing him."

"Killing him?" It felt like he'd been ejected into the cold of space. "I didn't—"

"Multiple witnesses say you did."

"Who?" he demanded. "Admiral—"

"Surrender to the force pursuing you. Lieutenant Commander Brandt is in charge."

"Hagan was on his knees, sir," he said between gritted teeth. "He was unarmed. His hands were visible. Someone on Brandt's team took him out." And Brandt's team was still pursuing them. Thirty seconds until Bayis would have a lock on their location.

"Find Hagan's assistant, Stratham," he said quickly.

"Surrender to the pursuit force, Commander."

"Question him," he went on. "He rewired Hagan. Make him tell you the truth."

"Damn it, Rykus." Exasperation shattered Bayis's professionally neutral expression. "I can't help you unless you turn yourself in. I can't help Lieutenant Ashdyn unless she gives us the cipher."

If the cuff hadn't been made from a strong metal, it would have crumpled in Rykus's hand. He felt Ash watching him, waiting for his words or body language to signal his decision: would he surrender or would he help Ash evade capture?

"I understand, sir," he said. "Rykus out."

He ended the call.

"That went well." Ash's tone was light and amused. It juxtaposed with the ready-to-flee tension in her posture.

"Telepaths," Kalver said. It wasn't a question; it wasn't a statement either.

Rykus shifted his gaze to the anomaly. "Yes."

Kalver scratched his beard. When he lowered his hand, he gave a small shrug, and Rykus could almost hear him drawl out an *All right*. No doubt. Just acceptance. Rykus said telepathy was real, so it was.

It grated against his conscience. It didn't help that he was certain Kalver should have been elsewhere, somewhere with his team, aiding the search-

and-rescue operations occurring throughout Ephron City. But he'd abandoned his team, his duty, to respond to Rykus's Mayday.

It was wrong.

This whole goddamn situation was wrong.

"The pursuit force will be crawling up our six soon," Kalver said.

He still felt Ash's eyes on him, still sensed how close she was to bolting. He didn't blame her. Until recently, he hadn't been worthy of her trust.

He would be worthy of it now.

He turned to Kalver. "Take us to the nearest outpost."

"Yes, sir." The anomaly unslung his rifle.

"Kal." Ash's voice hadn't shaken, it hadn't cracked, but it stopped Kalver mid-turn.

He scanned her head to toe, and understanding moved across his face. He looked at Rykus, eyebrows raised for permission.

Permission to give her a booster. Anomalies always carried two extra injections.

Rykus had to fight his immediate reaction. There were complications if he said yes, complications that hadn't been there when they'd been on the *Obsidian*. Ash hadn't been so badly hurt, and Katie would have watched out for her patient, given her medicine to make sure her body accepted the chemicals. Ash would have been okay.

Ash might not be okay now. She was already experiencing withdrawal symptoms. If she injected the booster without access to medical care, it could kill her.

But if she didn't get the booster, it *would* kill her.

Rykus dipped his chin in a fractional nod.

Kalver pulled a small, black case out of a zippered pocket. "Interested in a boost, sweetheart?"

Ash stumbled forward so quickly the other anomaly barely had time to take the syringe out. He chuckled when he pushed up her tattered sleeve and then plunged the needle into her arm.

Ash's knees buckled. Kalver snaked an arm around her waist. Her hands gripped his biceps, and she went limp. Not unconscious, but the chemicals always hit anomalies hard. Their coordination left, their strength too, as the concoction burned through their bloodstream. It wasn't an unpleasant sensation the anomalies said. It was a potent one.

Rykus turned away. *He* wanted to be the one holding Ash. He couldn't get her body out of his mind, the way she'd felt in his arms, the sound she had made when she'd come undone.

"How long has it been?" Kalver demanded.

"Three weeks," Rykus answered. He glanced back at Ash, saw her back arch.

"Just three?" Kalver lowered Ash to the ground. "She shouldn't be reacting like this."

"No, but she's been through hell."

"Then she needs medical care. You should have given the admiral our location."

"She would have run."

The expression Kalver gave him said *She would have tried.*

"And she still wouldn't have lasted long enough for the bureaucrats to approve an injection. Plus, you heard my transmission. The forces pursuing us took out Hagan when he told them Ash was innocent. A telepath got to Ash. One got to the war chancellor, and another to the soldiers sent to bring us in. We don't know how far the enemy's influence goes. We don't even know who the enemy is."

"But you trust the admiral," Kalver pointed out.

"We've worked together for a long time. He's risked his life for the Coalition, and he's a friend." He kept his expression firm as he held Kalver's gaze, but his mind cycled back to his last hours on the *Obsidian*. Bayis hadn't kept his promise to give Rykus more time before sending the interrogator into Ash's cell.

Suspicion clawed at his spine, but he forced the sensation away. They had to trust somebody, and if all the Coalition's top brass were compromised, they were screwed anyway.

"All right," Kalver drawled, accepting his words. Rykus could have told him humans had learned how to breathe in space, and the anomaly would have believed him.

Rykus turned his attention back to Ash. Sweat beaded on her brow, dampening her hairline. He wanted to take her out of Kalver's arms, hold her until she pulled through this, but he forced himself to stay away. He wanted Ash more than he'd ever wanted any other woman in his life. He could admit that now, but he also had to admit he never should have acted on it. He hadn't intended to. When she'd broken down, he'd seen her spiraling farther and farther away from sanity. The kiss had been instinctive, and he'd intended to end it with just that one touch, that one taste, but Ash had responded, and then *he'd* lost his sanity. He'd forgotten about the loyalty training, forgotten that he had authority over Ash, and he'd forgotten that any relationship between them wasn't just wrong, it was impossible.

He ran a hand over his face, then focused again on Ash. He watched her chest rapidly rise and fall, and as the evening darkened into the black of night, he wished his life had taken a different course, a course that hadn't taken him to Caruth, a course that hadn't made him Ash's fail-safe.

⊓I⊓ETEE⊓

ASH WAS alive.

Really alive.

The chemicals in her bloodstream ricocheted in her veins. She bounced on her toes, waiting for Kal to reappear. He'd gone ahead to scout their path. He and Rykus had decided she needed a few more minutes to recover. She hadn't. She was good and ready to move.

"Stay still," Rykus said behind her.

"Can't."

"Thought you wanted to avoid Coalition troops. You keep moving, you'll draw them all here."

"Not a problem, Rip." She could take on the six-man pursuit force. Hell, with the way she was feeling, she could take on twice that number.

"Commander. Sir. Or Rykus."

She looked over her shoulder.

"That's what you can call me, Lieutenant."

Holding his gaze, she said, "You're in a great mood. Sir."

The pause between "mood" and "sir" made Rykus's jaw clench. Normally Ash would have smiled or made another quip to get under his skin, but she didn't like that he and Kalver had decided she should stay here. The trees and boulders provided good cover, but she felt like a target.

It felt like *Rykus* was a target. That's the other thing that was bothering her. The soldiers who'd attacked them had claimed he'd killed Hagan. Ash couldn't tell if Admiral Bayis believed that to be true, but what if he did? Did the pursuit force have permission to kill them on sight? If they were captured, would Rykus end up in a cell?

"If this goes to hell, Rip, I'm taking the blame for Hagan." She wouldn't let her fail-safe go down with her. This was her problem, her epic clusterfuck. She'd get Rykus out of this mess.

His face, which had been like granite since Kal had shown up, softened. "You're not taking the blame for anything."

"I will. You wouldn't be involved in this if it weren't for me."

"I won't allow it, Ash."

"You—"

"No."

Her teeth snapped together. She almost stepped backward. It took far too much willpower to stand where she was. The booster had saved her life, but she still wasn't herself. If she had been, Rykus's *no* wouldn't have so easily snuffed her protest.

She bounced on her toes again, this time just to piss off her fail-safe.

"You got some excess energy to work off?"

Ash didn't spin toward Kal's voice, didn't jump or tense, but it was hard to hold back a curse. She hadn't heard him, probably because Rykus was right, she should have been stationary and alert. Injecting boosters in a combat situation was never a good idea.

"You volunteering to help me out?" She peered over her shoulder.

Kal smiled and let his gaze rove over her. "Anytime, sweetheart."

"Is the route clear?" Rykus's abrupt question cut through the air.

"The main force is east of us," Kalver said, his drawl shifting into a rigid staccato. "But we'll need to stay invisible for a while."

Rykus looked at her. "That means quiet and stealthy. Do you think you can handle that?"

"I can handle it." She choked back the *sir* that wanted to claw its way to her lips. Rykus's movements, his tone, and the way he loomed made the air seem thick. He was doing it on purpose, putting distance between them. She didn't regret sleeping with him, but... did he regret sleeping with her?

Well, that would certainly be a new experience, she thought with a soft, self-deprecating laugh.

The sound drew Kalver's attention. She shrugged at his raised eyebrow, but when he turned away, she was almost certain she caught a faint smile behind his beard. He was used to her laughs and not-quite-appropriate behavior. She'd gotten him and the other anomalies loaded with extra physical training for it dozens of times back on Caruth.

She stretched sore muscles and let Kalver take the lead. He set a slow, steady pace for the first hour. Several times they stopped. They kept immobile in the dark. On two of those occasions, Coalition soldiers stalked past them. One had come close enough for Ash to reach out and touch. It had taken all her concentration to remain stationary and concealed in her camouflage of shadows and leaves. Her limbs felt like they were filled with lightning, and her hand had itched to confiscate the soldier's weapon. Everyone but her was armed.

After the last encounter, Kalver had increased their pace. The forest thickened, but she still caught a glance of the relief cruisers that passed overhead every twenty minutes. Some of them came from the outpost they were headed for. If they were lucky, the stress of the bombardment and its aftermath would make the soldiers at the outpost tired and careless. She could hop on one of the cruisers and ride it into Ephron City, where she could disappear until she decided the best way to track down Jevan. He had a copy of the Sariceans' files. She'd kill him, decrypt the stolen data, then decide who else she needed to destroy in order to preserve and protect the Coalition.

Her hands, no longer shaking since she'd injected the booster, clenched at her sides.

Soon.

Soon Jevan and everyone associated with him would pay for what they'd done.

Kalver slowed until he maintained pace beside her. "You doing all right?"

She forced her fists to relax. "I'd be better if you'd let me borrow that rifle."

"Not a chance." His quiet drawl didn't disguise the threat in his voice.

Ash smiled. Kal had always been uptight about his weapons.

Kal eyed her. "You really can't talk about anything?"

She kept her gaze straight ahead and said nothing.

He chuckled. "The shit you get yourself into…"

She wished she could say this wasn't her fault, but it was. She'd let Jevan snake his way into her life. She hadn't loved him, but she'd liked him. He'd claimed to be like her, a street kid who'd benefited from the Coalition's humanitarian programs. He'd said he went into politics to help the weak, and he'd supported her not-quite-legal efforts to protect the aid workers on Glory. That's why she'd always made herself available when he'd called and wanted to grab a drink, but she should have seen through the façade, known he had other motives. He'd always asked about her schedule, her missions. She'd never told him anything, but he'd learned the information anyway, and that's how he'd been able to intercept her team and…

"How long have you been on this rock?" she asked, using the words to loosen up a throat that suddenly felt raw.

"Six months," Kalver said. "I'm with the QRF. Gamma Team."

Ash would have whistled if the sound wouldn't have carried. Quick Reaction Force: Gamma Team was legendary. Any time the impossible was pulled off, it was attributed to the Gammas whether they were involved or not. She'd heard they'd conducted urban warfare on Daden, simultaneously boarded three pirate vessels outside the Yolan System, and rescued high-level hostages in the Aberdonian Revolt. That last op had been a work of art. Zero casualties.

"Does the team know what you are?" she asked.

"Just my lead. He's smart enough to keep it to himself. Too many hotheads would want to test me."

Ash nodded. Most anomalies kept their identities to themselves, especially if they came into contact with members of the other special forces. The QRF teams were made up of highly trained, physically fit soldiers who thought they were tougher than everyone else in the KU, and they had a habit of trying to prove it. Problem was they weren't tougher than anomalies. One day they would realize it and stop picking fights.

Kalver stopped.

"Outpost is ahead," he said when Rykus caught up with them. "It's a storage depot and training grounds. Most personnel will be reassigned to search-and-rescue ops, so it won't be well guarded. I can get past the checkpoint with my ID, but you two will raise alarms."

"Can you get us over the wall?" Rykus asked.

"Yes, sir." Kalver unstrapped his comm-cuff and handed it to him. "Once I'm inside, I'll recon the area, find an invisi-line, then send you the location where I drop it."

"Good," Rykus said. "We'll circle to the north."

Silently, Kalver proceeded ahead.

She and Rykus started their trek around the outpost. It took over an hour, an hour in which the insects of the forest decided it was time to eat. They buzzed around Ash's head, landed on exposed skin, and flew into her nose and mouth. They hadn't been this bad before. Either she'd been too exhausted to notice or the smoke from the forest fires had kept them away.

Ash kept her mouth shut and trudged on. Rykus took them on a path well away from the outpost for most of the journey, and he checked his borrowed comm-cuff from time to time. Kalver had decrypted the pursuit force's chatter. They were searching for them along a route to Ephron City, not to the outpost. A lucky break.

After a while they veered closer to the outpost. Ash caught glimpses of a black, towering wall.

"I thought this wasn't a sensitive complex," Ash said, keeping her voice low. "Why the massive wall?"

Rykus kept his gaze on their path. At first, she thought he might not have heard her question, but then she saw deliberateness in his movements, in the way he didn't glance her way, that told her he had.

She stopped walking. He took another few steps, then stopped too. He was still close enough for her to hear him sigh.

"The stone's imported from Mikassia," he said quietly. "The indigenous vegetation doesn't like it, so it's effective in holding back the forest. A wall surrounds Ephron City too."

"How long were you stationed here?"

"Almost two standard years. The Corps had me data-punching before I transferred to Caruth."

She looked at him, at his grim expression, as he stared down at the forest floor. Then she focused on his reconstructed shoulder. "While you were recovering."

"Yeah."

"I remember your father visiting you here," she said. "The media wouldn't stop talking about it. They thought Javery would finally join the Coalition."

"Not a chance of that." He wrapped a hand around a thick green plant by his foot and pulled it up.

"Why did you join?" Ash asked, watching him break the plant's stem. "To piss him off?"

He snorted. "No. I joined because I believed in the collective safety the Coalition offers. Everything else I did to piss him off."

"Everything else?"

"My father is the grand general of Javery's armed forces." He peeled the outer layer of the stem off. "Every success I had, every accolade, promotion, and medal... It was all a personal affront to him. I could have been commanding Javerian soldiers. I could have been saving Javerian lives. It infuriated him every time I made the news."

"So that's why you're always perfect."

"Perfect." He let out a bitter laugh. "If I was perfect, I wouldn't have..." He stopped, looked at her. His mouth opened like he was about to finish the sentence. Then he closed it and swallowed.

"Here." He handed the stripped plant to her. "Rub this on your exposed skin. It will help with the mosquitoes."

The inside of the stem was wet with a gel-like substance that smelled like acid. It stung her scrapes and cuts, but it dried quickly, and it did seem to keep some of the insects away.

"What's this called?" she asked, noting the plant's smell and the shape and color of its leaves. She had thousands of herbs, roots, weeds, and other vegetation memorized—botanists taught anomalies the most common and useful plants in the KU—but Ash had never come across this one in her studies.

"We called it trip-weed," he said. "It has a hallucinogenic effect."

She looked up.

"When you ingest it," he added. "Not when you spread it on your skin."

She let a smile curve her lips. "Did you ever ingest it?"

He gave her a look that said she should know the answer to that question.

"Of course you didn't," she said with a quiet laugh.

A deep, buzzing sound reached her ears. She almost dismissed it as another flying insect, but then Rykus looked down at the comm-cuff on his wrist.

"Kalver's dropped the line," he said. "Shouldn't take us more than ten minutes to get there. Ready?"

At her nod, he led the way again.

They wouldn't have found the rope if Kal hadn't sent the location. Ash had spotted invisi-lines before, but those few times had been in situations where she'd been staking out an area for hours and either the wind had blown the rope or something else had moved it, making its digital fibers blur when they reset their translucent colors. The wind wasn't blowing tonight though, and even with the marker on Rykus's cuff, they had to drag their hands across the wall to find it.

Rykus motioned her to go up first. Climbing the rope was easier than climbing out of the DFC. Her broken pinky still hurt, but it was a bearable pain, and the booster in her system gave her extra strength. She made it to the top quickly, flattened herself on the wall while she waited for Rykus, then, after throwing the rope down on the other side, she rappelled down.

Kalver waited for them at the bottom.

"Outpost is virtually abandoned," he whispered. "Minimal security and personnel are rotating in eight-hour shifts to load up relief cruisers. There's one in the landing zone now. Emergency supplies are almost depleted, so it could be the last one for a while."

Rykus looked at her. He didn't know her plan, and she couldn't tell him. He was following her on faith alone.

The heat that flared through her stomach was unexpected and strong. She bit the inside of her cheek, trying to ignore the sensation.

"Let's move." She had to keep her thoughts focused on her goal.

Avoiding the personnel left behind was easy. The outpost was running on backup power, which meant the grounds weren't lit up as brightly as they'd otherwise be, and few guards were on patrol. Ash followed Kal and Rykus through the shadows and made it quickly to the landing zone on the east side of the complex.

Two soldiers stood outside the relief cruiser. Its side bay door was dropped open, allowing it to easily be loaded. She, Kalver, and Rykus headed to the crew-access door at the front of the cruiser. The two men stood guard while she hacked into the security pad.

Ten seconds, then the door clicked unlocked.

It should have taken her twice that amount of time to break in.

Taking her hands off the security pad, she stepped back, then slowly turned her head.

CHAPTER

TWENTY

THE ONLY WARNING RYKUS had was the sudden tension that shot through Ash. Then Kalver tossed a pistol to her, spun, and took aim at the soldiers encircling them.

"*Hold your fire.*" The command left Rykus's lips without a conscious thought. All he saw was the bloodbath that would occur if the two anomalies pulled their triggers.

"Put the weapons down," a soldier ordered. "Put them down!"

The words were taken up by other men, coming from other directions. All directions.

"Disarm," Ash yelled at the same time Kalver shouted, "Drop them!"

Anomalies were trained to lay their lives down for the mission. They'd go down fighting, taking out the opposition until they breathed their last breaths.

Rykus couldn't let that happen.

He put his hands in the air, well away from his holstered gun. "Ash—"

"Everyone hold your fire." Admiral Bayis's booming voice came from the now-open door of the relief cruiser. He stepped to the threshold, a sidearm in his hand. "Commander, they have sixty seconds to lay down their weapons."

Bayis had personally come dirtside to recapture Ash. The significance of that wasn't lost on Rykus. Neither was the significance that these soldiers hadn't killed them on sight. They weren't Brandt's men.

"Ash, Kalver," he said, his heart hammering against his chest. "These are Coalition men. Friendlies. No blood needs to be shed here."

Kalver's breathing was deep and regulated. Ash's was shallow and rapid. Her hand clenched on the grip of her pistol.

"Put the weapons down," Rykus said.

Kalver's jaw clenched, but he removed his finger from the trigger and laid the rifle on the ground.

"Ash." Rykus wanted to step between her and the soldiers who threatened her life, but he feared any movement would set off a massacre.

"Did you walk me into this ambush?" Ash demanded.

The accusation sliced through him. "No. I swear I didn't know."

"You were monitoring communications on the cuff."

"And Kalver was monitoring them on his voice-link," Rykus said. "All chatter indicated the pursuit force was heading toward Ephron City."

"Then how did they know we'd be here?"

"We slipped a slave code into your comm-cuff when you contacted me." Bayis's voice was serene compared to Ash's.

"You can't do that in a two-minute window," she said.

"I didn't do it. A crypty did it," Bayis said. "A crypty who happens to also be an anomaly. Twenty seconds."

Sweat trickled down his back. "Ash, put down the gun."

Her gaze flickered to his.

Kalver said something to her. Rykus couldn't hear the words, but whatever they were, they made Ash flinch. A moment later, she set down the gun.

Soldiers surged forward. Rykus lost sight of her in the swarm. Men confiscated his weapon, shackled his hands, then pushed and shoved him into the relief cruiser.

He jerked his shoulder out of one soldier's grasp, then rammed into another. "Ash?"

"Settle down." Bayis's voice rang out. "All of you."

The tight panic in Rykus's chest didn't lessen until he saw Ash. She knelt in the middle of the small bridge, hands cuffed behind her back, gaze locked on the deck in front of her. He wanted her to look up, to meet his eyes and give him some sign that she was okay, but her jaw was clenched and he could see fury radiating from her with each breath she drew in.

Every soldier on the cruiser had their weapons pointed at them. Rykus needed to keep calm and steady. He couldn't let this situation get out of control.

The bridge was lit. He scanned the faces behind the guns and recognized most of them. They were from the *Obsidian*, men and women under his command.

Or they had been under his command. Rykus identified the man now in charge, Brookins, Rykus's executive officer and the anomaly Ash had shot during her escape.

Hell, maybe Rykus was wrong about anomalies being mortal. That bullet had dropped Brookins less than a day ago and he was already out of med bay and back on the job. If the situation had been different, Rykus would have clasped his XO on the shoulder and told him how damn relieved he was to see him alive.

But the situation wasn't different, and Brookins was pissed. The anomaly rarely showed emotion, but the set of his jaw, the glare in his eyes, the way his attention was completely locked on Ash—it all betrayed how much he wanted payback.

"We could use more breathing room in here, Brookins," Rykus said.

The anomaly didn't take his eyes off Ash, and the gun he held remained aimed at her head. He didn't have to listen to Rykus's suggestion.

"Dismiss your men," Bayis said. He must have seen how precarious this situation was too.

"Henel, Markins, stay," Brookins ordered after only a slight hesitation. "Everyone else, out."

The soldiers moved, following the command. As they filtered off the cruiser, Kalver met his gaze. Rykus shook his head. No, he didn't want the anomaly to make a move. He wanted to decrease the tension on the bridge, not ratchet it up.

He turned back to Bayis. "Kalver was following my orders. No charges should be brought against him."

"His actions will be reviewed." The admiral stepped toward Ash. "I have authorization to terminate you, Lieutenant."

Ice replaced the blood in Rykus's veins. Bayis could kill her, right here in front of him.

"If Commander Rykus wasn't a soldier with an impeccable record," Bayis continued. "If he wasn't a damn good officer. If he wasn't *the* Rest in Peace Rykus, I'd use that authority and have you killed immediately. But he is a good soldier, and he's my friend. You have one chance to prove that you'll work with us. Decrypt the files."

Still kneeling on the floor, Ash lifted her chin and met Bayis's eyes. "No."

Bayis looked at Rykus. His grim expression said he had one last chance to get control of his anomaly.

Control. Shit. Rykus could do that. He could command Ash to enter the cipher. If he got his tone and cadence right.

"Ash—"

Ash glared at him. Fury radiated from her green eyes, and her expression held a vehemence he'd never before seen on her face.

His heart staggered backward, but there was no way out of this. If they fought, they'd die.

He moved toward Ash.

"Rykus," Brookins said, his voice filled with warning.

"Wait," Bayis said.

Rykus knelt in front of Ash, putting himself between her and Brookins. She stiffened and leaned away from him, still angry, still distrusting.

He needed armor to protect him from that venom. "Lieutenant—"

"Lieutenant." She let out a scalding laugh. "That's not what you were calling me a few hours ago."

In his peripheral vision, he saw Bayis straighten. The admiral was perceptive. He likely knew what Ash alluded to. Rykus didn't care. Ash was trying to hurt him, push him away, set him off so she could wiggle out of the command she thought was coming. But he couldn't do it. He couldn't violate her free will. All he could do was try to get her to see reason.

"I know you think you're doing the right thing," Rykus said, "but... Ash, it's the loyalty training. I know you don't believe that, but it's true. Only someone who has been indoctrinated would keep the files to themselves through all this, especially when those files can clear your name. You think you're fighting for the Coalition. I understand that—I admire it—but even if the telepaths' reach goes farther than Hagan, it won't permanently damage the Coalition. The Coalition will come out stronger and... Damn it."

Bayis stepped forward. "What is it?"

Rykus's hands were still shackled behind his back. He couldn't reach out and touch Ash, but he was certain she wasn't seeing him anymore.

"A blackout." He leaned to the right. Ash's gaze didn't follow. "This is why she wouldn't answer our questions. She can't."

"This isn't proof—"

"She's not a traitor."

Bayis held up a hand to calm him. "I'm just saying it's not proof. I wouldn't have personally come dirtside if I didn't think there might be some truth to your claim. How long will this last?"

"Around a minute." He watched her, wanting so damn badly to take her into his arms.

A few seconds passed. Ash blinked rapidly, then her eyes found him.

"You okay?" he asked. Stupid question. Of course she wasn't okay. She was back in shackles, hurt, exhausted, and telepathically handicapped.

"I must have access to the files," Bayis said, his tone thawing. "My hands are tied otherwise."

Rykus understood. Bayis had superiors to report to, and I-Com was probably breathing down his neck already. He couldn't blame the admiral for doing what he had to do.

"Ash," Rykus said, trying one last time to get through to her. "Even if you're right about the damage the files might do, it's not your choice to make. You're a soldier. You took an oath to follow the orders of your superior officers and... And you can't preserve and protect the Coalition if you're dead."

The thought of her dying, of being executed there on the spot, made his throat turn raw. He swallowed, then he said a silent prayer asking for Ash to listen.

Something in her expression changed. Her shoulders hunched, either in defeat or acceptance. Rykus hoped it was the latter. He hadn't commanded her—he'd done everything he could to let this be her choice—but the loyalty training was always present, urging Ash to do what her fail-safe wanted. On Caruth, Ash had fought against that pressure. The more Rykus had pushed, the more she'd pushed back. It was her way of maintaining control, of showing herself and the rest of the universe that the loyalty training didn't own her. Rykus had to believe she was strong enough not to let it own her now.

She looked away from him. Her nod was slow, shaky. Her gaze followed Bayis as he walked to the cruiser's command console. He inserted a device slightly smaller than a flattened comm-cuff into a port, then punched in a series of commands, turning the system into a secure communications gateway. The only way to access anything input into the station was by using the device's twin, a similar relayer which was likely under the control of Bayis's second-in-command. He'd be on the *Obsidian* waiting with the Sariceans' files.

Bayis motioned her to the chair in front of the console. Rykus rose when she did and stayed close when she walked to the console and lowered herself into the seat.

"I need my hands," she said, her voice monotone.

Brookins holstered his firearm, unlocked her restraints, then relocked them in front of her, allowing her to reach the keypad. Her jaw flexed once, then she brought up a generic scripting program. She typed in a long string of code as if she was recounting a nursery rhyme, not entering in a virtually unbreakable cipher she'd undoubtedly created back on Caruth. That algorithm was the reason none of the Coalition's security experts would have ever been able to hack into the files. No one could guess the timing of her equations.

Finishing the code, she then ran the Sariceans' files through the cipher using her encryption key.

Rykus straightened, let out a breath, then watched the files unwrap.

And unwrap.

And unwrap.

With the encryption and the compression of the data, the Coalition had no way of knowing how much information Ash's team had taken from Chalos II. He'd read the op specs. The plan had been risky and had relied on her entire team remaining undetected. Ash hadn't said a word about the op—she *couldn't* say a word about it—and as far as they knew, they'd executed it well. This amount of information though… This amount of information indicated the op had gone perfectly.

Standing on Ash's other side, Bayis let out a quiet curse. "You had a two-minute window. How did you steal all this?"

Ash didn't respond. She slumped back in her seat and stared at the screen.

The file names were written in the Sariceans' language. Rykus couldn't read it, but Ash could. Anomalies learned languages the Coalition deemed strategically important. If Trevast had verified the stolen data and come across the evidence that telepaths existed, he had been able to read it as well, and somewhere in all that data lay the information that would prove Ash's innocence.

The tension in his chest unwound. He knelt at Ash's side, putting him eye level with her. "Thank you," he whispered.

A mix of hesitant trust and trepidation etched her expression. It vanished when Brookins moved behind her.

Ash swung out of her chair with a soul-shredding battle cry. Her shackled hands went for Brookins's throat.

"Ash!" Rykus charged forward the same instant Kalver did. They reached Ash at the same time. Rykus knocked her away from Brookins while Kalver took the other man on.

Ash landed on her back. She tried to surge upright, but Rykus kept her down. Bayis and the two soldiers had their weapons trained on her.

"What are you doing?" Rykus demanded.

Ash's wide, rage-filled eyes locked on him. She started to say something; then her eyes rolled back and she went slack beneath him.

"Ash." He shook her gently. He had no fucking idea what had just happened. Had she snapped? Had decrypting the files broken something in her?

"Ash." This time fear leaked into his voice. They were close to getting out of this hell. Ash couldn't—

"Sir."

He'd lose it if he stared at Ash's unmoving body another second, so he made himself turn toward Kalver, who stood in front of Brookins. Both anomalies were facing each other, ready to attack and kill. Kalver was handicapped by his restraints, Brookins by the still-healing bullet hole in his chest, and Rykus by a fear that threatened to send him over the edge.

"It's just a sedative," Bayis said. "I have orders to keep her sedated."

Rykus blinked. Then he stared down at the floor. Beside Brookins was a small metal injector.

He looked back at Ash, saw the pinprick of blood on her neck.

Heart pumping, he rose to his feet and turned his fury on the admiral, grinding out, "She's innocent."

"I can't risk another escape."

"I'll take responsibility for her."

Bayis sighed. "Frankly, Commander, that's an additional cause of concern for I-Com. They want you on Meryk for a full debriefing."

"I'll tell them what they want to know, but she doesn't need to be sedated."

"She *will* be."

"Until when?" Rykus demanded, his control slipping. "Her trial six or seven months from now?"

"Until we have evidence of what's been done to her." Bayis stepped closer. "I'm trying to save your career, Rykus. There are questions—"

"I don't give a damn about my career."

"I do. I-Com does. Like it or not, you're important to the Coalition's image. If Rest in Peace Rykus violates the command and authority of the Fighting Corps, if he betrays the trust the senate placed in him, it will damage the integrity of the Coalition. You're an icon."

Rykus shook his head.

"Sir." This time Kalver's *sir* was a request for permission. His muscles were tight, and his breathing was war-ready rapid. He wanted to fight, to free Ash, to kick Brookins's ass. By the time the anomalies graduated, they were family. They'd survived hell together, and they'd do anything for each other, even break the law to get their brothers—or sister—out of the shit.

Rykus closed his eyes. He had to turn off his emotions, maintain control of this situation. He had to put himself in a position where he could help Ash later.

"Stand down, Kalver." He sounded like a fucking robot, but the anomaly relaxed out of his poised-to-attack stance. So did Brookins.

"Take her to the back," Bayis said. "Tell the crew to come in. We're returning to the *Obsidian*."

Brookins walked past Kalver, picked up Ash, then hoisted her limp body over his shoulder. Rykus wanted to slam his fist into the now-black computer screen. He wanted to feel the glass break, see the sparks fly. Instead, he let Brookins take Ash away without protest. He'd find someone to help her, to get her out of that cell and off the sedative as soon as he could.

When the crew came back in, Bayis retrieved the relayer from the command console's data-port. Rykus watched him pocket it. How long would it take to translate the files and find what Ash's team lead had seen?

A thought occurred to him, another route to the information they needed.

"Stratham," he said. "Hagan's assistant. Where is he?"

Bayis didn't answer immediately. He watched the three-man crew take their seats. His expression remained unreadable until he let out a sigh. "Stratham has disappeared."

"He was on your ship." It felt like he'd been locked in a pressure chamber. Someone was turning the dial up and up and up, squeezing his chest until it felt like it would implode.

"We searched for him," Bayis said. "We've had dozens of shuttles dock and fly since the Sariceans' attack. He could have been on any of them."

Or Bayis could have put him on one of them.

Goddammit. He was growing paranoid. Bayis was doing everything within his authority to help him and Ash.

"That's another one of the reasons I came dirtside," Bayis said. "His sudden absence was unexpected. We'll investigate it and your claims. If they are substantiated, everything will work out."

If they weren't substantiated…

There had better be clear evidence in the Sariceans' files. It was the only way Bayis and I-Com would believe him.

He nodded his acceptance of Bayis's words, but he couldn't escape the feeling that he might have just betrayed the woman he loved.

TWENTY-ONE

T HE TIME ON RYKUS'S COMM-CUFF blurred. He rubbed his eyes, forced himself to focus—1200 ship time. It had officially been three days since Ash had been sedated and thrown back in a cell. He hated not seeing her, not knowing if she was hurting, if she was trapped in nightmares.

Not knowing if she blamed him for all this.

He blamed himself. If he'd trusted his gut instinct before she escaped and had dug harder into the evidence, he might have discovered something significant. He might have been able to avoid the crash on Ephron, the assassination of Chancellor Hagan, and the fall down the DFC. He might have been able to avoid marching them into an ambush.

He fisted his hands on his desk. He should have known the trek to the outpost was too easy, but they'd been overconfident and desperate, and they'd relied on fabricated transmissions sent to them by, ironically, one of the cryptology officers assigned to Operation Star Dive. At least they'd been beaten by an anomaly, not by a rank-and-file crypty.

Rykus's chair squeaked when he leaned forward to rest his elbows on his knees. His room felt smaller than usual, but this was the only place he could be alone. Everywhere else, he had an escort.

His official designation was "person of interest," but all his authorizations had been revoked. He couldn't access his correspondence, couldn't send or receive any type of video or voice message without it being analyzed by security, and half the ship—the brig, the weapons locker, even the *Obsidian's* gym—was marked No Entry to him. The Coalition wasn't trusting him with something as minor as the mess hall's menu; it certainly wasn't letting him anywhere near the Sariceans' files. He didn't know why it was taking so damn long to find the evidence. Ash's team lead had found it without a problem.

Rykus stood, checked the time again, then paced his quarters. His duffel bag, always kept packed in case he had to leave quickly on an op, hovered at the edge of his vision. He felt its pull, just like he had every minute he'd been in his quarters these past three days. This time though, he didn't fight its lure. He turned toward it.

It was shoved onto the top shelf of his small closet. In addition to his combat gear, survival supplies, rations, and water, it contained an unregistered comm-cuff linked to an anonymous credit account. Possession of the unregistered cuff wasn't exactly illegal, but using it outside an op was. That's why he hadn't touched it yet, but the voice in his head—a voice that had grown louder and more paranoid every time Bayis denied him permission to do anything—argued that this *was* an op, possibly the most important one of his life.

Someone executed Hagan. Someone could execute Ash, especially now when she was a defenseless target sedated and strapped down in the brig.

Turning away from the closet, he clenched his hands into fists. The reasons Bayis had restricted his clearances made sense. Rykus had violated numerous rules and procedures, but it didn't feel right, and as much as he tried to push the feeling away, suspicion clung to him like dust to a hull.

What if Bayis was being influenced by a telepath?

His door chimed, cutting off his thoughts. When the automated voice said Dr. Katie Monick stood outside, Rykus turned. But before he could say "Enter," the door opened without his permission.

The admiral had changed his damn privacy settings.

Katie stopped before she crossed the threshold. "Admiral Bayis sent me to check on you. I take it you're not doing well?"

"Does he expect me to be doing well?"

"I don't think he expected you to glare a hole through my head."

He was scowling—had been scowling for the past three days—but none of this was Katie's fault. Forcing his muscles to relax, he erased any hint of an expression from his face.

"How is the search and rescue going?" He wanted to ask about Ash again, but every time he did, Katie's answer was the same—Ash was sleeping comfortably—so Rykus forced himself to clamp down on his concern while he pried for other information.

Katie finally stepped inside his room, her mouth tightening into a thin line. "Ephron's orbit is a death trap. Only heavily armored, authorized transports are allowed through. I don't know how bad it is on the surface, but SAR crews are bringing in body bags now. A few escape pod beacons are still sending out pings, but they're hard to get to, and there's not much hope for survivors."

"I'm sorry."

She gave him a pinched smile. "From what I've heard, it's not Ash's fault."

"Bayis told you…" He hesitated. Everything he believed about Ash was classified, and he didn't want to give Bayis another justification for revoking his clearances. "He told you what's wrong with Ash."

"He told me your theory, yes," Katie said. "He wanted my opinion."

"And?"

She shrugged. "In the three millennium of recorded history among the Coalition worlds, telepathy has never been confirmed. There have been hacks and frauds, but every time a claim has been investigated, it's been disproved. The most credible claims had implants, but the implants had both medical and operational consequences, and Ash has been scanned. There are no physical devices in her head."

"Ash and Hagan communicated. They spoke to each other."

"I'm not saying it's impossible. I'm saying it hasn't been proved, and no one's going to believe Ash's story until there's evidence."

"It's not her story, it's Hagan's."

"Hagan's dead, by your hand according to some."

"I didn't—"

"I know that," Katie said. "But it looks bad, Rhys. I'm surprised Bayis hasn't put you in the brig."

"The Coalition isn't ready to put its hero in chains." Bitterness laced the words, and once they were said out loud, a fist twisted in his gut. He'd rather be in chains than stuck with that damn label. The Coalition loved it. After reports of the disaster at Gaeles Minor, enlistment in the Fleet and Fighting Corps tripled, and for an interplanetary organization starving for a way to enforce its laws and treaties, they celebrated the increase in recruits.

Katie silently sank into his desk chair. Too silently.

"What is it?"

She looked away, obviously not wanting to say something.

"Katie," he growled out.

Her bright blue eyes met his. "Your name made the news."

Great.

He stared at the stars outside his window. The view was fabricated of course. It was a re-creation of what he would see if only a pane of glass stood between him and space. If a window had stood between him and the citizens of the Coalition, the view wouldn't be half as accurate. "What are they saying?"

"The media is asking questions. Coalition representatives are telling them you have knowledge about an ongoing investigation and that you're staying aboard the *Obsidian* for security reasons. They're only flashing your image across the news vids once or twice an hour."

His face twitched into another frown. The Coalition wouldn't release information about Ash, her mission to Chalos II, or the assault Rykus had been planning. He shouldn't be a news story. "They're twisting it, aren't they?"

She shrugged.

"What the hell are they saying?"

"It doesn't matter."

"What are they saying, Katie?"

"The media is just speculating."

He held her gaze the way he'd hold that of one of his soldiers if they'd screwed up.

She sighed. "They're saying you're the reason the Sariceans left the system."

"What?" He bolted off the bed.

Katie rose too. "Like I said, they're speculating. All they know is that the Sariceans attacked us, and that Rhys 'Rest in Peace' Rykus was involved in some way."

"That's fucking ridiculous." He grabbed his comm-cuff off his night-stand, fastened it around his wrist. He'd survived Gaeles Minor by making a decision that killed thirteen good soldiers. He might have saved hundreds of lives, but no one should be lauded for sacrificing their men.

"Where are you going?"

"I won't let that stand." Back then, if he'd known which transport the enemy would target, he would have made sure he was on it. He'd guessed wrong and he'd lived.

"Rykus."

He tucked in his uniform. He needed a target for his anger. The media would do just fine.

"Rhys."

He started for the door.

"The tachyon capsule is here."

He stopped and frowned over his shoulder. I-Com wanted him to go to Meryk for a debriefing, but he hadn't expected them to request his presence this soon.

"Ash is scheduled to be transferred in two hours," Katie said.

"They're transferring her?" he asked the question carefully, a sick feeling circling through his stomach.

Katie nodded. "I wanted you to know I've asked to be assigned to her profile. I'll watch out for…"

She must have noticed something in his expression. She pressed her lips together.

He moved toward her. "Where are they transferring her?"

"No one told you?" Katie grimaced. "I thought you knew. Shit. *Shit.*"

He grabbed her arm. "Where are they transferring her? Why? And whose decision was it?"

She pushed his hand away, then shook her head, muttering something under her breath before she met his eyes again. "They've analyzed every im-age and line of text in the Sariceans' files, and there's not one reference to telepathy or the corruption of Coalition officials. There's nothing to clear her name. So she's being sent to the institute."

He shook his head, retreated a step, shook his head again.

"No." He slammed his fist into the wall.

"They don't have a choice," Katie said. "And it's the best place for her."

"It's her hell!"

"We might be able to undo the telepathy—"

"The telepathy you don't believe exists."

"I didn't say I didn't believe it."

"You're putting her in the institute," he snarled.

Katie's expression went blank, and when she spoke, her tone was cold. "I'm not putting her anywhere, Rykus, and I didn't come up here to get yelled at. I came up here to tell you I'd be there for her."

He unclenched his fists. He was taking his anger out on Katie. She didn't deserve that, but Ash didn't deserve what was being done to her either. He ran his hands over his face, trying to calm down, trying to think.

"I'll make sure Ash is okay," Katie continued, her voice softer again. "I'll keep her off the drugs and away from the researcher's tests as much as I can. I'll work with her to try to prove the telepathy theory. Now that I know what might be wrong with her, I'll be able to try some new tests. But the most important thing is that I'll be there with her, and I'll be on her side."

He stared at the wall he'd slammed his fist into and nodded. Not agreeing with her. Not disagreeing. Just nodding.

"Bayis has authorized my request for the transfer," Katie said. "He's worried—we're both worried—you're going to do something stupid."

It took him a long time to realize she was asking a question. He turned away from the wall. "A child has more authorizations to move about this ship than I do. How could I do something stupid?"

Katie eyed the duffel bag in his closet. He didn't.

He kept his gaze on her and said, "I'm not looking for an official arrest."

The pinch to her mouth told him she wasn't quite convinced.

He flexed the hand he'd thrown into the wall, then sat on the edge of his bed. He needed to distract Katie. He needed to distract himself. "Do you know why she wouldn't decrypt the files?"

"She didn't want a telepath to gain access to them."

He rested his arms on his knees and stared at the floor. "It's more than that. She doesn't want the senators to learn that telepaths exist. She thinks they'll grow more suspicious of each other. They'll start pointing fingers, throwing around accusations. Eventually, they'll use it as an excuse to leave the Coalition."

"The Coalition is stronger than that," Katie said.

He looked up. "Is it?"

"I believe so," she said. "Yes, it could create problems, but the chance of planets withdrawing is slim. We see the benefits of working together."

"Ash believes she's 'preserving and protecting' the Coalition."

Recognition registered in Katie's eyes. "You think it's the loyalty training."

"You know what she's been through. She resisted my commands, tried to piss me off and send me away so I wouldn't use compulsion to get those files. She was hurt and threatened and tortured. She didn't have to be."

"Yeah, but it's very unlikely the Coalition would fall—"

"But there's a chance. Ash didn't sign up for the anomaly program for money or for glory. She signed up because she believes in the Coalition's mission. She believes in what it stands for. Add the loyalty training to that, and it's screwed with her judgment."

Katie sat beside him. "Even if that's the case, Rhys, you've done everything you can for her."

No, he hadn't. Not yet.

"I need to pack my bag," Katie said. "I'll let you know how she's doing."

He gave her another noncommittal nod, then stood and walked her the three steps to the door. Katie meant well. She wanted to help and Rykus trusted her, but he didn't trust everyone else. When Ash had sat in the *Obsidian's* brig before her escape, his gut had told him she was innocent. He hadn't listened until Hagan gave him evidence. He would listen to it now, and now it was telling him Ash would never make it to the institute.

"Thanks, Katie."

She gave him a small smile. "You're a good man, Rhys. Take care of yourself."

He waited until the door closed behind her. Then he went to his closet and pulled down his duffel bag. He took out the unregistered comm-cuff. Katie couldn't protect Ash. He could, but not from the *Obsidian*. He had to get off the ship and onto the tachyon capsule, and there was one person he could call who might be willing to pull some strings to get that done legally.

He tapped on the comm-cuff. "Contact Grand General Markin Rykus. Authorization Code 583910. Bypass Code 5."

CHAPTER

TWENTY-TWO

ASH FOUGHT THE DARK. She kicked and clawed and snapped her teeth at it, but it didn't retreat. It was damn stubborn. Damn impenetrable. And damn confusing. She didn't know why it existed.

She suspected it was poisoning her. She felt sluggish, mentally clouded. Was she under an ocean? Was she stranded in space? She didn't feel the pressure of a life-suit on her body, didn't hear filtered air circulating in a helmet. And wouldn't she see *some* light? The hint of a moon's glow on the water's surface? The flicker of a distant star?

She hated the confusion. Hated not being able to think.

She kicked at the darkness again, but it smothered her. It crept over her skin and chilled her blood, defeating her from the inside out.

Poison. Definitely a poison.

What motherfucker had poisoned her?

A face almost formed in her mind. She thought she heard a vaguely familiar voice. She needed to know who it was, if the person was there to help or hurt her, if the person was really there at all.

Her neck muscles strained. She swore she heard her tendons creak as they tightened and bent, and she was almost certain she turned her head to the left. It was a gargantuan feat, but it didn't impress the voice. The voice went silent.

She was alone again. Alone with the toxin. She had to cleanse it from her system. Sweat it out. Drink it gone. But the turning of her head had been a mistake. It had drained her energy, her strength. The poison was winning. It was beating her. Killing her.

She succumbed to the venom again.

CHAPTER

TWENTY-THREE

R YKUS ALMOST MISSED THE LAST TRANSPORT to the cap-
sule. He'd had to agree to a meeting with his father "sometime soon."
Rykus had been home exactly two times since his supposed death at the Battle of Gaeles Minor, and both trips had been to see the other members of his
family, not the man who'd done everything he could to sabotage Rykus's career. The Javerian general might have finally forgiven Rykus for joining the
Coalition's Fighting Corps, but that didn't mean Rykus and his father needed to be on the same planet together. They hadn't gotten along before Rykus
resigned from Javery's Home Guard. His father's mind-changing grief hadn't
changed that.

It took twenty long, frustrating minutes to convince the general to make
a call, and only after a promise to discuss events more when Rykus visited.
Of course, if the tachyon cruise went badly, he wouldn't be visiting his family on Javery; they'd be visiting him in a Coalition prison.

The transport's dock-clamp doors clanked open, and Rykus stared out
the window at the huge, oblong, garishly painted tachyon capsule. From the
outside, capsules were the ugliest vessels in the Known Universe. This one
was owned by Starlight Lines, a pleasure-cruise company who took the rich
from system to system on multiday vacations. It was painted bright green
and pink, a combination of colors that was guaranteed to make anyone not
from the company's home planet of Esyll sick.

But Starlight Lanes had offered the capsule to help with refugees and other humanitarian services, and even though it wasn't as big as the military capsules Rykus was used to traveling on, it was capable of holding a dozen full-size, capital-class ships in its hollow interior. In addition to transporting ships, capsules transported individuals, and the inner walls of this capsule would be lined with boutique shops, high-credit restaurants, first-class recreation areas, and of course, the most elaborate hotel accommodations of any vessel in the KU. It was a mobile civilization.

But it was a *civilian* civilization. Security wouldn't be as tight as a military capsule's, so if Rykus's instinct was right and someone tried to hurt Ash, they should be able to disappear, either into the crowds or onto one of the ships in the hold.

He felt a tug on his pants leg and looked down. A boy of about five standard years peered up at him.

"You're Rhys Rykus," the boy said.

Ah, hell.

The kid didn't wait for his response. He took off the comm-cuff encircling his small wrist and held it and a stylus out, his eyes wide with expectation.

Rykus stared at him. The boy couldn't have been born when the Coalition had pinned medals on him. He shouldn't know his name, let alone recognize him.

But the boy knew. Everyone in the transport knew. He felt their eyes suddenly, and his shoulder ached.

If the boy had been an adult, if there hadn't been other kids around, and if people weren't staring at him with so much damn appreciation in their eyes, he would have turned his back on the request. But he didn't have it in him to hurt a kid's feelings, and he wasn't allowed to discuss the details of what had happened over Gaeles Minor.

He took the stylus and comm-cuff.

"You got rid of the Sariceans?" a man, presumably the boys' father, asked.

It was a good thing the media wasn't on board. Rykus would have killed someone.

"Not me," was all he said, and he quickly signed the band of the boy's comm-cuff, then handed it back.

He turned to the window again. He wasn't a hero, never had been, and he was walking the edge of treason with his current actions.

"Please take your seats and strap in for docking." The pilot's voice came over the transport's speakers. Rykus sank into the nearest empty chair, thankful for the distraction. Five minutes later, the transport latched onto the capsule.

"We've docked," the pilot announced. "For those of you who've lost friends and family, our deepest sympathies are with you. Please depart, and know that we're going to get those Saricean bastards."

Some of the refugees let out cheers as they stood. Others muttered quiet agreements, but no one moved toward the door. They remained in their places. It took Rykus another second to realize they were waiting for him to depart first.

Seeker's God, he hated this.

Grim faced, he moved down the aisle.

The pilot met him at the door. "Thank you, sir."

Muttering something that wasn't quite an acknowledgment, Rykus fled the transport.

Half an hour later, he located Ash. The Coalition hadn't taken her to the capsule's detention center. She was in the medical bay, slotted into a room at the end of a hallway that needed more than a few lights replaced. Unconscious, Ash was harmless. It was more important to monitor her vitals than to make sure her chains and room were secure. He told the two men guarding the corridor that's all he wanted to do, but they weren't buying it.

"The authorization is from a highly respected general," he told them.

"General Rykus isn't a member of the Fighting Corps, sir."

"General Galmon is."

The younger of the two men, a corporal, kept his expression neutral. "General Galmon's orders state only that you are granted a transfer to capsule security detail. This is a special assignment. You shouldn't be here. You should be receiving your orders from Security HQ."

The muscles in Rykus's neck and shoulders tightened. He wanted to take out his frustration on the corporal, but the man was doing his job. He was following orders, sticking to procedure. It wasn't his fault that Rykus's father hadn't pushed Galmon for a more thorough authorization. Rykus was lucky his father had agreed to ask for the favor at all.

He stared at the corridor that led to Ash's cell and tried to convince himself that she was perfectly fine.

"Who are you receiving your orders from?" He asked the question out of a dim hope that he might know their CO, but a suspicious silence came from the two guards.

"Who's your CO?" he asked again, scrutinizing their expressions.

The other guard, a Sergeant Mullenz, answered. "Lieutenant Hastings, sir."

"Call him."

The two men exchanged a glance. Rykus's hand drifted toward his hip. His weapon wasn't holstered there. This was a gun-free capsule—only a very select few were allowed to carry—but the guards noted the movement.

"One moment," Mullenz said. He stepped to the computer terminal to the right of the corridor and waved his comm-cuff over the sensor. It took less than a minute for his CO to pick up. The soldier kept the conversation private. All Rykus got was a few glances and a sprinkling of "yes, sirs" and "I understand, sirs."

Mullenz ended the connection and turned to face him. "Commander Rykus, I've been ordered to take you into custody."

Rykus stared at the man. He couldn't have heard him correctly.

"You shouldn't be on this capsule, sir. You're AWOL."

"AWOL? You have my authorization right there on your comm-cuff." He jabbed his finger toward the man's wrist.

"It's fraudulent, sir." Mullenz took out a pair of restraints.

What the hell was this?

"Get your CO back on the comm."

"Turn around, sir."

Rykus shouldered his way past the man to look at the screen, hoping to glimpse the last connection. The comm screen wasn't up though. Instead, it showed a small white room with a bed in its center and a black medical tower to its right.

Ash's eyes were closed, her face relaxed. All lights on the med-tower were green, and its screen was idle and dark. The sedative was doing its job. It hung inside a recess near the top of the tower, dripping a clear liquid into her bloodstream.

Mullenz grabbed his arm. Rykus was about to let himself be pulled away when a man stepped inside Ash's room. Rykus couldn't see his face, but he was in civilian clothes.

"You said no one was permitted into her room." His tone didn't betray the sudden pounding of his heart.

"Medical personnel only." Mullenz pulled at his arm.

"That's not a doctor. Not even a medic."

"Your hands, sir. Before we have to use force."

"He's a threat." He fired the words in the guard's face.

The idiot drew his baton and swung.

Ducking beneath the blow, Rykus yanked the weapon free, then slammed it into the man's temple.

The second guard was already moving. Rykus laid him out too. He grabbed Mullenz's restraints, cuffed the men's hands together beneath the bolted-down desk, then sprinted down the long hall, praying he'd make it in time to save Ash.

CHAPTER

TWENTY-FOUR

THERE WERE COLORS in the blackness now. Dark blues, darker reds, and even the occasional streak of something that might be called orange.

Ash felt her chest moving, filling with air. That was good. And there was a prickling sensation in her hands and feet. That was better. She might be able to make her muscles work.

She started with her eyes, because that should be easiest. She told them to open—a simple order—but they squeezed shut instead.

At least they did something.

She lay there a moment longer, listening to the silence. She waited for something, some noise or rattle to give her a hint about where she was. When none came, she focused inward again. She needed to get the stardust out of her brain. She needed to remember.

Remember what?

Something important. Something big. Something…

Her body jerked. Memories assaulted her one after the other, bright and vivid and painful. Jevan blowing a hole in Trevast's head. Kris begging for his life. The rest of her team, slaughtered. More blood. More death.

Rykus.

His image eased her panic until more memories came. The ambush. The cipher. Rykus's cooperation with the admiral.

Son of a bitch. He'd tackled her when she tried to prevent his XO from sticking a needle in her neck.

Jolting fully awake, she opened her eyes.

Just in time to stop a man in midstep.

He stared as if she were a razorwolf clawing the ground. That almost made her laugh. She could barely lift her head, and her wrists were restrained, albeit with strong, self-attaching straps, not metal shackles, but she was in no condition to attack.

"You're supposed to be unconscious," the man said. Then he *pushed* against her mind.

Adrenaline scorched through her veins. It was Hagan's legislative assistant, the telepath who'd spoken in her head on the *Obsidian*.

"Stratham," she said. "So nice to finally meet you in person."

Her voice wasn't as strong as she wanted it to be, but she couldn't manage anything more. Her mouth was dry, and her body wasn't fully functional yet.

Some of the surprise left his expression. It was replaced with anger. "Who woke you?"

That was a good question, one she didn't have an answer to, but he didn't need to know that. "I'm an anomaly, asshole. I woke myself up."

More pressure on her mind. She glared at Stratham and said as loudly as she could without actually saying anything, *Fuck off.*

He flinched.

She smiled. Looky there. More of her facial muscles were working.

Stratham's eyes narrowed. His hand clenched around something. A syringe.

She stared at it before she shifted her gaze back to him, her expression unconcerned. "You don't look like a killer."

He straightened. Then he strode to the side of her bed.

"What happens if I scream?"

His gaze flickered toward the door, then back. "You can't."

The simple words made her chest tighten. It was the same uneasiness she always felt just before she blacked out. Now was definitely not the best time to risk losing consciousness. She needed to stall. Stall until the drugs wore off and she had some chance of breaking out of the straps.

"Did you kill my guards?" she asked. "Did you disable the cameras?"

"The guards have been taken care of," he said, then he reached toward the bag of fluids in the recess of the tall black med-tower. That liquid was supposed to keep her hydrated and unconscious. It was still connected to the IV in her arm, but someone must have switched the bag.

Rykus?

She fought the flutter that grew in her chest. The loyalty training was responsible for putting it there. Rykus wasn't coming to her rescue. He'd condemned her to this fate.

"You ever kill someone before?" she asked, keeping her tone conversational. "You might want to rethink this. Delegate the responsibility to someone else. You know, so you can keep your hands clean."

She pulled against her restraints, felt one start to give, but Stratham saw the movement.

He spun, locked his hand around her wrist, and snarled, "Stay still."

"I need some help in—"

Stratham's other hand grabbed her throat, choking off her call for help.

Ash gagged.

She coughed.

She battled down a surge of panic. Then she funneled all her strength into breaking the straps.

Cursing, Stratham moved behind her. His elbow came under her chin. His arm tightened around her neck.

Bastard.

She arched her back and tried to turn her head to bite Stratham's arm.

He tightened the hold.

Her left wrist slipped a millimeter in its strap. She pulled hard. Got another millimeter, but black spots punched through her vision.

She would have screamed if she'd had air. Out of frustration, not fear. Death was something she'd accepted a long time ago, but she damn well hadn't accepted this kind of death. She could not, would not, be killed by this man, this weak coward of a politician. If she was going to die, she wanted to go down fighting. Killing. Beating the ever-living hell out of something.

She tried shoving herself into Stratham's mind, but nothing worked. She couldn't breathe. She couldn't fight. She...

She was still conscious. The idiot was only cutting off her airway, not the blood flow to her brain. She had some time.

She twisted her left hand, trying to reach the edge of the strap, trying to stay calm and conscious.

Then Stratham adjusted his hold.

Fuck.

She heard a roar, then her vision went black.

It returned when something thumped to her right.

It thumped again.

It took a ridiculous amount of effort to turn her head, to see Rykus on top of Stratham, slamming his fist into the man's face again and again and again.

Damn, her fail-safe was strong. Stratham tried to cover his head, but Rykus's punches broke and bloodied his face. Rykus was using his left arm, the one he'd injured at Gaeles Minor, the one that was mechanically enhanced. A political aide, even a telepathic one, didn't stand a chance.

"You might not want to kill him, Rip," she said as nonchalantly as if she were telling him not to order the special from the mess hall. Despite the lack of urgency in her tone, Rykus stopped immediately. His hand clenched into a fist above the unconscious Stratham.

He wanted to obliterate the man. Ash saw that in the way his muscles bulged beneath his dark gray dress-downs. That fact made a fuzzy, warm, and entirely inappropriate heat surge through her. Rykus had saved her life. He wanted to end the man who'd tried to take it. There was something undeniably attractive about that kind of heroism.

Rykus finally looked at her. She had to force herself to meet his gaze. She wanted to look away, to run away, because she felt vulnerable and she wasn't sure if the feeling in her stomach was lust or loyalty or some combination of the two. It shouldn't have been either. She should be pissed. She *was* pissed. Rykus had betrayed her.

"Are you okay?" he asked quietly.

Shutting down her emotions, she smiled at his blood-splattered face. She wouldn't let him know he'd hurt her. Wouldn't let him know his actions had fazed her at all.

"I'll be better when you get this needle out of my arm."

Rykus stood, wiped his bloodied knuckles on his shirt, then carefully withdrew the IV from her wrist. "What did he put in it?"

"I'm sure something harmless." Her voice was raspy.

Rykus glanced at her neck, which was undoubtedly bruised and red. That wasn't the only reason why she was hoarse though. She'd been sedated for too long.

She watched his face as he pulled hard on the self-attaching straps, noting the tension around his mouth, the shadow of the day's scruff over his jaw. All she could do was lie there as he freed her, wondering what he was thinking and why he'd come.

As soon as her hands were free, she sat up. The room blackened, but her vision cleared quickly. Her body was getting rid of the sedative they'd pumped into her.

She looked at the IV hanging toward the ground, then the bag of fluids in the medical tower beside her.

"You were here before?" she asked. Someone had switched out the bag.

He looked at the tower too. "No."

"Then who…" She searched her memories and remembered a low voice. A reassuring voice. It was also a familiar voice. It was…

"Oh," she said out loud.

"Oh?" Rykus echoed, watching her.

"Oh, nothing," she said, casual as could be. She remembered the voice she had heard. It hadn't been in her head. It had been Kalver. Her brother had saved her ass.

"Ash."

She stared at the opposite wall, ignoring the tug of the loyalty training.

Rykus sighed. "Kalver. I got him cleared of all charges, but he was pissed when he heard you were being…"

His expression went grim. For the first time, Ash looked around the room. She wasn't in a cell; she was in a med bay. The air smelled of antiseptic and clean, refiltered oxygen. The equipment wasn't military grade.

She replayed the words Rykus had cut off. "I'm on a tachyon capsule?"

He drew in a breath, looked away. "You're being transferred to Caruth."

A cold, bone-chilling sickness shot down her arms and legs. No. No fucking way was she going back there.

She jumped to her feet, took one wobbly step away from the medical bed.

Rykus steadied her with a hand on her elbow. "I couldn't let them do that."

"But you could let your XO stick a needle in my neck." She jerked her arm free.

"I didn't let him."

"You tackled me to the ground."

"I didn't know what he'd done."

"You made me disarm."

"We didn't have a choice."

"You convinced me to give up, to surrender." She advanced on him. "You made me give Bayis the cipher."

"I saved your life," he yelled.

Ash didn't flinch. She raised her chin and met her fail-safe's gaze with all the defiance she could muster.

"And I didn't force you. I *asked* you." His face softened, and his eyes searched hers. "I couldn't handle seeing you die."

She felt unstable again, as if the tachyon capsule had bent reality early, throwing off her sense of time and place. Rykus didn't want to see her die. A week ago, she'd been convinced he wanted to kill her himself. He was the man who'd thrown pictures of her dead teammates in her face, pursued her on a reckless race into Ephron's atmosphere, and marched her through a forest with her hands bound behind her back.

But he was also the man who'd pulled her out of a nightmare with a kiss. And after the kiss…

After the kiss, they'd had sex. That was it. It was physical only. Ash wasn't the type of person to get herself into an emotional tangle. Not with Jevan, and especially not with her fail-safe.

But what if Rykus wasn't her fail-safe?

That wasn't a safe question. It led to too many impossibilities, so she closed off those thoughts and the warm, fluttery feeling in her stomach, and she focused on the man lying half-conscious on the floor. Stratham's head lolled to the left, and his closed eyes strained to open.

Ash knelt beside him, then knocked her hand hard against the side of his swollen face. *Wakey, wakey, asshole.*

Stratham grunted. His blood-covered face twitched.

Wake up now, she singsonged the words into his head. The bastard's eyes grated open. They widened when he saw her.

You're going to answer my questions, she told him.

He looked to the left. She grabbed his face and made him focus on her. *You're going to tell me how to undo this straitjacket on my mind. You're going to tell me who you are and why your people murdered my teammates. You're going to tell me the fucking endgame or I. Will. Hurt. You.*

The way he trembled made a dark, overdue satisfaction seep through Ash. She finally had a target for all the rage she'd built up over the weeks, all the days she'd spent cooped up in a cell, all the times she'd blacked out, unable to defend her actions or avenge her teammates' murders.

She wanted to maim and kill and torture.

"No," Stratham mumbled, his head moving back and forth in slow, short shakes. "No. I wasn't there. I didn't—"

She dug her fingernails into his face. *I don't give a fuck.*

Stratham tried to slide away. She held him in place, centering her weight on his chest and using her legs to lock his left arm against his body. His right arm, she grabbed and twisted.

Stratham cried out when the pressure built at his shoulder. "It shouldn't have happened. It was a mistake! A stupid risk."

Rykus stepped forward. He stood by Stratham's head, crossed his arms, and loomed like a Caruthian glacier.

Stratham's gaze darted to him, and sweat mixed with blood as it slid into his hairline. Rykus was big, intimidating, and he'd just beaten the hell out of Stratham. It made sense the bastard was terrified of him, but Ash needed him to be terrified of her.

She twisted the arm further, almost dislocating his shoulder. His face contorted in pain.

"She's an anomaly," Rykus said, his voice low but menacing. "She's the only woman who's survived Caruth. She's survived the hell you put her in, and she's pissed. I suggest you answer her questions."

Stratham's wide eyes stared. *I'm sorry. I… I had nothing to do with what happened to you or your team.*

"Answer her questions out loud," Rykus said.

"I—" He coughed, spraying blood into the air. He tried to rock to the side, but Ash didn't let him move.

"Let him sit up," Rykus said.

She kept the pressure on Stratham's arm. She wanted to break it, to snap his elbow, make him hurt.

He kept coughing, straining to breathe.

Rykus placed his hand on her shoulder. "Let him sit up. He can't talk if he can't breathe."

He could talk to her.

Ash wanted to reject Rykus's advice and let Stratham choke. Rykus had claimed he hadn't known about the sedative, but a part of her still felt betrayed. She'd put her faith in him, relied on him, and it had landed her in a tachyon capsule bound for Caruth.

But Ash made decisions based on logic and experience, not on emotion, so she released Stratham and stood.

He rolled to the side, spewing more blood.

Rykus grabbed a fistful of his shirt and yanked him upright. He dragged him to the wall as easily as if Stratham was in a zero-g bubble.

"Start talking," Rykus said.

"I… I don't know… where to start."

"Who do you work for?" Rykus asked.

"Hagan—"

Rykus slammed his fist into Stratham's stomach.

"You're a telepath," Rykus said. "Where are you from? How many of you are there?"

A warning pressed on the back of her neck. It was so sudden and severe she almost stumbled forward. She squeezed her eyes shut and blocked out Stratham's next words. She wasn't the one talking about telepaths, but she had to be careful. She drew in a breath, then stared at a black scuff mark on the floor. She didn't let her expression change. She didn't let her body move. She didn't do anything that her mind might construe as being an acknowledgment of Rykus's accusations.

Stratham shook his head. "Nowhere. Everywhere."

Rykus shook him, knocking the back of his skull on the wall.

"We don't have a home planet. We just… we're elite. Supreme. We… we rule the people."

"The people?" Rykus asked.

"Yes. The people. All of them."

"Explain."

Stratham licked his busted lower lip. "We're telepaths. We influence the leaders of the people we encounter. We control them."

"Who do you control?" Rykus asked the same time Ash did, only Ash's words weren't spoken out loud.

She gritted her teeth. She and Rykus had the same training, the same thought patterns when it came to conflict situations. It made sense that they would pursue the same line of interrogation, but it pissed her off that Rykus could put a voice behind his question and she still couldn't. She didn't want him to be her mouthpiece.

"I was assigned to Hagan." Stratham strained to breathe. "We have people assigned to other Coalition members."

"I want names," Rykus said.

"I don't know any names. I'm not high level enough."

"You controlled the Coalition's war chancellor. You're high enough."

"He wasn't chancellor when I was assigned. I just do what I'm told."

"Who tells you what to do?"

Stratham's expression tightened. He let his head thump back against the wall. "I don't know."

Ash knew, but suddenly she didn't want Stratham to say Jevan's name. She didn't want Rykus to learn how big a fool she'd been.

"Give me a different answer," Rykus said.

Stratham flinched. "I don't know! I get my orders telepathically. The people who talk to me don't give me their names."

"Someone gave you an order to kill her." Fury rolled off Rykus. "Is that person on this ship? How close do you need to be to communicate?"

"Close. Around a hundred meters."

Around a hundred meters was *not* close.

"You can communicate with anyone?"

Stratham shook his head. "Only other telepaths." He glanced at Ash. "And individuals who are susceptible to telepathy."

What does that mean? Ash demanded.

"You're special. It takes work, but your mind can be unlocked. That's why you were targeted. I'm sorry." Stratham doubled over, coughing and spewing blood again. "This shouldn't have happened. None of it's my doing. None of it's my fault."

He started to say something else, but the sound of his comm-cuff vibrating made him snap his mouth shut. He stared at the device.

"Answer it on speaker," Rykus said.

Stratham closed his eyes. It was a defeated gesture, a relaxation of his face that said he knew he was about to die.

He tapped on his comm-cuff.

"Ramie." Ash shivered as her name came from the comm-cuff and slithered through the air. "It's time for a reunion, my love."

CHAPTER

TWENTY-FIVE

R AMIE.
The second the man on the comm-cuff said Ash's name, Rykus knew who it was. How he hadn't connected the points, seen the full constellation before, he had no idea. Bayis had given him the clue when he'd said Ash was engaged.

Rykus's cadet wasn't wife material.

"Jevan Valt," Rykus said.

"Commander Rykus," Jevan said, sounding jovial. "I know so much about you."

Rykus wished he could say the same. He should have dug into the man's past, examined every acquaintance, scrutinized every action and word that had made it into public record. But he hadn't. All he knew was that Valt was a legislative assistant for Charles Hahn, the senator from Rimmeria.

"You've made a mistake coming here," Ash said. If a tone of voice could murder, she would be up for conviction.

"Oh, I doubt that."

"Where are you?" she demanded.

Valt chuckled. "I… am with a friend."

A chill strafed up Rykus's spine, making the hair on the back of his neck rise.

"Her name is Dr. Monick," Valt continued. "She's a pretty thing. I'd hate to have to hurt her."

Rykus didn't move. He didn't let out the litany of curses that ran through his mind. Valt did know about him, and much more than his name and reputation. He knew about the anomaly program, knew that Ash was brainwashed to obey and protect her fail-safe and, as a side effect, everyone close to him.

"I need a favor from my fiancée," Valt said.

"What do you want?" Ash's voice was strong, steady, and something sparked in Rykus's chest. He was proud of her, proud she wasn't letting this bastard break her.

"You're blocking me," Valt said. "Relax your mind."

"Ignore him," Rykus ordered.

Valt's sigh came through the comm-cuff clearly. "Your fail-safe is giving you bad advice, Ramie. Just like Trevast gave you bad advice. I should have killed him the second I stepped onto the shuttle, but I gave him a chance to live. I gave *you* the chance. All this could have been avoided if you'd just handed over the files. *You* killed your teammates, Ramie. Their blood is on *your* hands."

Rykus ripped the comm-cuff off Stratham's wrist. He wanted to squeeze the device until the screen shattered and the electronics snapped. Instead, he ended the call, then met Stratham's eyes.

"Who's with him?" he demanded.

Stratham wiped the back of his hand across his bloodied mouth. "He has people. I don't know how many."

"Where is he?"

"I don't know exactly."

Rykus threw the cuff at Stratham's broken nose. "Give me another answer."

"I don't know," Stratham bit out. "The cargo area maybe."

"Tell him to come here." The cargo area comprised half the capsule, too large an area to search. "If he comes here, ship security will arrest him but he'll live. If I go to him, he dies."

"He says ship security won't do anything," Stratham said. "They've been told you shouldn't be here."

"I have authorization to be here." Even as he said the words, he remembered the reactions of the two guards. They'd claimed the authorization was a forgery. They'd tried to arrest him.

"Tell him to…" Rykus stopped. Stratham wasn't looking at him. He was frowning at Ash.

"Don't listen to him." Stratham rose to his knees. "You need me. You don't know who you're dealing with. They'll destroy you, all of you."

He scurried backward as if he were being pursued by a starving beast.

Ah, hell.

"I can help! I can talk to the right people."

"Ash." Rykus moved to intercept her, but she slipped past him.

"No," Stratham screamed. "No. Don't. The factions—"

Stratham crumpled to the deck, his neck broken.

The sound of it snapping echoed in Rykus's ears. He stood there stunned, staring down at the man Ash had killed, the man who had information on Valt and the other telepaths who'd possibly infiltrated the Coalition.

"What the hell did you do?" Rykus said. Stratham had been theirs, damn it. The idiot had screwed up his mission to kill Ash, and he'd broken. He would have told them everything he knew.

Ash drew in quick, shallow breaths. When she met his gaze, she did so with no expression. It was as if she'd wrapped her body in heat shielding to block herself from the inferno of his wrath. He wanted to unleash it. He wanted to break things and end this hell they were caught up in.

He paced past her. He needed somewhere to direct the rage burning in his chest, but he couldn't vent like he usually did. He couldn't run or fight or take his frustrations out in a shooting sim.

He grabbed the medical tower and shoved.

It crashed against the back wall in a cacophony that only made him feel marginally better.

Ash didn't move. Rykus wasn't even sure she breathed.

He rotated his reconstructed shoulder. Hell. This wasn't her fault. She wouldn't have killed Stratham unless she had to, and the only reason she would have had to was if Valt had threatened Katie. And the only way for Valt to have threatened her was if he was in Ash's head.

He walked back to Ash and put his hands on her shoulders. He made her look at him. He didn't want to use compulsion, but he wanted that bastard out of her mind. "*Push him out of your head. Don't let him back in.*"

He was certain his tone and cadence were perfect, but she didn't acknowledge his command. It wasn't until she shook that he realized she *couldn't* acknowledge it.

Hagan had said she couldn't give indication—any indication, verbal or otherwise—that telepaths existed. So she was standing there in front of him, doing her goddamn best not to react to his words.

She stared over his left shoulder, swallowed once, twice, then said, "You should leave before we capsule out."

"That's not happening." His words came out so quickly they cut off the end of hers.

She shifted her gaze to his eyes and lifted her chin a notch. "You need to leave. Sir."

He tightened his hands on her arms. It was the only thing he could do to keep himself from throttling her. "You need my help."

She shook her head, then stepped out of his reach.

"What are you going to do?" he asked. "Go after him on your own? You'd be walking unprepared into an ambush, Ash. I trained you better than that."

She glared over her shoulder. "Don't be an ass."

"Don't be a fool."

"One of us needs to live. Sir. And this is not your mission."

Her *sirs* were barbs, always had been, but the thing that really cut him was the fact that she didn't think he would see this through until the end. She thought he'd leave her behind. Abandon her. She really was a fool.

Standing at his full height, he took a step forward, then peered down into her beautifully defiant green eyes. "Get this into your head: you are my mission, Ash."

He didn't let her react to his proclamation. He palmed her face in his hands and kissed her.

She was as exquisite as he remembered, all strong and slender and unbelievably sensuous. The tension he'd sensed in her melted when he parted her lips with his tongue.

She let out a little moan, and he was gone. He couldn't have stopped kissing her then if the capsule had imploded around them. Despite the voice yelling in the back of his mind, despite what he'd sworn he'd never do again and what he knew was right and wrong, he pressed into her. Seeker's God, he wanted her. He'd do whatever it took to make sure she survived.

They finished the kiss in the same moment, with one last lingering, thrilling taste of each other's lips.

It physically hurt to break away, but they'd both endured pain before. An inch of space appeared between them. Ash's eyes opened.

And a throat cleared behind him.

He spun, shielding Ash with his body.

Jon Kalver stood in the doorway. His gaze lazily swung from Rykus to Ash to Stratham's corpse.

"This a bad time for a jailbreak?" he drawled.

Behind Rykus, Ash let out a laugh. "I'm going to owe you till the day I die."

The anomaly grinned. "You know how I like collecting favors, sweetheart."

Ash moved forward, clasped his hand and pulled him close. In a soft voice Rykus just barely managed to hear, she said, "Whatever you need."

Their intimacy chilled the heat Ash's kiss had left in him. Kalver and Ash had been close on Caruth—their entire class had been close—but Kalver had just risked his career to save Ash from being sent into hell. And he'd made it to the capsule before Rykus had.

Straightening to his full height, Kalver turned toward him. "Sir."

The vehemence in that *sir* took Rykus off guard. Several seconds passed before he understood the tone. The anomaly looked like someone who'd just caught a man sleeping with his sister.

John Kalver had seen their kiss. He hadn't liked it, and not because he was jealous. He hadn't liked it because he didn't approve.

Condemnation from one of his anomalies. That proved how completely wrong Rykus's actions were.

"How did you get in here?" he asked. Despite his moral weakness when it came to Ash, he'd meant what he'd said to her. She was his mission now.

"Maintenance sheath behind the med bays," Ash answered for Kalver.

Rykus opened his mouth to say something but closed it quickly. Ash and Kalver both had the schematics for the capsule memorized, same as every other Caruth-trained soldier. A normal person wouldn't have been able to remember details from even one level of the gargantuan vessel. Ash and Kalver weren't normal. Not even a little.

Ash moved to the open doorway, more energy in her steps. "Any weapons?"

"Just my sidearm," Kalver said.

Ash glanced at where Rykus normally carried his gun.

"Confiscated when I came on board," Rykus said. Kalver's should have been too—civilian capsules were gun-free vessels—but it didn't surprise him that Kalver had found a way to smuggle one in. The man loved his weapons.

Kalver's gaze shifted between them. "We have an hour before we capsule out. Seems like we should be able to stroll out of here without blowing something up."

"We're not leaving," Ash said.

"We're not?" Kalver cut his question short and tilted his head. Ash turned hers slightly too, and a second later, Rykus heard it, the quiet buzzing of Stratham's comm-cuff.

Valt. Rykus didn't want to answer it, but he needed to know where Katie was and how he could secure her release.

He looked at Kalver. Ash's situation was still classified. Rykus wasn't supposed to talk about it to anyone, but hell. He'd already broken protocol. Might as well break a few more.

"Jevan Valt is a legislative assistant for the senator from Rimmeria. He's the telepath who screwed with Ash's head. He doesn't know you're here." He hoped that was true. "Don't make a sound."

Kalver nodded.

Rykus walked to Stratham's corpse, picked up the cuff lying on the floor, and handed it to Ash. His fingers brushed hers. She held his gaze only for a second before she docked the cuff in the medical tower he'd thrown to the ground.

She tapped it on.

"Ramie," Valt said, more agitation in his voice than there had been before, "you're blocking me again."

The tension in Rykus's chest eased some. That answered one question. His command had kicked Valt out of Ash's head.

Her fingers moved over the tower's keyboard. It would be quicker to hack through the cuff's security at a comm or classified terminal, but the tower was the only interface they had available. Ash had the skill to trace the transmission though. She just needed time.

"I've ordered her to keep you out of her head," he said, his voice low and even. "I assume you're familiar with the loyalty training."

"I am," Valt said. "Rescind the order. Ramie and I need to have a private conversation."

"No."

"Rescind the order or I kill Dr. Monick."

"No." He didn't take his eyes off the comm-cuff. Katie was one individual, one member of the Coalition's Fighting Corps. Ash's knowledge, the knowledge of what Valt was capable of doing and what he wanted from the files, was bigger than one person.

"I don't bluff, Commander."

"Neither do I." Sweat trickled down his spine. His dress-downs clung to his skin. Valt needed Katie alive for leverage. He wouldn't kill her. That one fact, that one belief, was the only way he kept himself from breaking the long silence that followed. But God help him if he was wrong. Katie might be a member of the Corps, but she was a good soul, a humanitarian. She shouldn't be caught up in this.

"I'll trade Dr. Monick for you and Ramie," Valt said, breaking first.

"Me only," Ash said. The tower's screen went black, then reappeared with an unwinding stream of code. She'd made it past the cuff's external security.

"You and your fail-safe, my love. You both know too much."

"You'll kill us on sight," Ash said. "Then you'll turn around and kill the doctor."

"I'll kill Rykus on sight. You, Ramie, get to live yet again. I need the cipher."

Rykus moved closer to the tower's microphone. "Having trouble getting it from Hagan?" He paused, waiting for an answer. When none came, he knew he was right. He'd let Ash live because he thought another one of his resources could get him what he needed. "You fucked up, asshole."

An Access Denied message flashed on the tower's screen, highlighting Ash's face in red light.

"I have things under control." For the first time, Valt's voice had an edge.

"You're sure about that?" Another Access Denied message appeared on the screen. Ash needed more time.

"Ramie's destroyed you," Valt said. "You know that, don't you?"

If the bastard called Ash *Ramie* one more time, Rykus would lose it.

"You had a promising career," he continued. "You had respect and were regarded as a hero. You've lost all that. Capsule security is searching for you. I've spoken with the right individuals in the Coalition and in the media, and speculation will soon spread about your mental condition. You have no evidence to support any of your claims."

Rykus let a ruthless smile invade his tone. "You're running scared, Valt. You're scrambling to cover your ass. The number of people who know the truth about what you are is growing by the hour. You can kill Ash. You can kill me and Dr. Monick, but you won't be able to stop the others."

"Everything you know is classified," Valt said. "Admiral Bayis will be taken care of. So will the few individuals who aren't under our influence."

"Who else is under your influence?"

"We have many assets within the Coalition. It would take too long to list them all, and I'm not planning to give Ramie the time to track my location."

Ash's fingers paused over the keyboard. She tightened her hands into fists, then took up her typing again.

Rykus wished Valt was an idiot, but he knew exactly what they were doing.

Another Access Denied warning flashed across Ash's screen. He had to stop himself from pushing her aside and tracing the transmission on his own. He had the training and experience to do what she was doing, but he wouldn't be able to do it as quickly. Neither would Kalver. Ash had excelled at hack-sig.

"I need proof of life," he said.

"I'll send it to you along with the meeting location after we capsule out. In the meantime, I'd avoid ship security. They have orders to arrest you on sight."

"Wait!" he said before Valt could end the transmission. He searched his mind for some way, some hook, to keep Valt's attention. "I want you to unlock Ash's mind. I want you out of her head. Permanently."

"How do you know I'm not in her mind now?" A smile crept into Valt's voice.

"Because I've made sure I'm there." He leaned in so close to the microphone his lips brushed it. "I'm her fail-safe, you son of a bitch. You couldn't undo the loyalty training. You couldn't undo her love for the Coalition. You couldn't undo *her*. She's stronger than anyone in the KU, and you were a fool to think you could beat her down. You messed with the wrong woman."

The screen flashed red again. Rykus felt red on the inside.

"Your opinion of your anomaly is grossly overestimated, Commander."

Ash's fingers flew over the keyboard. Access Denied.

"I've been in her body and in her head," Valt said.

Ash backed out of the coding, went back in. Access Denied.

"I know her better than she knows herself."

Access Denied.

"I'll send the proof of life and meeting location."

Access Denied.

Access Denied.

Access Denied.

Damn it. Ash needed more time.

"Valt—"

"See you soon, love." Valt cut the transmission.

CHAPTER

TWENTY-SIX

ASH'S HANDS FROZE when the comm-cuff went silent. She focused on the Access Denied warning, but there was no ignoring the fury radiating from Rykus. She could practically see the waves of his heat signature blurring the air around him.

It was his typical silent simmer. She countered it with her typical flippant smile.

"Have a little faith, Rip." She tapped the exit key. The warning vanished, and a cross section of the capsule appeared. Her fail-safe stared at the bright blue dot sitting in the center of one of its cargo bays. He breathed in a lungful of air. Then another and another. By the time he took in a fourth breath, he'd calmed down. His gaze shifted from the screen to her.

She fought the urge to step backward. Rykus saw through her shields and her smiles. He knew her, respected her, and that knowledge made Ash feel far too vulnerable, too attached.

Pulling her into his arms, Rykus squeezed her in a tight embrace and whispered in her ear, "You're amazing."

The butterflies that sprang to life in her stomach had jetpacks attached to their wings. They ricocheted inside her hard enough to screw with her equilibrium. For one brief moment, she let herself imagine what it would be like to be with him. To really be with him. To have him whisper other words in her ear, to feel his touch in times when they weren't likely to die, to go places where they would be safe and could laze around and just be with each other. No stress. No frustrations. No anger.

No chance.

"I should… I need to…" She needed to get it together. He was her fail-safe. He was a war hero. He was Rest in Peace Rykus, for God's sake. She'd pledged her life to the Coalition. She'd be a soldier until the day she died—so would he—and if they survived this, the Fighting Corps would assign them to opposite ends of the universe.

Focusing on the capsule cross section, she said, "Luxury cargo bay."

Rykus let her slip out of his arms. Whatever he was thinking, he kept it to himself. "We need a plan."

"We need more people," Kalver said, approaching to look at the tower screen.

"If capsule security is looking for me, others might be too." He glanced at her. "Does Valt know we tracked him?"

She almost answered the question, but the pressure at the base of her skull warned a response could lead to a blackout, and she couldn't risk that right now. That's how Jevan had pried his way into her mind the last time. He'd threatened to kill Katie if she didn't kill Stratham. She hadn't had a choice.

"Not a chance," Kalver answered for her. "She broke through his security quicker than I could have." His gray eyes appraised her. "Nice work."

She didn't acknowledge the compliment. She'd come too close to failing. The only reason she'd located Jevan was because he'd underestimated her.

"We have less than an hour until we capsule out." Rykus scowled at the screen. "How long will it take to reach that bay?"

"Twenty minutes," Kalver said.

That was Ash's estimate too. If they didn't encounter resistance and if Jevan stayed where he was. If he moved…

She could locate him if she tried. If she relaxed her mind like he said. But that was risky. He'd almost undoubtedly be able to locate her then too, and she did *not* want him inside her head again. She didn't know his capabilities. If he could sift through her thoughts…

"Hold on," she said. "I can't know your plan."

Rykus slowly shifted his gaze to her. "You're compromised?"

"We're operating independently," she said.

"No." The change in his tone was abrupt. "We've already had this conversation. You're not going in alone."

Rykus's will closed around Ash. It grabbed her puppet strings and pulled. She fought against the tugs and maneuvers, then met her fail-safe's gaze. "We're operating independently."

"If Valt can get back inside your head, you shouldn't go at all."

"I'll make sure Katie escapes."

"*We'll* make sure she escapes."

She lifted her chin.

Rykus's scowl deepened. "You're not—"

"She's right, sir," Kalver interrupted.

Rykus looked at the other anomaly, giving Ash the chance to breathe.

"'Keep your enemy ignorant,'" Kal said, quoting words Rykus had drilled into them on Caruth. "If Valt learns our plan, we die."

She didn't want Rykus involved in the rescue at all, but he wasn't the type of man who'd stay out of the action.

Rykus crossed his arms. "We go together or we don't go at all."

Ash let out a short, humorless laugh. "You're not leaving your fiancée behind, Rip."

He opened his mouth. Closed it. She was almost certain he was going to say "*ex*-fiancée," but it didn't matter. Rykus still cared for Katie. Ash used that fact to resist her fail-safe's will, to twist the invisible hands that manipulated her strings into making her care more about Katie's safety than his command to stay together or stay behind. Nothing short of outright compulsion would keep her from going after Jevan.

Standing to her full height, she met Rykus's gaze. The pressure of his presence made the air in front of her seem thick, the air behind her thin. She wanted to step back. She made herself step forward instead.

"She's an anomaly, sir," Kalver said. "She can handle the situation."

"Being an anomaly gives you an edge," he said. "It doesn't make you bulletproof. I'll contact capsule security."

"They'll arrest you," Ash warned.

"I'll explain what's happening."

"They won't listen."

"One of them might. I'll convince them to check on Katie. Valt won't be able to hurt her then."

He was wrong. Valt would kill Katie. Then he'd kill Rykus. They had to make this work on their own.

"The Coalition trained me to do the impossible," she said. "This is my job. I survive what others would never be willing to risk."

"You survive because you work as a team. You don't run off solo with no plan and no intel." The words were angry, but there was a note of resignation in them. He was breaking.

"Damn it," he whispered, fists clenched. "I don't want you to do this."

Or she'd thought he was breaking. The gravity in his words, the worry, ordered her to stay as effectively as a direct command. She spun away from her fail-safe, breathing hard and battling the grip of the loyalty training.

"Ash?" Rykus moved toward her.

"I have to do this." She forced the words out of a tight throat. She hadn't been prepared for the tender fierceness of his voice.

"I said I don't want you to, not that you can't."

She braced her hands on her knees. "Your words always have a pull, Rip."

Kalver watched silently from the doorway. She stared at him, hoping to find her resolve again, but his stony face offered no support. If their fail-safe didn't want her to leave, Kal wouldn't allow it.

Rykus let out a breath. "I know. I'm…" He stopped, gently gripped her arm and made her straighten to meet his gaze. "Just make sure you survive."

Pure, sweet oxygen entered her lungs again. His permission liberated her, but underneath the new freedom was a resentment, not toward her fail-safe but toward herself. She was usually mentally stronger than this. She didn't know if this weakness was because she'd slept with him or because she still wasn't one hundred percent mentally and physically. Whatever the case, she didn't like it. She couldn't let it continue.

So she reverted to the strategy that usually worked when her fail-safe was too demanding, too pissed off, or too intense. Tilting her head slightly, she smiled and let her gaze suggestively rake over him. "When we survive this, Rip, my offer to skinny-dip in the Liera River still stands."

If they'd been back on Caruth, Rykus would have had her counting comets. If he'd still believed her a traitor, he would have thrown her to the floor. If he'd reacted in any of the ways he should have, there would have been no hint of hurt in his eyes. But it was there in the brief tightening of the muscles in his face. He knew she was pushing him away, and he didn't like it.

She turned away before she apologized. On her way out of the small room, she met Kalver's gaze. "I'm heading in the front door."

That was all the planning she was willing to risk. They'd have to wing this op.

Kal acknowledged her words with a nod, then he held out his sidearm, a Berick 910. It was an accurate, durable, and easy-to-conceal pistol. "No fear. No failure."

Ash took the weapon. "No fear. No failure."

She stepped into the corridor, on her way to kill the bastard who'd murdered her brothers.

———◆·◆———

RYKUS ACHIEVED THE IMPOSSIBLE. He stayed still and silent as he watched Ash leave. Every instinct screamed this was a bad idea. He wanted to go with her, to watch her back, to protect her. He didn't want to use her as a damn diversion.

"I can get us into the weapons locker," Kalver said.

Rykus drew in a breath, held it, then released it through his teeth. The decision was made. All he could do now was focus on building a plan and be there when she needed him.

"How?" he asked. He would be there armed and ready to kill.

Kalver nodded toward the comm-cuff still docked in the medical tower. "I'll break the locker's inventory system, then show up to repair it. The problem is time. We need to move quickly if we want to help Ash. Best way to do that is via the public corridors. If capsule security is looking for you—"

"They're not," Rykus said. "Valt was bluffing. If security was looking for me, they'd be here already. How long to get to the locker and then to the cargo hold?"

"Without any problems, half an hour."

Rykus moved closer to the tower's screen. The capsule cross section was still there, that blue light blinking with Valt's last known location. Half an hour gave them little time to locate Katie before the capsule entered the time-bend and Valt contacted them via the cuff again. That was assuming, of course, that Valt stuck to the schedule he'd given.

He undocked the cuff and stuck it in his pocket. "Let's get to that locker."

Kalver didn't move, and the way he stood there staring past Rykus indicated he had something to say.

Rykus waited.

"Sir, what are your intentions, sir?"

Two *sirs* in one sentence; Kalver was angry enough about the intimacy he'd seen between Rykus and Ash that he was fighting the loyalty training. Good. He should be pissed off about it. There should be zero intimacy between Rykus and his former cadet.

"You can kick my ass later, Kalver. Right now, my only intention is to keep Ash alive. Get moving."

The response was good enough to appease Kalver for now. He ducked his head in a short, rigid nod, then led the way out.

TWENTY-SEVEN

ASH DIDN'T GO DIRECTLY to the cargo bay. She risked a short detour to a server closet to make a small, almost insignificant tweak to one of the capsule's minor settings. It wasn't a well-protected area of coding, and it didn't take too much finesse to make it in and out without raising an alarm. They'd see her digital footprints later if they looked, but she couldn't worry about that. She didn't have time to tiptoe through the sequences.

The capsule's med bays were located near the VIP suites, which happened to be located two levels above the luxury cargo bay. If Ash had been thinking clearly, she would have guessed that's where Jevan would choose to meet. He was VIP enough to gain access to the area, and it would be deserted this close to the time-bend.

Half an hour passed between the time she left Kal and Rykus and the time she reached the lift marked Capsule Personnel Only. The doors closed behind her, sealing her inside alone.

Ash stared at her blurred reflection. She should never have gotten involved with a politician's aide. She hadn't wanted to, but she'd needed a favor once. One of Glory's precinct bosses had threatened someone Ash cared about, and Jevan had been able to get that person to safety. Ash had met him often after that, and she'd liked him enough to keep her word when he'd called her bluff during a game of Vortex Six. She'd been all in, and he'd raised the stakes, betting her a marriage contract. The six cards on the table all pointed to her having the best hand. Any sane person would have backed out, especially considering the hand Jevan had been dealt. The odds had been blatantly against him, but he'd won with one of the weakest hands ever played in the game.

Playfully, she'd accused him of cheating. He'd denied it with a laugh.

That laugh had been a lie. He'd been in her head even then. She just hadn't realized it.

The lift doors slid open. Ash started to exit, but froze.

Jevan was there, leaning against a data-desk in the center of the reception room, his arms folded over his muscular chest, his legs crossed at his ankles.

A cold sweat swooped over her body. She almost let the lift door slide shut. She was there to kill him. She was prepared to see him again, but the bored expression on his face reminded her of the bored expression he'd worn when he'd murdered Trevast and the others. The same horror she'd felt then seeped through her veins, but this time her brain wasn't rattled by a stun grenade. This time he wouldn't slip inside her mind. This time she wouldn't be the one left in a pool of blood.

Meeting the bastard's gaze, she stepped off the lift.

The corner of his mouth quirked. His posture didn't change. It didn't need to. Two men had Grath pistols trained on her from the right. Another two had them trained on her from the left. Graths contained ship-safe-caliber bullets—they'd put a hole in a person but not in a hull. The men on the left stood in a way that said they knew the capabilities and limitations of the weapons, but the other two were faking their bravado. They were political aides or personal assistants most likely. Or maybe cheap hired thugs.

"I underestimated you," Jevan said.

She took a few slow steps forward. Yes, he'd underestimated her, but not enough. He'd known she was coming early. "Where's Dr. Monick?"

The men on her left moved enough to make sure the lackeys on her right wouldn't get caught in the cross fire if they had to shoot. The former definitely had military experience. She'd have to be careful with them, take them out first.

"Stay where you are," Jevan said.

She obeyed, stopping a couple of paces away from him.

"Where's your fail-safe?"

"He's unconscious and restrained in a maintenance closet." Her voice was stronger now that she'd been awake for almost an hour. Her body felt stronger too.

Jevan sniffed. "You didn't knock out your fail-safe."

"Better than letting him travel down here and get killed."

Uncrossing his ankles, he pushed away from the desk. "Which maintenance closet?"

"You want me to answer your questions then you answer mine." She let her gaze inventory the room. Six dingy plastic chairs lined the left and right walls. A door lay behind the reception desk. That would be the cargo-bay office, and the room's other two doors led to opposite ends of the bay itself. With less than fifteen minutes to go before they capsuled out, all the cargo was checked in and stowed and personnel would be taking a break. Jevan must have taken care of the check-in crew. There was little chance of somebody stumbling across them, and an even smaller chance of her taking down Jevan and his four henchmen.

A small chance here at least. If she could get into the cargo area, she could stage something. There would be plenty of obstacles and shadows to get lost in there.

Her gaze found Jevan again. He was quietly studying her. There was a deep intelligence in his eyes. She'd always recognized it, respected it. He might have made a colossal error in his underestimation of her, but she couldn't count on him doing the same thing twice. Jevan was smart and cunning, and she didn't really know a damn thing about him or his capabilities.

She'd learn though. Right after she saved Katie and took out Jevan's backup.

"I want proof Dr. Monick is here," Ash said.

"I want proof that Rykus won't come rushing to your rescue."

"I don't need rescuing."

Jevan laughed. It was a laugh that pulled people in, open and, on the surface, honest. "You did on that shuttle."

She sent the clammy cold that covered her skin to her heart, numbing herself on the inside. She couldn't let him provoke her. Anger and fear would lead to mistakes. She had to feel nothing if she wanted to accomplish her mission.

"What do you want?" she asked.

He gave her a thin smile. "Disarm."

She held her arms out to the sides. "We're on a civilian capsule, and I've been unconscious in med bay."

"Apparently not unconscious enough," he said. "And I know you. You wouldn't come here unarmed. So you can either drop your weapons, or I can very thoroughly search you for them."

"You'll search me anyway."

"You could let me in your head instead."

She almost fell for the trap. Her mouth opened to say he'd never again touch her mind, but the pressure at the base of her skull made her snap her teeth together.

Jevan gave her an unapologetic smile. "I had to try."

And she had to be careful. No blackouts. No mistakes.

"Put your hands on your head, Ramie. Dr. Monick is nearby. If you try anything, my men will put a bullet in her."

She could kill him. She could snap his neck before his henchmen fired. Most of the bullets from their Graths wouldn't penetrate all the way through Jevan's body. She could use it to block their attack, maybe even take one or two of them down with Kal's gun. Still, the probability of making it out of the room alive would be slim.

Good thing she'd often worked with slim.

"Hands on your head," Jevan repeated.

She complied. She needed him closer, and it was almost time to act.

He kept his eyes on hers as he approached. His were gray with a confident rim of blue. They'd always seemed to see too much, and now she knew why. Despite her brush-offs and vague responses to personal questions he'd asked, he'd learned more about her than she'd ever intended. She'd never let him in while they were dating, never fully shared her thoughts and feelings. He'd complained about it, told her she was keeping their relationship superficial, and she'd just given him her I-am-what-I-am smile and shrugged. She should have given him that smile and slugged him.

It took an effort not to throw her fist in his face when he placed his hands on her shoulders. Two more minutes, her mental clock told her.

"Relax, Ramie." He slid his hands down her arms, then stepped closer to pat down her back. At the small of her back, he found Kal's gun.

He raised an eyebrow. "Not armed?"

"Oops," she said.

He hemmed, then tucked the weapon into his waistband. If she stayed close, it was within her reach.

"This isn't the way I wanted things to play out," he said, continuing his search. "I wanted us to be allies, but you never let me in enough to see if you were open to the idea, and I ran out of time. It's a shame, really. You could have been such a valuable asset. We would have made a great team. But circumstances forced me to make you a sacrifice."

He paused his search. She held his gaze, making sure her expression said nothing except *Your time is limited.*

One more minute.

"I was upset when I learned what you went through on the *Obsidian*," he continued, glancing down at her right hand. "Stratham told me what they did to you. Torture. To one of their own. They've added more scars to your body."

He ran his hands under her arms, then pushed against her mind as if he was seeking a response to his words. It wasn't going to happen. She wouldn't rise to the bait.

Twenty seconds.

"If you let me into your mind," he said, leaning close to her ear, "I'll take off the muzzle. You'll be able to say anything you want."

She allowed herself one tiny weakness, a slight rise of her shoulders and a cringe away from his mouth. He pressed closer, and that little half inch put him between her and the experienced guards to her left.

"I've missed you," Jevan said.

So little room to work with, but she'd always vowed she would die fighting. If this was it, she was ready. No fear. No failure.

Lowering her voice to an icy whisper, she said, "You'll miss me more in hell."

The capsule entered the time-bend. There was no alarm—Ash's tweak had disabled it in the bay—and without the warning, only she was prepared for the spiraling darkness that erased their vision. Stomach steeled against the deep nausea in her gut, she forced her body to move, blindly grabbing for Jevan's throat.

She missed.

If she could have talked during the time-bend, she would have cursed. Instead, she switched to plan B and sprinted to her left.

Hell if she knew where she was going. Moving during a bend was like trying to run after you had spun in a thousand little circles. It was impossible to move in a straight line—she was lucky to stay on her feet—and when reality finally straightened out, she stood between the idiots on the right side of the room.

She grabbed a pistol out of the nearest man's hand when he doubled over and vomited. There were curses behind her. She started to turn, her raised pistol leading the way.

A bullet slammed into the wall near her head. She returned fire. Missed. Shot three more rounds.

Two of those hit, killing the target, but the other experienced lackey recovered his equilibrium and centered his gun on her.

She grabbed the man she'd disarmed, used his body as a shield as she backed away. One round passed through his body and struck her collarbone.

She squeezed off a dozen more rounds, causing the gunmen to dive behind the check-in desk. That had to be where Jevan was hiding. It would be suicide to rush the target now. She'd have to kill him later, after she located Katie and took out the rest of his men.

Shoving her human shield away, she disappeared through the cargo-bay door.

◆ ◆ ◆

IF RYKUS HAD EATEN ANYTHING in the past twelve hours, it would have ended up on the deck.

On his knees, he gripped the metal shelf hard enough to dent its edge, willing the nausea to pass.

Beside him, Kalver chuckled. "Clever girl."

Those weren't the words Rykus was thinking. A long, blasphemous string of profanities raced through his mind. Ash could have told them she was planning to disable the capsule's siren. Moving while entering or exiting the time-bend sent most people to the infirmary. That was the point of the alarm. It gave folks a chance to find a seat and brace themselves.

"You going to keep it down, sir?" Kalver asked.

"Yes." He grated the word out and forced himself to inch to the edge of the shelving unit. Ash had told them she was entering through the front door, so he and Kalver had come in through the metaphorical back, a crate elevator that had been locked down for the time-bend. Kalver had made quick work of splicing into the system, and he'd also disabled the trip wire someone had left just outside the door.

That trip wire, and the fact that no one had greeted them with bullets, was a good sign. Valt didn't have enough manpower to cover both entrances.

Rykus moved forward in a low crouch, keeping his head below the crates on the shelves to his left and right. Kalver stayed behind, covering him with one of the pistols they'd stolen from the weapons locker. Rykus had a new, unmodified Covar in his hand and another one strapped to his left leg. It wasn't the normal gear he packed on an op, but it was a hell of a lot better than nothing.

And it was a hell of a lot better than what Ash had.

Clamping down on his worry, he continued on, footsteps silent on the dura-steel floor. The bay wasn't one of the capsule's largest, but it was still massive. Valt could be hiding anywhere. If he and his men remained still and silent, it would take hours to find them.

Rykus reached a cross section, stopped, then carefully peered both ways down the aisle. Nothing. A quick glance over his shoulder didn't reveal any signs of life either. Kalver had disappeared, but he was back there somewhere, covering his six.

With a quick burst of speed, Rykus darted across the aisle. He slowed when he reached the other side, then continued on with cautious steps.

So many shadows here. So many places for an enemy to hide. If he'd been setting up a defense instead of moving in on the offense, he would have ordered his men to lie down in those black voids and wait for the enemy to approach.

He could almost feel crosshairs on his head.

He wiped his sleeve across his sweaty brow.

No fear. No failure. It had never been his motto, but he made it one now. Hesitation would get him killed. It would get Ash and Katie killed.

He stayed in his low crouch and increased his pace.

CHAPTER

TWENTY-EIGHT

THE MAN'S ELBOW SLAMMED into Ash's side, cracking a rib that hadn't had time to heal. She gritted her teeth and kept her arm locked around his neck, doing her best to keep his thrashing legs from squeaking across the deck.

His face turned from red to blue. Then he went still.

Ash lowered him to the floor, broke his neck to make sure he wouldn't rise again, then confiscated his pistol.

She crawled into the shadows between two crates and listened. Jevan and the two men who'd survived the brief fight in the lobby had followed her. They were somewhere in the bay. So was Katie. As much as Ash would love to hunt down Jevan, she needed to secure the doctor first.

Closing her eyes, she strained to hear something. Instead, she felt something. A shadow. It was somewhere to her left and edging closer. She wished she could stay in the darkness, wait for whoever it was to move into her sight, but if she felt him, then he undoubtedly felt her too. She needed to keep moving.

Tightening the makeshift dressing she'd placed over her collarbone, she retreated from the darkness to climb up the shelving unit. She'd made it halfway to the top, the fourth shelf, when Jevan's voice reached her.

"Ramie," he called out. "I'm getting tired of this game. Come out of the shadows and talk."

He was closer than she thought. She moved to get a better view of the aisle below.

"I'll be the gentleman and apologize first," Jevan said.

She still couldn't see him, but she was almost certain he was the shadow she felt.

"I'm deeply sorry for your wounded feelings. If it makes you feel better, it wasn't easy getting into your head. It took time. It took finesse. It took quite a bit of fucking."

Jevan had always loved to hear himself talk. He was an idiot to do so now. She couldn't pinpoint his location using only the pressure in her mind, but she'd be able to pinpoint it using his voice. If he wanted to be an idiot, she was more than happy to let him.

"That's the only way I was able to get inside your mind," he continued. "You were open to me when you came. Your defenses were down, and I crept inside you, thought by thought."

She slipped into the shadows between two crates, inching closer to his location.

"We had some good times." His voice sounded more distant, like he'd turned away from her. "I was using you, but it wasn't a burden. We could still work well together."

She stopped before she peeked into the lighted aisle.

"I'm being patient, Ramie, but my tolerance for your games won't last long."

Instinct told her to remain still and silent, and in a few seconds that paid off. She heard a footstep, and when she leaned the slightest bit forward, she glimpsed the top of Jevan's head. He still wasn't looking her direction.

Raising her pistol, she took aim at his left temple, the lowest part of his head she could see. Her hand ached to squeeze the trigger. She wouldn't miss. She'd take him down, spill his brain across the floor like he'd spilled her teammates'.

But the Grath was a loud weapon. Any shot she took would alert Jevan's colleagues. She couldn't risk them getting trigger-happy and shooting the doctor.

She closed her eyes, drew in one long, slow breath. Soon. She'd kill him soon. She just needed to find—

A scuffle of feet came from below. A man moved between her and Jevan. Ash kept her finger on the trigger, waiting, watching, listening. She risked leaning forward into the light so she could get a better view of the aisle.

The man shoved Katie to the ground in front of Jevan.

"You want proof of life," Jevan called out, pointing a pistol at Katie's head. "Come find me."

The man who'd brought the doctor also drew and aimed his gun. So did a third man who stepped into view.

Ash swallowed down a curse. She couldn't take down all three of them before they had a chance to squeeze off a round.

She sat back on her haunches. At least she wasn't hunkered down with Rykus and Kalver. Stratham's claim that Ash was special, that it took work to pry into her mind, implied that Jevan couldn't locate everyone like he could locate her. He didn't know when Rykus and Kal would show up or where they'd come from. Hell, he didn't know they were a *they*. Ash still had a chance to get Katie out of this. Rykus and Kalver just needed to get their asses there.

Stall. That was one hell of a plan.

"Say hello, Doctor," Jevan crooned.

A few seconds passed. There was a thud, a quiet gasp, then Jevan ordered, "Say. Hello."

"Go to hell," Katie snarled.

The woman had backbone. Nice.

"Come out, Ramie," Jevan said.

Ash pulled her lower lip between her teeth—

"No!"

Gunfire cut off Katie's scream, and Ash bit through her lip.

She fell back as if she'd taken the bullet in the gut. It felt like the capsule had collapsed around her. Fear tightened her body, and the muscles in her neck and shoulders cramped. The edges of her vision turned black from lack of oxygen. She was panicking. She never panicked.

Tightening her grip on her gun, she ordered herself to relax. It didn't work. She was still shaking, still hearing the echoes of bullets. That sound had reverberated in her ears even after Jevan had shot her teammates. It had banged around inside her head as Trevast whispered his last words. But back on that shuttle, her heart had eventually slowed down. It was speeding up now, battering her chest like solar wind on a damaged hull. She'd been through more firefights, more stressful situations than this. She shouldn't be reacting this way, but Jevan had shot her fail-safe's fiancée. Ash had failed. Again.

"Last chance, Ramie," Jevan called out.

A tendril of air slipped into her lungs. Her ears picked up a sound, a quiet, pain-filled moan.

Katie was alive.

"Time's up," Jevan said. "This is your fault—"

"I'm here." She stuck the Grath into her waistband, then scurried from the shadows.

Jevan and his two men looked up, but their pistols didn't move away from Katie's head.

"What the hell do you think you're doing, Lieutenant?" the doctor demanded.

Ash's gaze shifted from Jevan to Katie. She was sitting with one bloodied leg stretched out in front of her. Her lip was busted, and a bruise purpled the skin under her left eye. Craning her neck, she glared up at Ash.

The sight almost made Ash smile. The blackness that edged her vision faded, her heartbeat slowed to a steady, deliberate thud, and she could see the situation clearly again.

"I'm attempting to save your life," she said.

"You think he's going to let me go?"

Ash ignored the question and focused on Jevan again. "Let her walk away."

He looked down at Katie's leg. "That might be difficult at the moment."

"She'll manage."

"Climb down," he said, filling his voice with an exaggerated exhaustion.

Ash swallowed down a retort that was likely to get both her and Katie killed, then she carefully—and more importantly, slowly—descended the shelves. She listened for Rykus or Kalver. Ash didn't know their plan, but they should be there by now. There's no way they'd waited in the medical unit for Jevan's call. They were targets there. They'd likely left soon after she had, so what was taking them so damn long?

She reached the floor, counted to three, then turned and faced Jevan.

"Hello again, Ramie." Jevan's smile made her more nauseous than the time-bend had. He'd smiled like that on the shuttle from Chalos II.

"Can I help her?" She nodded toward Katie, who'd unfastened her belt to tighten it around her leg, just above the hole in her thigh. Jevan's men didn't stop her; they kept their guns aimed and ready.

"You can help by placing your gun on the ground," Jevan said.

"How will you explain her death if she bleeds out?"

"Gun on the ground, Ramie. It'll be harder for her to treat a hole in the head."

Ash took the Grath out of her waistband, leaned over, and placed it on the ground.

"Kick it this way."

She did that too.

"That's a good girl. Now let me in your head."

That she wouldn't do. Ever. She kept her mouth shut and looked away so she wouldn't trigger a blackout. The warning was there, pressing against the back of her skull. She needed to end this. To do that, Katie needed to be taken out of the equation.

"You said we could work well together."

Jevan's eyebrows went up. Whether the interest was feigned or real, she didn't know.

"If you'd cooperated with me from the beginning," he said, "we wouldn't be here. Your teammates would be alive and I'd have a decrypted set of the Sariceans' files."

"You didn't have my fail-safe's fiancée then. You have her now."

"*Ex*-fiancée," Katie said between gritted teeth. The skin around her mouth was pale, but the rest of her face was flushed red. She was pissed that

Ash was supposedly considering switching alliances. At least, she was acting like she was pissed about the possibility.

Ash shrugged. "Rykus still cares about you. So I care about you." She focused on Jevan again. "I don't have a choice. I have to do whatever it takes to keep her safe."

Jevan's eyes narrowed. She didn't think he'd buy it. Sure, she felt the influence of the loyalty training, but she could fight it if she tried.

"We would make a good team," Jevan said, his tone turning contemplative. "Tell you what. You give me the cipher and let me inside your head for thirty seconds, and I'll consider it."

He lowered his gun. His two men didn't—they kept their weapons pointed at Katie's head—but they took their fingers off the triggers.

"What do you want from the Sariceans' files?" Ash asked.

The corners of his mouth lifted into a subtle, sly smile. "Schematics for a tachyon drive."

She opened her mouth to say something, then closed it when her mind registered his words. Hagan had said there was speculation the Sariceans had built a new technology. He'd assumed it was a weapon or upgraded defense device. If Jevan was telling the truth, it was both.

"They've developed it," he said, misinterpreting her silence as disbelief. "How do you think the Sariceans launched a surprise attack at Ephron?"

"I wouldn't know. I was in the brig at the time." Troops and ships had to be transported via capsules. If the Sariceans had found a way to give individual vessels interstellar travel capabilities, it would revolutionize the way wars were fought.

"That's how they got close," Jevan said. "Their tachyon-driven ships emerged from the time-bend right on top of Ephron. Your command is scrambling to find out how they accomplished that. They're contemplating the existence of a tachyon drive."

"There are other ways to launch a surprise attack," she said because she needed to keep him talking. "The Sariceans could have sent in scouts, powered down and coasted, cloaked transmissions."

"They didn't."

She inched forward.

"Okay. Let's assume a tachyon drive does exist," she said, shifting slightly to the right. "What would you do with it?"

"My faction would control it."

Ash ceased her slow advance.

Faction. Stratham had uttered that word right before she broke his neck. And faction... It sounded so very much like *fashion*.

Will destroy Coalition, Trevast had said right before he'd whispered, *The fashion. Fight.*

The factions. Trevast hadn't uttered nonsense. He'd given her a clue, a clue that now sounded like a dire, desperate warning.

"You weren't supposed to change the encryption on the files," Jevan said as if she weren't reliving the hell of losing her team. What had Trevast seen? What had he known? Hagan had assumed he saw a list of names, but would a list of names have been enough to convince Trevast that telepaths existed? Ash had only believed his words after the confrontation with Jevan. Why would Trevast believe so easily?

Everything had happened so fast. It had become muddled in her head, and the only things she had focused on were escaping, protecting the Coalition, and killing Jevan. She had never questioned her team lead's belief in telepathy.

"I had a copy," Jevan continued. "Your copy would have been lost when we destroyed your shuttle. That little stunt you pulled saved your life, but just barely. I was this"—he held up his thumb and forefinger—"close to ending your existence, but the last tweak I made to your mind silenced you. That tweak allowed me to let you live. You owe me your life, Ramie."

"You sent Stratham to kill me," she said. Her voice sounded weak to her ears. She was still reeling, still trying to see if she'd missed something else.

Jevan shrugged. "You became too much of a liability. You were supposed to decrypt the files. I had people in place to copy and corrupt them. You would have been transferred to a prison and quickly executed."

She needed to focus, to keep him talking and swing the conversation back around to where she wanted it, but could she risk a blackout? It would incapacitate her and let Jevan back into her head.

Her heart slammed against her chest. A warning crawled across the nape of her neck. She couldn't say the word *faction*, she was sure of it.

"You will give me the cipher, Ramie," Jevan said. "I've invested too much to let it go."

Her shirt clung uncomfortably to her chest. The bullet that had passed through her human shield and hit her collarbone hadn't done too much damage, but it bled as if it had passed all the way through. Maybe she could convince Jevan to let Katie help her.

"I need to know what's in it for me." She edged closer.

"Your life and your freedom to begin with," he said, taking the bait she dangled. "And information, Ramie. Power. You could be one of us. You want to be one of *us*. The alternative is far worse." He looked at Katie. "For everyone."

The temptation to let him talk hung there like a star within reach. Ash could say the right thing, encourage him to continue, and learn everything. But she was close enough now. She would bludgeon the rest of the information from him soon.

The kick she sent to Katie's chest was quick and hard.

The doctor flew back. Ash grabbed the nearest man's gun and aimed it at Katie's other captor.

She fired, shifted her aim to Jevan, but he charged from the left while the other man wrapped his arms around her from behind.

Jevan got a hand on her weapon.

"Run!" Ash ordered. She didn't see if Katie complied. Jevan put his full weight into controlling the pistol.

Ash stopped trying to keep the gun raised. The sudden change of momentum made it easy to redirect the line of fire. She squeezed the trigger, putting a bullet in the gut of the man holding her, then she slammed her head into Jevan's nose.

Cursing, he jerked back, giving Ash the inches she needed to plant a solid kick in his stomach.

She brought the barrel of her gun to point between his eyes.

This is for Trevast and the guys, she thought and squeezed the—

"*Hold your fire*," Jevan hissed, both out loud and in her mind, and she felt the *tweak* in her head.

Panic made her eyes widen.

Fury made her hand shake.

She couldn't pull the trigger.

She tried harder, straining against Jevan's mental hold. It didn't help.

A sick realization slid over her. She hadn't been the only one stalling for time. Jevan had been stalling too.

Sweat glistened on his forehead. He wiped his sleeve across his bloodied nose, but managed a smile. If she could have moved enough to hit him, she would have made his white teeth scatter like pebbles on the floor.

"Gotcha," he said.

TWENTY-NINE

Rykus gave up all pretense of stealth and ran, weapon raised as he sprinted toward the sound of gunfire.

A movement to his left. He swung his weapon, tightened his finger on the trigger—

The man fell before Rykus fired, a hole in his chest.

Kalver's work.

Rykus didn't signal his thanks; he kept moving.

He rounded an aisle, shot down two targets, and sprinted to the next aisle. Kalver fired from behind him again, one deadly shot that dropped a man from the top of the shelving unit. They'd sprung the trap Jevan had set for them. If Rykus hadn't had an anomaly watching his six, he'd be dead.

"Ash," he called out. No sense in being quiet now. Valt and his men knew he was coming.

He should be close. The gunfire hadn't been far away.

Weapon held ready, he took the next corner and found Ash. She was on her knees, hunched over in the center of the aisle.

"Are you hit—" Bullets erupted all around him. He ducked behind the shelving unit. Took a breath. Then fired two times blindly before peeking back out and aiming.

His target was in the shadows between crates. Rykus's next shot hit.

Gunfire went off behind him. He didn't look back—Kalver would take care of the rest of the combatants. He kept his head on a swivel and approached Ash.

"Are you okay?" he asked.

Ash looked up, and his breath left his lungs.

She wasn't there. Her green eyes, always so bright and defiant, were dull and lifeless. There was no smile on her face, no slight tease on her lips, no arrogant lift to her chin.

"Ash?"

She stood, her movements robotic. Rykus took a slight step backward and flexed his fingers around his Covar. Ash was armed too.

"Ashdyn," he said, regulating his tone, his cadence, his entire demeanor. "*Push him out of your head.*"

A vein on her forehead stood out. Her blinks were long and exaggerated. "*Push him out.*"

She looked over her shoulder. Then she turned and walked away.

"*Stop.*" His commands weren't working. Either he wasn't getting his voice right or Jevan was too solidly in control of her.

Or maybe it was both.

She stepped over one of the bodies on the floor. He'd have to tackle her, physically subdue her. He could. She wasn't herself. She was unfocused and moving as if she were in heavy atmosphere.

He hurried after her, stepping over the same body she had. But the body didn't remain still for him. It lurched up, grabbing his leg and flipping him to the ground.

Rykus cursed his carelessness, brought his gun across his body to take aim, but the man plunged a knife deep into his shoulder.

His artificial shoulder. It didn't hurt as much as it should have, but his entire arm went numb.

His attacker knocked the gun from his hand.

They both lunged for it. The blade dislodged—that should have been a blinding pain—and Rykus locked his legs around the other man, holding him in position until he saw the opportunity to switch to a choke hold. He grabbed his useless left arm with his right hand, slipped it under the man's chin and squeezed, collapsing his airway.

A movement pulled his attention away. Katie. She stumbled into the aisle. Fresh blood ran down the side of her face. She didn't move, not even to straighten from her crouch. Rykus didn't understand why until he saw Ash. She'd turned her cold, dead stare on Katie.

"Kill her." Valt's voice came from where Katie had emerged. "Then kill your fail-safe."

The man struggled in Rykus's choke hold. He was reaching for the gun. His fingers touched it. Rykus couldn't let him go, couldn't move, or the man would get the millimeter he needed to grab the weapon.

"Kill her, now, Ramie," Valt said.

"*Put down the gun, Ash,*" Rykus commanded. He wanted to take her in his arms, shake her until she listened and her mind became her own again, but the asshole he was fighting wouldn't fucking die.

Ash raised the gun. Her hands shook.

Rykus put everything into tightening his hold.

"Ashdyn," Katie said. "Listen to your fail-safe."

The asshole he was choking kicked one last time then went limp.

"*Lower your weapon,*" Rykus yelled as he grabbed his gun and took aim.

"You don't want to do this, Ashdyn." Katie sounded calm, in control, but the arms she held away from her body were shaking.

"*Put it down!*"

He saw the moment Ash lost the battle. Saw her exhale, her shoulders relax, her aim steady.

He had to take her out. *He had to. He had to. He had to.*

His bullet hit her chest, knocking her backward, but she didn't go down. She brought her gun back up as if blood wasn't drenching her shirt, and she pointed the gun at him.

"Please, baby. Look at me. Talk to me."

She aimed at his forehead. He could feel the crosshairs between his eyes. One of them was going to die.

Sweat ran down his face. His insides felt raw and tortured.

"I don't want to do this," he said.

Seeker's God, he couldn't do it.

He dropped his weapon to the ground and waited for her to pull the trigger.

KILL YOUR fail-safe.

The command severed the puppet strings Ash had lived with for years. She dangled in space, disoriented and spinning as the words echoed in her ears. When she stopped spiraling, she stared at the man in front of her, the man she no longer had to obey and protect.

Kill your fail-safe.

New manacles clamped down on her free will. These had no give, no mercy. They demanded she obey and removed the obstacle from her path. The loyalty training was gone, swept out from under her as if it had never existed, and the man begging her to drop her weapon, to listen, to fight, was just that: a man.

Kill your fail-safe.

Her fingers tightened around the cold weapon in her hand, and she focused on the target. Anguished eyes stared back at her over the barrel of his gun, and something fluttered in her stomach.

No. The man was an enemy, an obstacle, a mark.

Kill your fail-safe.

She had no fail-safe. No reason not to pull the trigger except…

The man dropped his weapon.

Rip.

Kill your fail-safe.

His name tasted of memories, and something inside Ash broke.

Kill your fail-safe.

No!

She threw her gun to the ground. The universe roared around her, dangerous and deafening, and Ash's mind shattered.

"ASH!" RYKUS ROARED as he sprinted to her side. Her eyes rolled back in her head. Her body shook, spasmed.

He took her into his arms, held her as she lurched again and again. Her face contorted into a silent scream. The sight ripped through him, more painful than any bullet wound.

Her spine arched, and she bucked so hard she jerked free from his arms. He reached for her again, but she stiffened, becoming board-straight. Her eyes shot open, bloodshot and staring at nothing. She was pale. So pale.

"Ash?" He touched her arm, and she went limp.

The air pressed in on him, heavy and stifling. He couldn't think, couldn't breathe. All he could do was crouch by Ash's side, waiting for her to move, to speak, to blink.

No.

No. He wouldn't let her die.

He placed his hands over the hole he'd put in her chest. It didn't stifle the blood flow. The dark red liquid ran everywhere.

God, he'd done this.

He'd killed Ash.

Someone landed beside him. Rykus had no strength, no willpower, to defend himself.

"Chems. Field congealment." Kalver dropped the items beside Ash's body. "I've got your six."

Rykus grabbed the syringe. He had to focus on something. If he didn't, he'd lose any sense he had left.

He flicked the top off the needle, then plunged it into Ash's thigh.

"You shouldn't have come here, Ash," he grated out, tearing her shirt to peel it away from her chest. "It was stupid. We were stupid."

He squirted the tube of clear gel on the wound in her chest. It congealed—barely—but Ash didn't react to its sting.

"Katie!" he bellowed.

"I'm here." Katie crouched beside him.

"You have to help her." He could barely get the words out of his raw throat. His chest felt like it would collapse.

Katie stared at Ash's body.

"Damn it, Rhys," she whispered. "This was close range, center mass." She shook her head as she assessed the damage he'd done. She sounded like a doctor who was seeing her patient in a body bag.

"She wouldn't listen."

"I know," Katie said. "Just go. Kill him."

She grabbed Ash's wrist, feeling for a pulse. When Katie's shoulders sagged, his hope disintegrated.

His hands clenched into fists.

He stood.

He headed in the direction Valt had fled.

Rykus shut down his thoughts, his feelings; he shut down everything except his combat instinct. This had turned into a bloodier disaster than Valt had intended, and the only way he could begin to hide his involvement was to make sure Rykus and everyone else in the cargo bay was dead. Valt would be nearby.

Rykus stopped, listened. His hearing didn't pick up a sound, but his battle sense told him to stay in place. It paid off.

Valt stepped into the aisle. He didn't see Rykus.

Rykus aimed. Fired.

The single bullet dropped Valt to the deck.

Rykus approached and kicked the bastard's gun away.

"I can undo the muzzle on her mind," Valt said, blinking rapidly, face squinted in pain.

Rykus holstered his gun.

More blinking. "I can help you. I can—"

Rykus hammered his fist into Valt's face.

"Wait—"

He hit Valt again.

"Ash—"

And again.

Valt had hurt and abused and mentally assaulted the woman he loved. Rykus would let him live so he could pay for those transgressions for the rest of his goddamn life.

He felt bones shatter, blood spray, but he slammed his fist down over and over, beating Valt until he lay as still as Ash had.

One more hit.

One more.

And another.

A hand rested on his shoulder. "Sir."

Rykus stopped with his fist in the air. He wanted to hit Valt one last time. Wanted it with every cell in his body, even if it would kill the man.

"Ash has a pulse, sir."

THIRTY

THE DOOR TO RYKUS'S CELL clicked open. He raised his head.

"Bayis has authorized your release," Katie told him, stepping inside.

He stood. He didn't care about his release. "How is she?"

"She's the same. Sit back down."

He glanced at the open door.

"You can see her soon," Katie said.

"I-Com will let me?"

"Yes." The word sounded hesitant.

Rykus tried to force his exhausted mind to make sense of her tone and expression. He'd expected to have to fight to get permission to see Ash. "What's wrong?"

Katie toyed with the strap of her comm-cuff. "We're taking her to Caruth."

Anger flashed through him.

"She'll pull through on her own," he said, attempting to keep his emotions in check. "She doesn't need anyone fucking with her mind again."

"We think we might be able to fix her," she said. "We think *you* might be able to fix her." When he didn't react to her words, didn't respond in any way, she added, "We want you to re-indoctrinate—"

"No." He turned away.

"Jevan broke the loyalty training. Her mind went from one set of instruc-tions to another, and if we—"

"I'm not re-indoctrinating her." He couldn't.

"It's the only thing we have left to try."

"Get someone else to do it," he ground out.

"You really want that?"

He cut her a look over his shoulder.

She stepped closer. "Don't you think she'd want her sanity back? That she'd want to live?"

Ash was a fighter. Of course she'd want to live, but re-imprinting himself as her fail-safe... "I won't do it."

"The loyalty training was designed to prevent mental breakdowns. That's why some anomalies sign up for it. This has a chance to work, and you would be saving her life."

He wanted to save her life; he just didn't want control over it.

"You're worried about her free will," Katie said. "But you don't have to be. You just have to accept never seeing her again. If this works, Ash will be like she was before, voluntarily fighting to preserve and protect the Coalition and whatever new team she's assigned to."

"Voluntarily." He snorted at the word.

"She *chose* to join the Fighting Corps. She *chose* to go to Caruth."

He ran a hand over his face. Katie's words made sense, but putting Ash through the loyalty training again felt like an abuse. A betrayal.

"I can't make this decision for her," he said, lowering his hand.

"You can." Katie unhooked her comm-cuff and passed it to him. "She gave you authority over her life if she became incapacitated for any reason. Look at the date."

He swiped down the screen, saw Ash's digital signature.

"It's the day before she underwent the loyalty training," Katie said. "She trusted you with her life then. I think she'd trust you with it now."

Why? On Caruth, he'd been a cold, heartless instructor. He'd pushed her beyond her capabilities, punished her for major and minor transgressions, sentenced her to weighted runs through hellish terrain. Only once had he been... different with her. That night before Drop Day when he'd caught her in the shower. There had been a moment then, a moment when he'd allowed himself to see Ash as a brave, beautiful woman.

And a moment when she might have seen him as something other than her bastard of an instructor.

He closed his eyes. He couldn't allow that memory to be significant. He couldn't allow *any* moments to be significant.

"I'll do it," he said. It felt like he was putting another hole in Ash's chest.

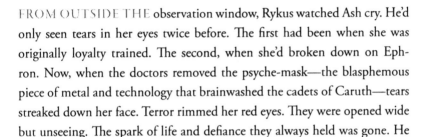

FROM OUTSIDE THE observation window, Rykus watched Ash cry. He'd only seen tears in her eyes twice before. The first had been when she was originally loyalty trained. The second, when she'd broken down on Ephron. Now, when the doctors removed the psyche-mask—the blasphemous piece of metal and technology that brainwashed the cadets of Caruth—tears streaked down her face. Terror rimmed her red eyes. They were opened wide but unseeing. The spark of life and defiance they always held was gone. He prayed to the Seeker's God that Ash was in there somewhere.

Blood dripped from her nose. A technician wiped it away. Another hemorrhage. The fifth so far. The tech injected her with a treatment, made a few adjustments to the electrodes inside the psyche-mask, then enclosed Ash's head in it again.

She thrashed against her restraints, arching her back in a silent scream.

"You don't have to watch this," Katie said from behind him.

"How much longer?" he asked.

A pause. "Another hour. Maybe two."

It had been ten already. He told himself to be grateful he was watching this. Ash was alive. She'd survived the bullet he'd put in her.

"You have half an hour before you go in again. Why don't you get something to eat?"

He shook his head. "Next time."

He'd said that during the last session too. Every hour, he entered Ash's chamber, and the technicians ended her nightmares. It was a temporary relief. It gave the doctors time to read her brain and body scans, and it gave Rykus time to plant his voice in her mind.

Pain pulsed behind Rykus's eyes. He wanted to reach up and rub his temples, but he deserved worse than a headache. He deserved eternal damnation.

Sweat glistened on Ash's skin. She wore only underwear and a thin wrapping around her chest to keep the bed's restraint strap from rubbing against her healing bullet wound. He wanted so badly to take her away from here. He wanted to hold her in his arms and watch the fires in the Camarnerie Clusters dance in her eyes. He wanted to relax with her on a beach and take her up on all those ridiculous offers to skinny-dip in the seas of Caruth.

He wanted to make love to her again.

It wouldn't happen. Each time Ash crawled her way to consciousness, she was deranged. Completely crazy until she saw him or Katie. When she saw one of them, her focus sharpened, and she tried to rip their heads off.

Valt's last command still controlled her.

◆ ◆ ◆

BRIGHT lights.

An incessant beep.

Something pricked her left wrist. She couldn't lift her arms.

She opened her eyes. Her vision was blurry, and everything was bright and white. Were her wrists strapped down? Her ankles? Something heavy crossed her chest.

She turned her head to the side, made out the image of a man dressed in light blue.

The beeping sped up with her heart rate. That shade of blue would be tranquil to most people, but not to her. Not to any loyalty-trained anomaly.

She squeezed her eyes shut, tried to get rid of the rough, sandy feel behind her lids, tried to see. There was a patch on the person's left breast. His deep voice spoke to a blur beside him. The second blur moved toward her, lifting a black, fully enclosed helmet.

A psyche-mask.

No! Ash tried to scream the word, but something was in her throat, cutting off her ability to make a sound.

Three men held her shoulders down. She tried to fight them, tried to kill them, hurt them, make them let her go, but two... ten... twenty hands gripped her. There were hands everywhere. Too many to count. They crept around her thighs, her stomach, her throat. They found their way inside her veins, pricking capillaries as she writhed on the bed.

No!

She was too weak. She couldn't free her arms or legs, couldn't defend herself against the psyche-mask as the demons lowered it over her head. Before they cinched it tight around her throat, she caught sight of the eerie, green shimmer of a hundred medicine-coated electrodes.

She shouldn't be here.

She shouldn't be here. She shouldn't be here. She shouldn't be here.

Someone shifted the mask, making sure the electrodes made contact with her skin. She felt them burrow into her scalp, attach to her face and lips.

A jolt of pain flashed through her. She gagged, convulsed, and then her sight, which had been blessedly black, lit up with a thousand overlapping images, and she screamed.

"IT'S TIME, Commander."

Rykus jerked awake. It took a second to orient himself, to realize he'd fallen asleep against the wall in the observation room and that this wasn't a nightmare. Ash was still strapped to a med-table on the other side of the one-way mirror.

He rubbed his eyes, stretched muscles that had grown tight from exhaustion and stress, then stood.

His knees creaked, an appropriate sound considering he moved to the door like an automaton. He'd lost count of the number of times he'd entered Ash's cell. The doctors had wanted to end the programming hours ago, but he'd ordered them to keep going. Ash was strong. She'd make it through this. She had to.

He tapped a command into a keypad in the wall. The door slid open.

Before Rykus stepped inside, a technician intercepted him. "It's been thirty-six hours," he said, staring down at his data-pad. "If she doesn't show signs of improving, this is it."

Rykus didn't throttle the man for his dismissive, uncaring tone. He waited until the technician sensed his silence and looked up. The man's mouth opened, then closed. He shifted his weight, glanced inside the cell, then, after one last, uncertain look at Rykus, he moved out of the way.

Rykus went inside alone. The doctors and techs had stopped coming in with him a few sessions ago. They'd given up on her.

He moved to her bedside. They'd stopped taking the psyche-mask off too. He'd figured out how to undo it himself. His fingers found the locking mechanism on both sides and pressed. A click and hiss indicated it had retracted the electrodes. Carefully, he lifted the device off Ash's head.

Her lips were blue. He'd asked the doctors for a blanket the last time he'd entered. They'd denied the request.

He wanted to slam the psyche-mask into the wall. Instead, he set the multimillion-credit device on its docking station, then turned back to Ash. Her eyes were closed, her hands clenched into tight fists.

Rykus wasn't allowed to touch her. Physical contact that wasn't preapproved with the doctors could damage the loyalty training.

Like that mattered now.

He placed a hand over her cold fist and sat on the stool beside her bed.

He swallowed, loosening his vocal cords. Sometimes his voice soothed Ash. Sometimes it made her scream.

Regulating his tone and cadence, he spoke the words he'd memorized almost half a decade ago: "Ramie Ashdyn, you are a soldier of the Coalition's Fighting Corps. You exist to preserve and protect the Coalition and all its citizens. You will sacrifice your desires, your life, and your freedom to complete the missions given to you. You will not fail. You will not falter. You will not disobey."

Her eyes squeezed shut.

"Ramie Ashdyn," he said again. "You are a soldier of the Coalition's Fighting Corps. You exist to preserve and protect the Coalition and all its citizens. You will sacrifice your desires, your life, and your freedom to complete the missions given to you. You will not fail. You will not falter. You will not disobey."

Her body spasmed as if a jolt of electricity had been sent through every one of her muscles.

"Ramie Ashdyn. You are a soldier…" His throat tightened up, cutting off the words.

He squeezed her fist.

"Open your eyes, Ash. Please."

He brought his mouth down to her fingers, kissed her knuckles.

She didn't react.

She wasn't in there any more than she had been when he'd shot her.

He slammed his fist against the metal headboard. "Open your goddamn eyes!"

He stared at the dented metal, was contemplating hitting it again, when he felt a change in the atmosphere.

He looked down. Ash's green eyes stared up at him.

She'd stared up at him twice before. Both times, fury had eclipsed the confusion and uncertainty in her gaze. He waited for it now, braced for yet another failure.

It didn't come. She lay there staring.

"Ash?" His voice was soft, his tone cautious.

"Sir." There was no punctuation to the word, no flippant tone or suggestive smile, but no threat to kill him either.

He wanted to kiss her, to unlock her restraints and pull her into his arms. He wanted to apologize for every time he'd been an ass and for ever questioning her loyalty. He wanted her to know how damn sorry he was for shooting her.

He brushed her hair away from her face.

Her brow furrowed. "Sir?"

Her soft skin was dented where the electrodes had pushed against her. Rykus's thumb traced a path over them, down the side of her face, along her jaw. He shouldn't touch her, not like this. Not ever again like this.

She turned into his hand slightly and her eyes hooded.

Behind him, the chamber's door slid open. Doctors and technicians flooded inside. They came between him and Ash, pushing him toward the back of the room.

She kept her gaze on him, only him, while the doctors checked her vitals. Then someone blocked their view. He tried to move, to see her again, but too many people were in the way. They pelted her with questions she didn't answer: How do you feel? What do you remember? Do you know where you are?

He couldn't see her, which meant she couldn't see him. She'd panic soon. All the anomalies did when their sanity returned. Their fail-safes always stayed close and quiet and in sight, but unless Rykus threw out every one of the assholes in here...

No reason not to.

He grabbed the shoulder of the nearest blue-clad technician. "Get out."

The tech shook free. "I have readings to take—"

"Everyone out." Katie's order came from Rykus's left. She was standing in the doorway, scowling at the dozen people crammed in the chamber.

The man in front of Rykus looked from Katie to him. Rykus gave him his grimmest expression and the technician fled.

"Out," Katie said again. "Everyone but Dr. Nedan and Commander Rykus."

Nedan, a white-haired man with a young face, turned away from the medical tower. "I need my tech—"

"They can come back later, when your patient isn't on the verge of panic."

"I don't panic, Doctor," Ash said.

Rykus's gut tightened at her tone. The words were something the real Ash would say, but there was a warning in her voice, a harsh whisper that made him want to reach for a weapon.

Katie must have heard it too. She glanced at him, a sympathetic look in her eyes.

He straightened his shoulders and shoved another technician toward the door. That started the others moving.

Nedan glared as Katie approached Ash's bed. "We don't know if the loyalty training reprogrammed her. I need more observation notes than just my own."

"You'll have mine," Katie said, staring down at Ash. "How do you feel, Lieutenant?"

Ash had claimed she didn't panic, but her eyes darted from person to person, object to object. Her gaze stopped on the docked psyche-mask. She knew where she was—the light blue lab coat Nedan wore gave it away—and her breathing rate went rapid.

Rykus moved closer.

"How do you feel?" Katie asked again.

Ash's gaze found him.

"Answer the question," he said, hating the look in her eyes, the request for permission. If the loyalty training took hold of her the same way it had in the past, the need for his approval would fade in time. And if Ash was herself again, she'd start defying him every chance she could.

Seeker's God, he wanted her defiance.

"I feel like I've been strapped to this bed for an eternity, Doc," Ash said, a clever way to ask to be released. Rykus wanted to fall for the trap, but if she wasn't fully herself, if Valt's orders were still controlling her, she was dangerous…

Hell, *he* was dangerous. If she still wanted to kill him, he'd deal with it.

"Leave," he said to Nedan and Katie. "She needs to sit up and move."

Nedan looked at him. "Despite what Dr. Monick might want you to believe, I'm the lead doctor here. Lieutenant Ashdyn will remain restrained until I clear her." He looked down at his data-pad and added, "It's for your own safety, Commander. If she still wants to kill you—"

"Of course I want to kill him."

A chill swept the room. In unison, everyone turned their heads and looked at Ash. Her green eyes found his, and the most acute anguish he'd ever felt kicked his heart into his gut. She still wanted to kill him. Valt's programming still controlled her.

"Ash." His voice broke.

"You shot me," she said levelly. "In the chest at close range. A bit over-kill, don't you think, Rip?"

Rip. The nickname she'd given him, a name he'd always hated. But the whole Known Universe could call him Rest in Peace Rykus now. He didn't care. He grinned like a soldier who'd just survived his first firefight.

"I was trying to teach you that you're not invincible."

"I'm still alive, aren't I?" Ash's mouth bent just perceptibly at the right corner in one of her subtle, infuriatingly tempting smiles.

Rykus moved to her bedside, grabbed the strap holding her right wrist, and unbuckled it.

Nedan almost dropped his data-pad. "Commander Rykus, I insist—"

"She's fine." He reached across her, released her left wrist.

"She wants to kill you," Nedan spluttered.

Rykus couldn't stop smiling. "I know."

THIRTY-ONE

THEY KEPT HER IN THE INSTITUTE for another day. If Ash hadn't spent the past month in her own personal hell, she would have said it was the longest day of her life.

But it wasn't the longest day. The hallucinations the psyche-mask triggered reminded her of that fact. The longest day, the worst day, was the half hour Jevan had been on board her team's shuttle. She'd failed to save Trevast and the others again and again. Each time, it hurt. Each time, she'd screamed.

Each time, the visions that came afterward screwed with her mind and deepened the nightmare.

Ash stumbled. She almost grabbed the fence to keep her balance but found her footing first. The blue sky was too bright. It spun above her as her heart rate picked up, and despite the chilly air, her skin grew damp. She squeezed her teeth together, forced her feet to move forward, and tried to keep the panic under control. She'd lived her life presenting a strong front. She was determined to do so now. The more she let her panic show, the longer the doctors would keep her here.

And she had to leave. The institute would break her.

She didn't look up at the tall, gray building. She did her best to pretend it wasn't there. She was finally outside its walls. Confined to the fenced-in field surrounding the complex, yes, but the doctors were still pissed. They wanted her in shackles. Just in case. Someone had to have broken arms to get her outside.

Ash hadn't seen that someone since she first woke up. Her fail-safe had freed her from the nightmares, freed her from her restraints, then taken her into his arms. He'd held her tight, kissed the top of her head, and then he'd said nothing.

Nothing.

He'd left without a word.

She tasted blood. Realizing she was biting her cheek, she made herself stop, made herself keep her gaze steady and straight ahead. Even though Rykus had left, she kept looking for him, glancing over her shoulder because she thought she felt his gaze. He was never there. His looming presence was embedded inside her mind, nestled in with her memories of Caruth, the Coalition, the whole KU. Every thought she had, every action she took, reminded her of him. The pull of the loyalty training was stronger than it had ever been. It was strong enough to make her brittle.

The only thing that had kept her sane these past twenty-six hours was that she could answer the doctors' questions. All of their questions. Once they realized she could talk about Chalos II and Jevan, they sent in an interrogator.

And Ash had promptly sent the interrogator away. She told them she would only talk directly to her fail-safe. She trusted him.

Ash breathed in Caruth's clean air. The fence surrounding the perimeter was clear except for a faint blue tint. The barrier was sleek and tall, and because the doctors here dealt exclusively with anomalies, it was incredibly secure. Ash hadn't found a quick way over it. A slow and tedious way, yes, but the guards would kill or capture her before she made it halfway to the top.

They were watching her now. They stood in their guardhouses, armed and ready to shoot. Every time one of them moved, she tensed. Reflex. She knew they wouldn't do anything unless she gave them a reason, but she feared this place. It toggled a switch in her mind that made her paranoid and panicky.

She continued her walk of the perimeter. She hadn't been cleared to run yet—Katie had made her promise to take it easy—but Ash wouldn't get stronger if she didn't push herself. She needed the mindless exercise.

The fence curved back toward the building, and she fell into a careful, slow jog.

Her injuries hurt and she grew winded quickly, but it felt good to move.

She was on her second circle of the field, just past the door to the institute, when she heard footsteps behind her. The fresh, clean smell of her failsafe's aftershave cocooned her. She slowed down, and Rykus fell in step beside her.

They walked half the perimeter without saying a word. Ash kept her gaze forward, afraid that if she looked at him he'd see how much she wanted him there. Showing need wasn't something she was good at, and she couldn't come up with a flippant quip to break the silence.

She really wasn't herself yet.

They passed a guard tower. In her peripheral vision, she saw Rykus glance up at the armed man watching them. When he looked back at their path, she realized why he was there.

"You're here to say good-bye." She made sure her tone was level. Emotionless.

Looking at the grass beneath their feet, he said, "I've been summoned to Meryk. My actions are under review."

"Your actions? The actions where you saved my ass?"

His mouth tightened into a humorless smile. "I bent rules to get to you on the capsule. I pursued you to Ephron without authorization and defied Bayis's order to surrender to the pursuit force. And there's some question as to why I couldn't get the cipher from you on the *Obsidian*."

"They have enough information to clear you," she said, trying to ignore the protective furor building in her chest. "I'll clear you."

"I'm not worried about that."

"What are you worried about?"

He glanced at her briefly before looking ahead again. "The Sariceans' files didn't contain any evidence of telepathy."

Ash almost stumbled back into a nightmare. Her hallucinations had mocked her with the possibility that nothing would be there. Sometimes it was because telepathy didn't exist. Other times it did exist, but the only evidence of it was in Trevast's mind. Trevast had said the word *faction*. Trevast had been certain telepaths were real. Trevast, the hallucinations told her, had known the boarders were coming. He'd invited them on.

No. Ash shook her head, clearing out the dark thoughts and the lies so she could find the grains of truth. "Trevast told us telepathy existed before Jevan boarded. None of us believed it, but he did. Completely. And he'd been… afraid. Just before he died"—Ash swallowed—"he said, 'Faction.' He was trying to tell me something."

"Admiral Bayis will look into it."

She clenched her teeth. Rykus must have noticed.

"He's done everything he can to help us, Ash. You can trust him. He's being careful with the information. He has a very select group of people analyzing the data. I-Com and the entire senate are raising hell about the secrecy, but he's used his command authority to get an interstellar security exemption."

An ISE. Good. Maybe they could contain the information. Ash was still certain the Coalition would fall apart if the public learned about the telepaths. She needed to prevent that, but she couldn't do that on her own.

Rykus's comm-cuff chimed. He didn't look at it.

"Is that your ride?" she asked.

"I leave in an hour."

"Any idea what will happen to me?"

"Officially, you've been reassigned to another special operations force. Your CO is Major Tanner Liles. He's a good man."

Rykus had to have broken a few extra arms to get her reassigned so soon. He knew her well enough to know she needed to get back to work. Needed the distraction and to put her skills to use. She wasn't sure yet how she felt about a new CO. She wanted her old CO, her old team, back.

"And unofficially?" she asked, stopping beside the door to the institute.

Rykus faced her. "You'll be debriefed on Meryk first."

"So, we'll both be there."

"Yes."

That heavy silence settled between them again. Not exactly awkward, but not comfortable either. Now that she could talk to him freely without any worry of a blackout, she didn't know what to say.

In fact, she really didn't want to say anything at all. She wanted to do things, like move closer so she could get a better smell of his aftershave, maybe press her lips against his jaw and find out just how close his shave was.

She shifted her weight and looked away. She wanted Rykus. She wanted him more than any man she'd ever met.

"You taking a military transport to Meryk?" she asked.

"Commercial," he responded.

She hated his succinct answers. She wanted more from him, more of his voice, more of his reaction, more of his...

Well, hell. She'd always been flirtatious and direct. No need to stop now.

"Do I get an invite?"

He looked behind her more than at her. "You're expected to be on a military transport."

"It wouldn't be the first time I broke a rule."

"Ash—"

"I'll say my brain was a bit scrambled." She moved toward him. "Wouldn't be a complete lie."

He placed his hands on her shoulders, stopping her from coming closer. "I'm re-imprinted in your mind, Ash."

"I'm aware of that."

"No, you're not thinking. You're letting the loyalty training control your feelings. I took advantage of that—"

She stepped back quickly, causing his hands to fall from her shoulders. "If you're saying I wasn't willing—"

"You were willing." He grabbed her arm, preventing her from moving farther away. "Seeker's God, you were willing. We both were, and... hell. I'm saying this wrong. What I did was an abuse of power. The Coalition has laws preventing fraternization between the ranks, but what I did was worse than that. I broke an ethical code—"

"If you want me to sign a statement of relationship, I will."

"That's not what I want, damn it." He turned away. "It would destroy your career. It would take you decades to rank up."

"I don't care about rank."

Glancing over her shoulder, he pinned her with his dark gaze. "Morally it's wrong."

Ash crossed her arms, lifted her chin. "You're afraid of me."

Rykus let out a chuckle that edged just this side of exasperated. "Terrified."

When she stepped closer, he turned toward her. He reached out and found the braid hidden beneath her hair. She'd finally showered, and she'd made sure she tightly rebraided it.

"There's a right way and a wrong way to do things," he said. "I went outside my chain of command, broke countless rules and protocols, and did it the wrong way. My feelings for you clouded my judgment."

"If the legendary Rhys 'Rest in Peace' Rykus has feelings, then why are you pushing me away?"

"Because you don't have a choice."

She eased closer. "Very noble of you, Rip, but I don't give a damn about chivalry. And I do have a choice."

He released her braid, and the air turned too cool when he dropped his hand to his side. "You never give up. I don't know whether to love or hate that about you."

She laughed. "It's okay if it's both."

He looked on the verge of smiling, but he had more control than she did. His expression settled into his customary scowl, and he said, "Valt is alive."

The words cut through her, dousing the little heat that lingered. Rykus's intent, undoubtedly.

She refused to let him see the shard of ice that speared her. She'd suspected Jevan had survived. She had a vague recollection of him running, and an even vaguer memory of Rykus shooting her. She hadn't asked the doctors or the interrogator about him. She'd spoken to them as little as possible.

"He wanted you," Rykus said. "He came across your name—the name of the only female ever to complete the Caruth training—when you graduated, and he was obsessed. He thought with a little more time he could turn you into a drone."

She had to force herself to breathe. That was one of her fears, one of the hallucinations she'd lived over and over again.

"You're not a drone," Rykus said.

She met his gaze. "How do you know?"

"He told us he was unsuccessful."

"And you believe him?" Rykus couldn't be that gullible.

"The Coalition has used... persuasive methods to make him talk."

"I'm familiar with those methods."

The skin around Rykus's eyes tightened, and she felt him withdraw. She wanted to tell him it was okay, that it wasn't his fault she was tortured and hurt, but she was pretty sure a reasonable, non-loyalty-trained person would be a little pissed about it. So she said nothing.

"No," he said after a long silence. "I don't believe everything he says. But I believe in you. You're free now." He grimaced. "Or you will be once you get away from me."

He reached for the door.

"Wait." She placed her hand over his.

"Ashdyn, I told you—"

"The braid," she said. "Back on Ephron, you asked why I still wear it."

His brow furrowed. "I did, but—"

"I wear it because it reminds me of you."

His gaze moved from her eyes to the braid draped over her shoulder, then back to her eyes. He didn't understand.

"It's reminded me of you for a long time, Rip."

His jaw clenched. He still didn't get it.

"Since *before* the loyalty training," she said, spelling it out.

His eyes locked on hers. His lips parted. He started to say something, stopped.

Ash moved closer, close enough to be wrapped in that strong, unique scent that was his.

He didn't back away. "Are you sure?"

She answered him with a kiss. He was taller than her, so she pulled his head down. If he'd tried to back away, she wouldn't have let him. But he didn't try. His mouth opened, his tongue found hers, and he pressed his body into hers.

He opened the door to the institute, that hell she never wanted to return to, but she didn't care when he swung her over the threshold. His right hand fisted her braid, his left circled to the small of her back, pulling her hips forward.

"There are a thousand reasons why this can't work," he whispered against her mouth.

Ash laughed and kissed him again. "I'm an anomaly, Rip. I obliterate the odds every day."

ABOUT THE
AUTHOR

Sandy Williams has lived and breathed books all her life. When she was a teen, she was always the first to finish her class assignments so that she could read as much as possible before the bell rang. Her grades didn't suffer (much), and she was able to enroll in Texas A&M University. She didn't sneak in novels there, but her college lecture notes are filled with snippets of stories. After she graduated, she decided to turn those snippets into novels.

Sandy writes books with high-octane action adventure infused with a strong shot of romance. She is best known for The Shadow Reader novels, an urban fantasy romance series about a college student who becomes caught up in a fae civil war. When she's not reading or corralling her twin boys, she enjoys playing EuroGames like Dominion, Castles of Burgundy, and Caverna.

To learn more visit
WWW.SANDY-WILLIAMS.COM

CPSIA information can be obtained at www.ICGtesting.com
Printed in the USA
LVOW07s0451190116

471180LV00001B/47/P